DOG'S TWILIGHT

Also by Roger Teichmann
THE ECHO DIES
Forthcoming, 2024

DOG'S TWILIGHT

ROGER TEICHMANN

DOG'S TWILIGHT

Published by Eucalyptus Titles, Oxford, UK

978-1-7384539-1-7 (paperback)
978-1-7384539-0-0 (ebook)

Website | contact information

Publishing services provided by AuthorImprints.com

AUTHOR'S NOTE

THE OXFORD OF *DOG'S TWILIGHT* is partly real, partly imaginary. The Marlborough Hotel, scene of more than one crime, does not exist but the Randolph Hotel and Godstow nunnery can be visited by any tourist and other landmarks and public spaces will be familiar to many. I'm happy to say that I have never encountered, personally or professionally, any student resembling Conrad Merrivale – nor any literary agent resembling Vince Parker.

I

'VINTAGE PORN ON THE WALLS in there,' the older man said as he resumed his seat beside the younger man. 'Why would you want to look at that while having a slash?'

'A case of divided loyalties.'

The older man snorted. 'You're a wit, Conrad. Did anyone ever tell you you were a wit? If wit were shit...'

He trailed off. The younger man downed his half pint and wiped his mouth with the back of his hand. 'Thirsty boy,' said his companion. 'It's only half twelve, we could have a couple more pints if you want.' The younger man merely nodded. With half-closed eyes he reached for some crisps.

The two of them were having a lunch break in a pub near their place of work. Near, but not too near; the hotel manager, for example, was unlikely to make an appearance. It was a pleasant enough drinking-hole, quiet at this time of day. As usual they occupied the oak settle crammed into one corner of the room from where you could look out at the passing show. A sticky carpet with a floral pattern lay underfoot, circular tables on metal legs were dotted round the premises and the ceiling was painted a dimpled red. From a wall-mounted speaker directly above them came the subdued throb of music.

The older man got to his feet and made for the bar. Conrad watched him. Three locals were standing there, colonising the space and forming a human barrier behind which a callow and ineffectual barman stared at his phone. Elbows, thought Conrad. You have to use elbows if you want to get a drink. Pete's hopeless, look at him dithering there. Ah no, the barman has noticed him at last. Lucky Pete. Lucky hopeless Pete.

'You didn't get yourself anything,' he said when Pete brought a single pint of beer back to the table.

'Oh, I'm all right,' said Pete sitting down. 'Mustn't breathe too much alcohol into the guests' faces, it might scare them off.'

Pete was a spindly man in his forties wearing a jacket and tie and sporting a small gold ring in one ear. Shaven-headed, large-lipped and with dark eyebrows meeting above the bridge of his nose, he could have been PA to a Russian oligarch rather than what he actually was, receptionist at a three-star Oxford hotel. His colleague, who was half his age, wore his blondish hair in a ponytail and had a red-tinged goatee. Watery blue eyes looked out from beneath heavy lids. The boy was wearing a leather jacket and scuffed jeans that he would have to change out of before his evening shift.

Pete sipped from his remaining beer and said, 'Got any plans for the weekend? Any jaunts lined up?'

Conrad shook his head. 'Not really. I might go and hear Meg at the Hedgehog.' He spoke slowly with an accent that was three parts Estuary to one part unidentifiable.

'Is that your girlfriend, then?'

'Meg is my partner, yes. She's a singer-songwriter.'

'Your *partner*. Silly me, and I thought she might be your girlfriend.'

'Don't be a twat, Pete. It gets on people's nerves.'

Pete smirked. 'Well, for you, poppet, I'll try not to be a twat. And I'll never call her your girlfriend again. Do you take her for spins on your motorbike?'

'Sometimes.'

'That must be nice, having her holding you from behind while you rev your engines.'

Lucky hopeless Pete, thought Conrad. Luckless hopeful Pete, more like. He's hopeful all right but I doubt he has much luck, unless you count rent boys. But what do I know, appearances can be deceptive and who cares anyway.

Conrad was staying in Oxford over the summer to make some vacation money, waiting tables four nights a week at the Marlborough Hotel as well as writing a novel in his spare time and getting stoned with Meg. With or without her, that is. The motorbike took him to Reading or London on those occasions when he needed to replenish his stock. Oxford was awash with drugs but he preferred to keep his distance from the county lines and the confusion and aggro they entailed. He looked upon himself as a freelancer, a connoisseur. Mainly he bought stuff for his own use, the dealing being more of a side show—really only to make ends meet, keep the wolf from the door. Sometimes as he prepared himself a bonus spliff he would intone *I hereby keep the wolf from the door*. Curiosity might one day get the better of him: it would be interesting, perhaps, to invite the wolf in and see what he had to say for himself. Make the wolf's acquaintance.

'Have you heard about this VIP who's turning up next week?' said Pete.

Conrad looked at him. 'VIP? What VIP?'

'Famous writer. Bernie's not letting on, wants us all to guess. A great honour for the hotel, you understand, red carpet treatment *de rigueur*, tips all round I hope. Apparently she's a millionaire.'

'She?'

'Yes, they do write books, Conrad. *She* was all Bernie would give away. I'm polishing my best smile in preparation, cheek exercises in front of the bathroom mirror every morning.' He giggled. 'So to speak.'

'When's she turning up?'

'Monday or Tuesday. She's flying in from Italy where she has a villa *of course*. Plus swimming pool I don't doubt.'

'Why's she coming to Oxford?'

'God knows. Maybe she wants to do some literary research in the Bodleian, though I thought writers made do with Wikipedia these days. Anyway, be prepared. This'll be your chance for a brush with celebrity.' He looked at his watch. 'Tempus fugit. Might have to love and leave you, young man. Can't stay for lunch today, I have to see a man about a dog. Don't glug it,' he added, standing up. 'Take your time. Savour the hops. See you back at the ranch.'

Conrad watched him leave, a thin figure in a dark suit ignored by the other customers, slipping out into an Oxford side street. For a moment or two he wondered if Pete had a private life. Then he decided to look at the menu.

*

Tessa leant over her laptop. The sunlight made it harder to read the screen, with or without dark glasses; she had already several times shifted from one position to another on the balcony with the sun now behind her, now in front of her, now to the side... She could have gone indoors but why have a balcony in Tuscany if you weren't going to use it? Well, this would do. Vince's email was legible enough.

> I have attached your itinerary. Please let me know if you have any queries concerning the details. I have booked the taxi to pick you up from Il Tramonto at 10 a.m. sharp. This should mean that you arrive at the airport with plenty of time to spare...

And more of the same. Vince had a team under him but with one or two valued clients he preferred to do the legwork, probably on the principle that if you want a job done well you should do it yourself. And he had special reasons for valuing Tessa as a client. She after all was the goose that had lain the golden egg. From being her agent Vince had evolved into something more like a factotum, organising her professional life as well as her publishing deals.

Odd to think that in not many hours' time I'll be miles away from here, she thought. Flying through the air towards a probably rainy England, land of my birth and scene of my chequered past. *My chequered past*: that ought to mean discrete areas of light and dark equally distributed, like a chessboard or a quilt. It was much messier than a quilt, that's for sure, a whole lot messier. However, none of that's to the point. You should be focusing on the positives, Tessa—think of all your English readers and especially all those fans on tenterhooks for volume four of *The Quest*, having apparently had their lives changed forever by volumes one to three: now they'll be able to see you in person, or some of them will, and you'll be able to see them, and more to the point see a number of old friends whom you haven't seen for too many years. Not to mention the quiltlike city of Oxford.

And Ben. I will see Ben again.

It still seemed improbable, in the way that a dream is improbable. But it was true. He had emailed to confirm the date and time, a certain fixed point in the future when they would actually encounter one another. They would look into each other's faces for the first time in twenty-three years, she a 48-year-old woman, he a young man of –

Of twenty-three, of course.

Butterflies in the stomach. Stage fright. Why such nerves, what did it mean? Impending joy or fear of catastrophe? It was like a first date.

Six months ago a letter had arrived with unfamiliar handwriting on the envelope. It had been placed on the kitchen table by Emilia along with a bill and a doctor's appointment. When Tessa got round to opening it, assuming it to be fan mail, she barely understood the sentences she was reading and skipped to the signature for enlightenment. For a moment she felt only numb incomprehension and this moment of stasis was, she later realised, a plateau or ledge dividing two existences, before and after. Now reading through the letter properly she wept for joy, smudging his words with her tears. The joy was mingled with sorrow, naturally—sorrow at the last twenty-three years, empty of him. It wasn't all the fault of Ben's father. Alex had, it seemed, told his son the truth when the boy was thirteen, but something—pride, resentment, something—had inhibited Ben from contacting her. Until six months ago.

Tessa looked down into the valley where the village nestled among the trees. The church tower caught the light and the pink of terracotta-clay roof tiles mingled with the heavy green of vegetation. As she watched, a flock of birds descended from the sky into the foliage of a huge elm, sending ripples of shadow through its leaves and into the leaves of its neighbours. Beyond the village a glint of sunlight showed where the river, more of a stream really, continued its journey to the ocean. It was almost ridiculously pretty, this scene. Fame brings money brings a room with a view, that is the way of the world. She would bring Ben here—this villa would be his one day, after all. Her career, her writing, could no longer be regarded as a purely self-interested activity, it was raised to a higher level by his existence, it would be a source of wealth and comfort to him in years to come. Closing her eyes she turned her smiling face towards the sun.

*

A hotel kitchen is a place of controlled chaos. Several different activities, carried out by several different kinds of person, proceed simultaneously and in parallel as if unrelated to one another while being in theoretical lockstep, each symbiotically connected with all the others and all serving the same end, namely the pleasuring by means of food and drink of a bunch of largely unappreciative customers. This at any rate was how Conrad viewed the matter. Why such sweat and bother should be expended on satisfying other people's basic animal appetites was obscure. Or rather it was absurd, laughable. Each of us may, indeed must, attend to his or her own pleasure, but there was something degrading in seeing to it that another human being had arrived at a state of glassy-eyed repletion.

But he was good at his job. Those chewing swilling diners were charmed by his repartee and his ready smile, and the management noticed and approved. He reserved his critique for private soliloquy or the occasional barbed comment to Pete. From his fellow waiters he remained largely aloof and the kitchen staff he looked upon as skivvies. Pete in fact was his only friend in the hotel, mainly because Pete had made overtures and shown himself willing to buy Conrad drinks.

That evening a hen party was in progress on table nine. The belle of the ball or sacrificial victim was a large unit (as Pete would have described her), name of Karen, whose squiffy giggles indicated how much her friends had already plied her with. The night being young Conrad could only guess where she would be by ten-thirty. It was all good for business and Conrad saw his role in simple terms, to play preux chevalier to the bride to be on this her not-quite-last evening of liberty, helping her to focus her roving libido for a final instant on a comely stranger, if only for the vicarious delight of her friends. The other waiters wouldn't sink, or rise, to this level—Conrad knew it and they knew it. He could act the part, they could not.

'And may I see the ring?' he enquired (Estuary tones discarded for the evening), pausing in his job of refilling people's glasses. Karen lifted up a pudgy hand. Diamonds winked in the candlelight and Karen blushed becomingly.

'A girl's best friend,' sighed Conrad.

'That's something else, isn't it?' squealed one of the party. 'Something you've got and we haven't!'

Lewd hilarity rocked the table. Conrad smiled indulgently. 'If you say so.'

'We do!' shouted an anaemic brunette.

'Just ignore them,' said Karen rolling her eyes. Conrad leant over her to pour her some pink prosecco then continued on his way.

Half an hour later the noise levels had risen to the point at which fellow diners cast amused or irritated glances. Conrad observed the proceedings with detachment. When a female hand groped him as he removed dishes from the table he slapped it gently as you might an over intimate dog.

'What's your name?' a girl with glasses and a shoulder tattoo asked him.

'Conrad. Like the author. What's yours?'

'Katie. What author?'

'*Lord Jim. Nostromo.* Novels and short stories. He was Polish.'

'Oh...' Katie paused. 'My hairdresser's Polish.'

'Is she?'

'Yes.' She paused again. 'I don't read novels much. Except fantasy and stuff. You know, like *The Quest.*'

'I don't think I know it.'

'You're kidding me?' She stared at him. 'You haven't heard of *The Quest*? Tessa Wainwright?'

''Fraid not.'

Katie turned to her neighbours. 'Conrad here hasn't heard of Tessa Wainwright!'

'Maybe it's because I'm a student of English literature,' Conrad said, so impassively that no one noticed.

'Isn't Tessa Wainwright coming to Oxford?' asked one of the girls.

'Yes, I read that,' another said. 'Apparently she hasn't been to England for years. She's staying at an undisclosed location but I bet they...'

'I could get her autograph!' shrieked Katie—then, 'Oh shit... I can't, I won't be in Oxford...'

'What are you all talking about?' Karen's voice came from down the table, strident and slurred. 'What's so interesting?'

'Apparently Tessa Wainwright...'

Conrad didn't stay to hear the rest. The couple at table five were beckoning for the bill and a well-dressed woman was hovering by the entrance waiting to be shown to a table. He was beginning to get a headache. Nothing that a few lines of coke wouldn't sort out, washed down with a little whisky, with the headphones on and Richard Wagner carrying him to a higher plane.

*

By the standards of his contemporaries Conrad's artistic and intellectual tastes would have to be called highbrow. The poems of Donne, *Tristram Shandy*, Otto Weininger, Musil, Ezra Pound and above all Wagner were his sources of spiritual sustenance. Musically not much else moved him, apart from Glenn Gould's renditions of Bach and some Frank Zappa.

'You like weirdoes, don't you,' a friend of his at school had said.

'Donne was no weirdo,' he had replied, 'he was Dean of St Paul's. And Wagner was the sanest man of his time.'

As for the books he had to read for his degree, he had dipped a desultory toe into some of these but relegated most of them to low priority status, counting on his capacity to wing it in tutorials or exams. Lectures he avoided. He supposed he would get a First. Meanwhile in college he was regarded with awe by people who took indolence and reclusiveness as signs of brilliance. Others thought him stuck up. His tutors disagreed among themselves; when they compared notes it was almost as if they were discussing different students. 'One must be all things to all men, Pete,' he once said to his friend, quoting St Paul. 'You charmer, you,' replied Pete. 'Merely versatile,' corrected Conrad.

And the novel. Ah, the novel. All anyone knew was that he was writing it. Even Meg knew nothing about it, neither its theme, nor its title, nor how much (if any) had been written. Conrad was secretive about the whole thing. Sometimes he would disappear from view for several days, hunkering down in Bwthyn Onnen, the Welsh cottage his family owned to which he had a set of keys. Later he would explain that he'd been working on the book. If quizzed too much about it he was liable to snap, and Meg had learnt to be encouraging without being curious and not to raise the subject herself but let him raise it if he wanted to, which wasn't very often. When he did mention the novel his face assumed a far-off expression as if he were glimpsing his destiny.

That a famous writer was coming to stay at the Marlborough was vaguely annoying. He, whose literary talents he was sure were considerable, would have to kowtow to her, who evidently wrote 'fantasy' and was read by people like cretinous Katie. For it was pretty clear that Pete's VIP was none other than Tessa Wainwright. Of course I might end up only viewing her from afar, he said to himself. That would mean I could leave it to others to tend to her needs and desires. Which might be the best plan, all things considered.

'It's Tessa Wainwright, isn't it?' he said to Pete a couple of days later in Pete's cubby-hole, a.k.a. the receptionist's office. Pete was wont to invite Conrad into his private den from time to time for a chat and a whisky, Conrad sprawling in the green armchair while Pete perched on the edge of his desk or paced around. A framed photograph of the late queen smiled down upon them and on a squat filing cabinet in the corner a pot plant was slowly dying.

Pete shrugged. 'Seems everyone knows by now, down to the hotel cat.' (He often invoked this mythical animal.) 'Yes, Tessa Wainwright it is. She's getting the Blenheim Suite. Arrives tomorrow evening. Are you excited?'

'Not in the slightest. Why should I be?'

'You're a literary type, aren't you? Reading Eng Lit at an Oxford college, or so I hear. If you're nice to her she might get you a job writing reviews for the TLS. Just flutter your eyelids a little.'

Conrad drank some whisky. 'She writes fantasy fiction. For kiddies.'

'Kiddies and the young at heart, my dear sir. Don't be disdainful, it's a very lucrative business. She's got them eating out of her hand, knows just how to get them coming back for more, lots more. My nephew's an addict. Three volumes out of four have already been published and everyone's guessing what's going to happen in the fourth—apparently some devastating plot twist is going to occur, the fan base is in a lather on Twitter, her publisher's feeding little titbits to the press to maintain the excitement. The whole show is extremely professional.'

'You seem to know a lot about it.'

'Only what anyone can read online. Plus what my nephew tells me.'

Conrad fell silent. He was mulling something over. 'How long's she staying?'

'Three weeks.'

Conrad mulled some more. 'I suppose she'll be working on her book while she's here.'

'Might be. What if she is?'

'Well... It wouldn't be hard to find out what's coming in volume four if she's brought her computer. You'd just nip into her room when she's out, armed with a memory stick.'

Pete's eyebrows went up. 'You'd have to be pretty desperate. Why not wait till the book comes out?'

It was at times like this that Conrad realised how different his thinking was from other people's. It seemed to him that he lived among a lot of myopic children, drifting or blundering around without seeing what was under their noses. He gave a half-weary sigh and said, 'Find out what the big denouement is and sell it to the papers. Let it go to the highest bidder.'

Pete examined his friend's face for signs of flippancy, detected none. 'But they'd know it was one of the hotel staff. Too risky. And anyway it'd be theft.'

'Not at all. Not even a breach of copyright. The stuff's unpublished. As for who was behind it, it could just as well be a remote hacker. Or one of her Italian servants—I presume she has a whole team of them.'

Pete shifted his position on the desk, drawing one foot up and folding his arms across his chest. An ambiguous smile hovered on his face. 'I might ask you why you're revealing this plan to me if you think it's such a good one.'

'Because you look after the room keys and can see when guests are leaving the hotel.'

'So why don't I do it on my own?'

'You'll need me as a look-out.'

'Hm. And is your idea that we go fifty-fifty?'

'If that seems like a good arrangement to you.'

Pete got down, walked a few paces and stopped under the gaze of Queen Elizabeth. 'What if she's a pen and paper person?'

'She's not ninety, is she? And even if she does use a quill and parchment, a quick flip through the later bits of the manuscript will get you to the right sections and then you just take a few photos. If your phone is capable of that.'

Pete shook his head. 'Let's hope it's on her computer.'

'The most likely hypothesis by far.' Conrad held out his empty tumbler. Pete went for the bottle.

'I take it you agree to my proposal?' Conrad said as the whisky was being poured.

'We'll need to see what her movements are,' said Pete. 'She might stay in her room all day. Or she might carry her device wherever she goes. Or the denouement might be in her head, not on her computer. There are a lot of unknowns.'

Conrad smiled, holding the glass up to the light. 'I have a good feeling about this one,' he declared. 'It'll be a cinch.'

'Have you done this sort of thing before by any chance?' asked Pete.

'Not exactly *this* sort, no.'

'What sort, then?'

'Oh, nothing much. Really, Pete, you seem a bit lily-livered about the idea. I would have hoped you'd have more fire in your loins.'

'Leave my loins out of it, *chéri*,' said Pete, pouring himself some whisky. 'They can look after themselves. It's our brains we need to keep in good order for this sort of racket. We need to be as sharp as acupuncture needles. Assuming I agree to do it.'

'Quite right. And prepared—we need to be prepared. I intend to read vols 1 to 3 so as to know what to look out for in vol 4. You might do the same.'

'That's going to take a lot of strong coffee.'

'I shall be using other stimulants.'

'I'm sure you shall,' said Pete primly. 'Naughty boy.'

*

On the evening before her departure Tessa put on her favourite Abba CD and made herself a pasta supper, taking the previous day's half bottle of Chianti out of the fridge in advance. Her bags were packed, her passport and tickets were in a prominent place, £100 in sterling in her purse. She had once been a frequent traveller but that habit, like some others, seemed to have been mislaid in recent years so that these preparations kindled an old feeling of excitement, the sense of new experiences just around the corner. This time the guise in which those future experiences appeared was less indefinite than usual, even if Ben's face remained a mysterious blank. She'd been too shy to ask him to send a photo.

Chopping an onion she hummed along to 'Dancing Queen'. This was the music of her youth—of her childhood, in fact. With a little wine inside her it still exerted its old power; she swayed in time, the floor was hers, *my kitchen is my disco*. What would her teenage fans think? She had no idea what sort of stuff they listened to. Abba would probably seem prehistoric. Or maybe the very fact that Tessa Wainwright listened to it would lend it glamour and sophistication. That was the sort of angle Vince would have taken, beaming the spotlight of his marketing mind on the issue. Let the two franchises promote each other, everyone's a winner! She wondered how he was, dear old Vince, with his bow ties and his iron handshake. She'd be seeing him the day after tomorrow: lunch at the Old Parsonage, one of the places Alex used to take her when he was feeling brave, after which they'd go back to his flat. Have some madeira, m'dear. No, it wasn't like that exactly, but near enough. And now he's dead and he can't even say sorry. And I can't say sorry. We can't say sorry to each other, it's too late, actually it was too late a long time ago, it was too late when he stood at the foot of my hospital bed and said in that croaking voice, 'What are you doing to us? Are you trying to destroy everything?'

Gently, gingerly, she put down the knife, closed her eyes. *Don't go there, Tessa. Think of something else.* Life is full of good things, joy is all around you and within you. Moreover there's no point in crying over spilt milk and Alex is ashes in an urn. Think of Ben. She took a sip of Chianti and resumed her chopping.

Yes, Ben. And Oxford and *The Quest* and your successful career and lots of other things. And tomorrow you'll be in an aeroplane looking down on the fluffy mountains of clouds as they move below you, slowly wise, the bright sun flashing on the wing of the plane and the comforting roar of the engines in your ears. Then from Heathrow to Oxford in a taxi (Vince again) to be set down at the door of the Marlborough Hotel, a quick smile and nod to any waiting paparazzi, a hot bath and a nice dinner. She hadn't bothered to check out the hotel online, as always relying on Vince's taste and discretion, but she assumed it was a high-class establishment and that the restaurant could be relied on.

'Nice food, nice drink,' she murmured, cutting into a red pepper. 'Soft bed, soft towels.' She could imagine the puff in the brochure: *Luxury in the heart of an ancient university town*. Somewhere Alex had *not* taken her, if only because it hadn't been around in their day.

'Dancing Queen' had given way to 'Knowing Me, Knowing You'. Tessa poured some olive oil into a frying pan. The last rays of the evening sun came through the kitchen window.

In another universe, one where Tessa spent many of her waking hours, Taskar walked hand in hand with Princess Lemula through the stony desert.

*

'It's a hypothetical question but it's not a hypothetical question, if you get my meaning.'

'No, I don't get your meaning.'

'Well, it's not hypothetical whether I can get the story but it is hypothetical whether your paper will want to publish it.'

'You mean whether we'll want to pay for it.'

'Same difference.'

Conrad was on his burner phone. His interlocutor, Mervin Carroll of the *Mirror*, was playing hard to get but Conrad sensed beneath the sceptical surface a fluttering, a tingling of excitement.

'And you say your source has direct access to Ms Wainwright's PC, is that right?'

'Correct.'

'How did he come by that access?'

'I'm afraid I can't divulge that.'

'Really. And I suppose you can't divulge the person's name either?'

"'Fraid not.'

'I don't see why I should believe any of this. Why should I believe any of it?'

Conrad was mute. It was a good question. Then inspiration hit: 'What if I gave you the serial number of Wainwright's device?'

'What good will that do me?'

'Phone her up as if you're the police and say you've retrieved a haul of stolen computers and are getting in touch with their registered owners.'

'But she'll say hers hasn't been stolen.'

'At which point you ask if she wouldn't mind checking the serial number on her computer since it would be strange if two computers had the same serial number. She goes off and checks, confirms the number, you say there must have been an error in transcription at your end, apologise for wasting her time and wish her good day.'

Silence. Mervin Carroll was obviously digesting this. As he did so Conrad looked up at the stars. He was on Port Meadow. On each side of him stretched turf, silvery-blue in the moonlight, and a few hundred yards off was a black mass of trees merging with the night sky. Above the city was a faint glow, yellowish smudge of electric light. The nearest human being was probably half a mile away; Conrad had supped a pint at The Perch then come out here for a stroll, a long stroll.

Finally Carroll spoke.

'Well, Mr—'

'Jones.'

'—Mr Jones, I think the best course would be for your friend to obtain what information he can—legally, of course…'

'Of course.'

'…and when that information is in your hands you can give me another call.'

'You want the serial number?'

'Why not.'

'I'll get back to you in a few days.'

'Goodbye, Mr Jones. Happy hunting.'

Conrad returned the phone to his pocket and stood awhile in contemplation. It was a balmy night; not far off stood the silhouette of a horse, grazing. Conrad felt pleased with himself. It was clear the press would bite. He would put off contacting the other papers till he and Pete had the gen—plus the PC serial number—and had talked a bit about the asking price. Ten thousand quid, five thousand each? He didn't have a clue what the going rate was. Overshooting was fine, the other party could always bring you down, what he didn't want to do was undershoot. Ten thousand sounded about right as a figure to kick off the auction.

And what of Tessa Wainwright? *I am but a poor innocent fantasy novelist! If you prick us do we not bleed? Have you no conscience, sir?* Not like other people's, no. Not your standard-issue, conventionally earthbound conscience. Mine is a free soaring bird, able to look down from a great height and take in the whole wide plain. Things look smaller from such a great height but that after all is how they really are. Small and insignificant is how things are. That goes for Tessa Wainwright, though goodness knows even a conventional conscience would feel hardly a pang at the prospect of Tessa's cat being let prematurely out of Wainwright's bag like this. Won't affect sales at all, I imagine. A little invasion of privacy is all it amounts to.

In the end you have to take what's yours by right if others are too stingy or stupid or sleepy to let you have it of their own free will. And some things became yours by right simply because their owners are stingy or stupid or sleepy. If someone leaves something lying around they effectively relinquish their title to it. Caveat possessor. There's a sense in which the world and all that's in it belongs to everyone, no? Let no one call me an egoist, I'm a high-minded egalitarian! What's mine is yours, what's yours is mine. I might be more adept at laying my hands on stuff, that's all.

The voice of his mother came to him: 'You'll share now, won't you, Conrad? It's nice to share your things.' Since he didn't have any siblings she will have been talking of his schoolfellows, his playmates. He didn't like to disappoint her. 'Yes, mummy,' he'd say. What mummy didn't see, mummy didn't know about. Then as later it would have grieved him to cause her pain.

He was ambling back the way he had come, back towards The Perch. I'll have another couple of pints, he thought, talk some nonsense to the girl behind the bar, then go home to read a bit of fantasy fiction before bed.

II

IN THE TAXI FROM HEATHROW to Oxford Tessa dozed. The Rumanian driver, excited to have in his car the author of *The Quest*, of which both his children were keen fans, soon ran out of questions. To fill the void he started on an account of his family, a complicated affair involving sick aunts and rich brothers-in-law. 'My sister, she don't wanna go to Dubai, she real happy in Bucharest but her husband—you know, he works in construction so...' When Tessa woke up they were coming into Oxford and he'd either cut short his narrative or completed it. She felt slightly ashamed.

'Here we are,' she said brightly as the car halted at another set of traffic lights. The Rumanian grunted. They were on a huge roundabout. Could this really be the Headington roundabout, eastern gateway into Oxford? If so, it had expanded threefold at least. As had the volume of traffic. One lane seemed to slice irresponsibly through the roundabout itself, resulting in a sort of choreographed contraflow, the whole turmoil being governed by an obscure system of lights. The London bus brought you in by this route and Tessa began to anticipate sights and sounds, the long stretch of houses and the bored voice of a bus driver calling out the names of stops: 'Thornhill park and ride…Headington shops…Pullens Lane…' A sort of poem, the lines interleaved with silences. The houses were still there, the poem was only a memory.

The traffic was moving again. A few minutes later they were going down the hill and into St Clement's, past the fish restaurant where Alex had taken her a few times, over the roundabout known as The Plain and onto Magdalen Bridge. From here it would be just five minutes to the hotel.

'You been here before?' asked the taxi driver, turning up Longwall Street.

'Oxford? Oh yes…a long time ago though.'

'Must have changed a lot.'

'Yes and no.'

Once arrived at the Marlborough the driver helped her with her bags, carrying them ahead of her into a brightly lit lobby. From behind a desk a shaven-headed man with an earring smiled at her with studied courtesy. In an armchair nearby a hotel guest was doing a crossword. Tessa thanked the driver and approached the smiling receptionist.

'Good evening, madam,' he said, head tilting deferentially. 'And welcome to the Marlborough Hotel. I trust your journey has been a pleasant one?'

Presumably he didn't say 'Can I help you?' because he knew who she was and that he could. But she wasn't going to not introduce herself. Fame couldn't corrupt her to that extent.

'I have a room booked in the name of Tessa Wainwright.'

'Indeed, madam, your arrival has been expected. We are honoured that you've chosen to be a guest at the Marlborough; I hope you'll have a very pleasant stay here. I know the manager will be keen to show you to your rooms himself so with your permission I'll just alert him to the fact of your arrival.'

She wondered if he'd prepared his little speech. He picked up the receiver of a nearby telephone and pressed a button. Tessa looked around her. *Luxury in the heart of an ancient university town.* Not quite luxury, more clean and comfortable. Perhaps Oxford doesn't do luxury, she thought—or it's simply that Vince is saving my pennies. That's one of the things I pay him for, I suppose.

'Good evening, Dr Wainwright! What a pleasure it is to meet you, you are most welcome, more than welcome...'

A bearlike man had materialised beside her wearing an awkward grin and rubbing his hands together as if on the point of carving a Sunday roast. This must be the manager. Tessa passed over the 'Dr' without comment, recognising in it the panicky substitution of something, anything, for more problematic forms of address like 'Miss', 'Mrs' and 'Ms', either impertinent or unworthy of a world-famous author, or both.

'Hello—good evening,' she returned, 'Mr...?'

'Oh, just call me Bernard,' he insisted, 'everyone else does, I like to be informal, life's too...'

'In that case you can call me Tessa. As you say, life's too short.'

Struck dumb, the manager reached down for her bags. Tessa noticed his bald patch and felt strangely sorry for him.

'Blenheim Suite,' murmured Pete. Bernie ignored him.

'Please follow me,' he said, turning on his heels. Pete handed Tessa the room keys and disappeared into his office.

Together they went up in the lift, Bernie discoursing of the hotel's amenities and Tessa smiling and nodding and looking at herself in the wall mirror. I still smell of aeroplane, she thought. Bad breath of grey plastic.

'There's a bath, isn't there?' she interrupted.

He stared at her. 'Bath?'

'In my room. Suite, whatever.'

'A bath, a bath, yes of course, the Blenheim Suite has not only a bath but a wet room with power shower, not to mention walk-in wardrobes, a mini bar...'

'The bath will do fine. And what time is dinner?'

'From six-thirty, madam.'

So I'm madam now, she thought. One's status can change so quickly in this world.

The lift doors opened and they walked in single file down a carpeted corridor the left hand wall of which was punctuated by touched-up photographs of Oxford colleges, turned a corner, went up three steps and arrived at the Blenheim Suite. Tessa squeezed past her companion, unlocked the door and entered a large sitting room with pink furnishings and a window that looked out over rooftops and chimneys. Set against a wall was a shiny mahogany desk underneath a picture of a punting scene, all willows and parasols and sun-dappled limbs. An archway led off to further rooms.

'It's lovely,' she said, turning to Bernie with a smile.

He blushed with pleasure and deposited her bags.

'If you need anything,' said Bernie gallantly, 'please don't hesitate to call down, reception will...'

'Thank you, Bernard, thank you so much. Till later.'

Still smiling she showed him to the door. Then it was unpacking time: clothes to be hung, toiletries disposed in the faux marble bathroom, laptop placed upon the mahogany desk. Superfluous pillows, cushions and bolsters chucked into a corner of the room. Mini bar checked for contents (complimentary bubbly, sauvignon blanc, mineral water). And finally taps set running for a hot bath, blue bath salts to be added later on.

Here I am back in the place where it all happened, thought Tessa as she undressed. I must watch out for ghosts. Ghosts and demons will be round every corner, lurking in doorways and smiling out from first floor windows. Just look them in the eye. Don't flinch. Hold your ground and they'll fade into their surroundings.

Naked she stepped into the steaming water.

*

An owl hooted and Meg turned her head towards the trees along the river bank from where the sound came. She was standing beside the ruined chapel, shivering a little. The owl hooted again. The voice of a departed soul, perhaps—of fair Rosamund herself, perhaps? *Sounds like an owl to me*, she could hear Conrad saying. Lovable sceptic, puncturing playfellow. He would be here soon.

Meg walked along the stone wall feeling the grass underneath her bare feet and humming softly to herself. In the evening sky one or two stars had already come out; the earth was giving up the heat of the day, in an hour or two it would be chilly. The air carried exhalations of herbs and grasses. This was Godstow nunnery, two and a half miles and a thousand years away from Oxford city centre—Meg's favourite haunt. The place was best when deserted: at such times it was possible to sense things that human presences drowned out. Songs would come to her here when she sat on the grass with her back against the wall, songs which she felt came up through the ground or out of the air, about the isle of Gramarye or a demon lover. Usually the words would come first, waiting to be clothed in music, though sometimes the story demanded a tune for a vehicle and couldn't be given birth to except by being sung so that Meg would have to bring it into the world by singing it into existence. Later, at home, she would give it a guitar accompaniment. Meg's songs were new buds on an ancient tree and if there was little originality in them she was content. A leaf that's different from all the others probably has something wrong with it.

But today she wasn't waiting for a song. She was here because this was one of the places they met, especially when Conrad had just scored and wanted to share a little dope with her, Godstow nunnery providing the perfect setting for altered states of mind. Drugs enhance the magic of this place, she thought—or maybe it's the other way around, these ruins magnify the neurochemical hit. Both statements are true, no need to prioritise. It's like those 'interactions' you're warned of when you've been prescribed painkillers: 'Alcohol to be avoided since the effect of the analgesic will be potentiated.' Does the booze potentiate the opiate or the opiate the booze? And why should any of that lead to your avoiding either? Don't you *want* them to work?

Well, there's such a thing as too much. Something she had tried to tell Conrad on occasion. There might even be too much Godstow nunnery, she supposed, though she couldn't remember ever having had a surfeit of that. Maybe her analogies were imperfect. But she was damn sure there was such a thing as too much skunk. She hoped Conrad would be bringing something milder.

'Penny for your thoughts.'

Meg cried out in surprise.

'Jesus, Con, you scared the shit out of me. Do you have to creep up on people like that?'

'I couldn't resist it, you looked so dreamy,' said Conrad, coming up to her.

'That's a reason?'

'Uh-huh.'

They kissed in the fading light, stones pressing into Meg's back, Conrad's hands on her shoulders. She moved away from the wall and pulled him down onto the grass. They kissed again.

'So?'

'So what?'

'So what were you thinking about?'

'So where's my penny?'

He felt inside his jacket pocket. 'No pennies this time, but I've brought something even nicer. A hemp derivative, the man told me.'

His deft fingers were already fiddling with rizlas, to be filled with loose tobacco and crumblings of hash, three parts to one like a gin and tonic as Conrad would say, the tobacco being the tonic.

'One for you and one for me.'

A lighter appeared and two spliffs were born. The owl hooted again, from further away now. There was a moon in the sky. Meg inhaled the sweet-smelling smoke and let her mind drift.

'There used to be nuns here, didn't there?' said Conrad after a while.

'Mm.'

'Funny sort of existence.'

'Why?'

She looked at him. In the darkness his eyes reflected the burning end of his reefer, two orange glints which blinked from time to time.

'Giving yourself in slavery to a higher power. Handing over your freedom. And then spending your days singing praises to the higher power you've just enslaved yourself to.'

'Maybe they thought that freedom wasn't such a great thing. Is it such a great thing?'

'What else is there? Doing what other people tell you to do? That was one of their vows, wasn't it—obedience, along with poverty and chastity. Ways of reducing yourself.'

'It's possible to reduce yourself by acting freely. It's possible to fuck up completely by acting freely.'

'If you're stupid. I guess if you're stupid you might need to take orders from others. And if you're really stupid perhaps you're better off not owning money or having sex. Don't want to give birth to a retard.'

Meg didn't like it when he talked like this. I should stop the conversation now, she thought, change the subject or just say nothing. But instead she said, 'So you think the nuns who lived here were all stupid?'

'Not necessarily. It might be the lesser of two evils—marrying some wrinkly old lech or taking the veil. It's free accommodation after all.'

He took a drag on his spliff, held it in for a few seconds, let out the smoke with a sigh.

'I can imagine wanting to be a nun,' said Meg softly. 'I think it might bring you closer to something.'

'Particularly if you're a lesbian.'

'Oh, shut up, Con,' she said, giving him a thump. 'You're so...'

He was gripping her by the wrist. 'Don't hit me, Meg.'

A silence fell between them. Meg felt cold.

'I...'

'Just don't do it. Don't hit me. Ever.' He let go of her wrist.

'Okay.' Her voice was small, she was shivering again.

'Let's change the subject,' he said. 'Have you ever read any Tessa Wainwright?'

The two orange glints shone at her amid the blacks and greys.

'Tessa... She wrote *The Quest*, didn't she?' Meg didn't know why they were talking about this but it was better than the other stuff. Her thoughts were hobbling, things were moving slowly. She felt heavy.

'She's written three volumes out of four. Crappy fantasy fiction. Anyway, she's staying at the Marlborough.'

'At the Marlborough?'

'Yes, madame echo, at the Marlborough. The hotel I work at. Everyone's very excited. I just wondered if you'd read any. But if you haven't I wouldn't bother, it's a pile of...'

He sneezed.

'No, I haven't,' said Meg.

'Fucking pollen,' muttered Conrad.

*

On the third day they arrived at a river. There was no ford or bridge.

'Canst thou swim, lady?' Taskar asked the princess.

'I cannot,' replied she. 'I have been brought up among the Hoshi, who swim not.'

'In that case thou must be borne by me: I will swim us both across. It were best for us to wrap our clothes in a single bundle and for thou to strap this bundle to thy back, for in this way our passage will be made swifter.'

Lemula blushed and said, 'Sir, do you ask me to go naked?'

'Blindfold me first,' replied Taskar, and he ripped a strip of cloth from his cloak and handed it to her.

*

Vince was sitting at a corner table reading a newspaper. As she approached he looked up and a smile appeared on his pockmarked face.

'Don't stand up,' Tessa said, too late. They shook hands; Vince was a bit old school for kisses and hugs. He was an ex-policeman after all.

'My dear Tessa,' he said as they sat down, using the form of address he had lit upon and stuck with since their first meeting. 'Very good to see you. I hope you had an uneventful trip? And that the hotel is satisfactory? Let me get you a drink.'

Not waiting for her answers he raised a hand and a young woman came over. It's all different, thought Tessa looking around her. They've changed everything, thank God. No ghosts here.

She asked for a glass of white wine. Vince was drinking water, of course. A bowl of olives arrived with the wine. You come all the way from Tuscany to Oxford only to find yourself eating Italian food; the olives had probably come over on the same plane as her.

'Cheers,' she said, raising her glass. 'The hotel's very comfortable, thanks. They've put me in something called the Blenheim Suite, very grand.'

Vince nodded and folded his hands in front of him on the table. He wanted to talk business.

'So how's the writing going? HarperCollins are prodding me about dates again, Tessa, it would be nice to give them a rough window. I know these things can't be hurried but if you did happen to have an idea...'

He'd once told her that his gingery moustache covered a scar and Tessa found herself as on previous occasions trying to imagine what it looked like, wondering how the hairless lip would carry the old wound. On the whole the moustache did suit him. At any rate it suited his persona, like the bow ties and the tweed jacket.

'I can't really say, Vince, but why don't you tell HarperCollins it'll be ready in time for the Christmas sales?'

'Christmas next year?'

'I think so. Look, I'll let you know how it's going—I'm hoping this trip will energise me, travelling can have that effect, you know, new scenes can stimulate the creative juices. The story's all mapped out but you'd be surprised how many details come in at the last minute.'

'Was that one of your reasons for planning this trip?'

Tessa had been vague about her reasons for travelling to England and vagueness was uncharacteristic of her. 'To see some old friends' and 'To do a book-signing or two' hardly covered it. Vince, a man of surprising penetration, sensed that something was going on inside her to which he was being denied access and this piqued him a little. But here perhaps was an answer.

'As a matter of fact it was,' replied Tessa. 'You know I don't like bothering you with the inner workings of my creative brain. I'm not totally aware of it all myself, a lot of it goes on subconsciously. And you might think it odd I should want to come to Oxford of all places, right?'

Vince knew about Alex but not about Ben. Tessa had shared only a part of that trauma with him—not even half the trauma, in other words. She couldn't yet bring herself to talk about Ben with anybody and certainly not with her agent.

'This very restaurant,' she went on, 'the one we're about to have lunch in—Alex brought me here three or four times and yet...' She held up a hand: 'No, it's fine, you haven't done wrong, I'm glad we've come here, really I am, because it's completely changed, they've completely altered it, so it's like a purging or an exorcism. To be here, I mean. Even the shapes of the rooms are different. Did they just knock down the old place and build a new one? A new Old Parsonage?'

'That'd be a good name for it,' contributed Vince. 'The New Old Parsonage.' He was trying not to sound disgusted. The thought of her affair with Alex always disgusted him. A married man having it off with a girl half his age then casually clearing out. And her own morals can't have been so pure. But so what, it was all water under the bridge.

'Well, I'm glad to think you'll be in a place where you can be inspired to write. And I'm sure millions of your fans would be glad also. The world is waiting with bated breath, Tessa.'

'I hope they don't suffocate. But tell me what you've been up to, Vince. How's life? How's publishing?'

'Publishing... The same old racket. No better than it should be. But there's still talent around if you have a nose for it.'

'Which you do?'

'You're witness to that, my dear Tessa. Yes, I flatter myself I have some powers of detection, some sort of intuition as regards—as regards...'

'As regards what'll sell?'

'I was going to say as regards the reading public, but it boils down to the same thing.'

Vince had taken early retirement from the police force about fifteen years ago, had tried this and that without much success and had seemed almost to have run out of options when an old friend introduced him to someone who ran a small-scale literary agency. As a favour to the old friend this person agreed to take Vince on in an apprentice role, in which capacity he had shown considerable promise. After a while Vince, always a restless man and by now having made the requisite connections, decided to go solo. Almost immediately he had the ridiculous good fortune of landing Tessa Wainwright as a client. She'd been turned down by six other agents before she approached him—how they must have kicked themselves! Vince thought he was taking a punt at the time and so he was, but it was the best punt he'd ever taken by a long shot and among other things enabled him to look former colleagues in the eye whose gaze he'd been inclined to avoid since the time of his departure in somewhat hazy circumstances from the Met. Look at me now, he'd exclaim to them inwardly, this is what success looks like. If there isn't room in the force for a man with initiative, that man will simply take his initiative elsewhere, shaking the dust from his feet. See if he doesn't. A man with initiative will carve out his own destiny. Spare me the timid legalistic types, officious with their red tape and their stupid regulations—I don't need them, I can go my own way. Have done, in fact.

So he felt grateful to Tessa, grateful and at the same time protective. Her talent, her brand, needed protecting for it was a cut-throat world out there: envy and malice lay in wait for the famous and successful, ready to pounce, especially when they were as innocent as he was sure Tessa Wainwright was. His job was to guard her. He was a sort of bodyguard, it occurred to him.

'You remember about tomorrow afternoon?' he said.

'Remind me.'

'You're giving a talk at a school. *How to Become a Writer* is how they've advertised it, but I imagine the children will want to know all about Taskar's adventures among the Hoshi. You'll be careful not to give too much away, won't you? They're to wait till the book comes out.'

She smiled. 'I'll be like the sphinx. What sort of age group?'

'Eleven to sixteen, I think.'

'Girls and boys?'

'Yes.'

'The girls will want to know about Taskar's sister.'

Vince winced. 'Do keep your voice down, Tessa. Even walls have ears.'

'I bet most of them have already guessed who Princess Lemula is,' she laughed.

'If they've guessed that they've guessed everything, haven't they?'

'Not *everything*. For instance...'

'Shall we order food?' he said firmly.

'Dear Vince, you worry too much. Anyway,' she said picking up a menu, 'this talk: what time does it start? And what's the school?'

*

Conrad generally parked his motorbike round the back of the hotel where it was 'out of the way'. The phrase was Bernie's. It meant 'won't be seen or bumped into by guests'. The trouble was, it might be bumped into by the guys taking the rubbish out since there was only just room for a wheelie bin to get past a Triumph Scrambler and sometimes Conrad found his bike a few feet or even yards from where he'd left it, undamaged, okay, but still moved. He didn't like the idea of other people touching his stuff, didn't like it at all, but there was nothing much he could do. Today he got off his bike and pushed it tightly in against the wall then, removing his helmet, made for the tradesmen's entrance (as Bernie called it). Just beyond the steps up to the door stood a large blue wheelie bin. Conrad gave it a vicious kick before entering the building.

'Hi, Conrad,' said Tina, one of the kitchen staff. She was heading for the door he'd just come in by, holding a packet of cigarettes. 'Pete's been looking for you.'

'Off for a cancer break?' said Conrad.

'You can talk, pothead.'

Conrad went to change out of his leathers and into his waiter's outfit. His evening shift started in half an hour. He might see the author of *The Quest* at dinner, unless she preferred the haute cuisine of the Cherwell Boathouse or something ethnic on the Cowley Road. Crossing the lobby to reception he spotted Pete through the open door of his office and since no one else was around whistled the opening bars of *The Ride of the Valkyries*. Pete turned his head with a frown and beckoned him in.

'I don't think Bernie would approve of that,' said Pete, closing the door.

'Doesn't he like Wagner?'

'He doesn't like members of staff drawing attention to themselves, as well you know. Sit down, I've got news.'

Conrad threw himself into the green armchair while Pete got out the whisky and a couple of glasses.

'Do you ever water that thing?' said Conrad, nodding towards the pot plant in the corner.

'Yes,' said Pete handing him a tumbler, 'but why don't you shut up for a minute while I bring you up to date? Wainwright will be off the premises tomorrow afternoon. The coast'll be clear. Have you got a memory stick?'

'Several.'

Pete looked at him. Legs stretched out in front of him, half-closed eyes lending his face an expression of boredom—a picture of self-satisfied ennui.

'Do you want to do this thing, Conrad? Or have you tired of the idea already?' Pete was evidently feeling twitchy.

'Take it easy, man. If my calmness distresses you, reflect upon the advantages of a regular heartbeat for those engaged in hazardous enterprises.' He drank some whisky. 'It's the nervous types who fuck up. And stop walking up and down, will you.'

Pete stood still.

'What time is she going out?' Conrad continued. 'For how long? And where's she going?'

'She came up to me earlier today to ask where Hillgrove Academy is and whether it was worth booking a taxi to get there. She said she's giving a talk there tomorrow at 2.30 so I've booked her a taxi to pick her up at 2.15. I imagine she'll be out for at least an hour.'

'Fine.' Conrad downed his drink. 'Let's meet outside her room at 2.30. The Blenheim Suite, right?'

'Yes, fourth floor.'

'It's the penthouse job, isn't it?'

'No, that's on the fifth floor.'

'I didn't know we had five.'

'That's because you're unobservant.'

'Is it easy to find?'

'Just turn left out of the lift and follow the corridor to the end. I can take you.'

'No, we should go separately. In fact, why don't you arrive a bit before me so that if anyone bumps into me I can say I'm looking for you—to lend you a book you were asking about, say.'

'And what's my story if someone bumps into me?'

'Somebody rang for Wainwright via reception leaving an urgent message which you wrote down and thought best to leave on Ms Wainwright's desk to ensure receipt.'

'Merrivale, you're a genius,' said Pete. The conference was over.

At dinner she appeared. Conrad was conveying two soups of the day (cream of asparagus) to table seven when he caught sight of her being conducted to table twelve by 'hipster' Hugo. It was eight o'clock. She was wearing dark glasses and a white bolero jacket over a blue dress. As she sat down she removed the glasses.

How did I know it was her? he later asked himself. I just did. Well, she was the right sort of age, intelligent looking, could easily be a writer... It was none of that. I knew it was her when our eyes met. It was as if we recognised one another—or rather recognised what the other person meant, what they signified. At that moment each of us was a piece of text that only the other could read.

He stood in the kitchen, eyes closed, a little dizzy. Maybe I need a toke of something, he thought. Or a line. This is ridiculous, it's just a middle-aged woman, fairly nondescript, dark hair streaked with grey, high cheekbones, nothing special. The image of her on my retina is nothing but an array of neuronal stimuli, without depth or meaning. Rods and cones, electrochemical buzzing.

'Conrad, are you all right?'

He turned around. It was Tina.

'You look kind of sick.'

'Tina, who's the woman at table twelve?'

Tina peered through the porthole in the door. 'That's Tessa Wainwright, you idiot.'

'I knew that, I was just testing you.' He smiled feebly.

'You need to do less drugs,' she said walking off.

That night he dreamt of his mother.

III

'THIS IS A PORTRAIT OF Taras Shevchenko—a self-portrait, actually. He was a Ukrainian poet and painter of the early part of the nineteenth century. And that's one of his poems translated into English, with a response by one of the ninth years.'

'A response?'

'Yes, they were told to write—to express whatever the Shevchenko made them feel, you know, about the topic or about the poet himself or anything else. This one's by Bella Freeman, she's very good, you'll see her at your talk.'

Tessa was being shown around the school by the Head of English, Mrs Adcock. I can imagine the nicknames, thought Tessa. Teachers' surnames come on a scale and hers is fairly near the top. One of Tessa's own teachers had been a Mr De'Ath. Children are cruel, hence the need to educate them in compassion by means such as this one: a project on Ukraine, the innocent victim of Russian aggression not so long ago, when news reports echoed with unfamiliar names, Mariupol, Bucha,

Kharkiv, and grave-faced pundits discussed the like-lihood of nuclear war. Along the walls of the corridor were posters, artworks, maps, poems, news cuttings. Tessa was impressed. If the ninth years absorbed all of this they'd be ready for the diplomatic corps. From the twelfth century to the present day the history of Ukraine was laid out, complete with depictions of Cossack dress and photos of a rock group called Boombox. Only de-scriptions of Ukrainian cuisine appeared to be missing and perhaps there was a reason for that.

The two women were alone in the corridor; students and staff were shut away in classrooms. Occasionally a murmur of voices could be heard or a muffled peal of laughter.

Mrs Adcock, tall and thin and wearing powerful lip-stick, pointed to another portrait and said 'Taras Bulba'.

'Another Taras.'

'It's a common boy's name. He was the Cossack hero of a novel by Gogol, semi-mythical.'

'What does he do? In the novel?'

'He and his sons go to fight against the Poles. The Cossacks were a very martial people. Are, I should say. That's his shashka, his sabre.'

Tessa inspected the picture. Looks good and sharp, she thought. Not sure if that'll teach the ninth years much compassion. Then it occurred to her that Taskar might carry just such a thing for use on Hoshi.

Mrs Adcock was looking at her watch. 'Well, I think we'd better be getting down to the hall now, Miss

Wainwright, if that's all right with you. I hope you've enjoyed this...'

'It's very impressive,' said Tessa, 'and obviously involved a lot of effort. Well done. I really think I could spend hours in this corridor.'

Mrs Adcock's smile was uncertain. I don't know if I meant it either, thought Tessa, it just came out like that. She followed the Head of English down a flight of stairs and across a sort of atrium to a large pair of double doors which when opened revealed the school hall. To the left was the stage on which a couple of lecterns kept their distance from one another. In the body of the hall were about two hundred and fifty empty chairs and at the back an upright piano looked out from the shadows. Huge windows let in the light.

'Where would you like me to be?' asked Tessa.

'It's totally up to you,' replied Mrs Adcock. 'Both lecterns have working microphones. They can be shifted if you want to be more central.'

'I think a lectern might be a bit formal—I don't have anything written down, you know, I'll just be ad libbing. Maybe I could sit on the edge of the stage?'

Mrs Adcock raised an eyebrow. 'I'm not sure you'll be heard at the back of the hall, the acoustics are quite—erm...'

Tessa had walked over to the stage and with easy athleticism hoisted herself up onto it. She sat in her jeans and jacket, hands on the edge of the stage, and looking out into the hall declaimed, 'The rain in Spain falls mainly on the plain.' Simultaneously the first trickle of students began to appear, entering through the big double doors: teenagers in green and grey uniforms, the boys wearing ties and trousers, the girls wearing skirts of varying lengths with black stockings. Two or three stared openly at the visitor—ogled might be a better word—others whispered and giggled as they took their seats. Over the next few minutes the trickle grew, turning into a stream and eventually into a flood which spread throughout the hall as over a flood plain, the sound of the deluge mounting by degrees until Mrs Adcock had to come up close to Tessa and raise her voice to say: 'I'll just say a few introductory words then it's over to you, is that all right?' Tessa nodded and Mrs Adcock retreated to one side. At this point Tessa made out several other teachers placed at strategic intervals, mainly along the aisles. Like sheepdogs, she thought.

How to Become a Writer was a topic she ought to know all about. In fact however she wasn't at all sure how it had happened; she hadn't really been paying attention. Vince would have been able to give a better account than she, of how the manuscript had first landed in his inbox, of how he'd told her which bits to tighten up and which to fluff up... eventually of how he'd instructed her what (not) to say to the press, when to demand a bigger percentage in royalties, which film adaptation proposals to listen to and all the rest of it. He'd have the whole story pat, would Vince. So it seemed obvious for her to begin her talk that way: 'My literary agent is a man called Vincent Parker and if he were here now he could do a much better job than me...' After which she just went with the flow, exactly as she did when sitting at her desk writing about Taskar's adventures with Princess Lemula. Don't think too much about what you're doing and the story comes of itself. Sure enough, the faces that looked out at her were rapt, the students of Hillgrove Academy were putty in her hands and she found herself wielding the magic power of the storyteller even though the story was simply the chronicle of a middle-class middle-aged writer of fantasy fiction, more than averagely successful and now visiting the UK for the first time in fifteen years, the fourth volume of a tetralogy in her pocket and a hope of love and reconciliation burning in her heart... Not that she said that last bit, she wasn't so incontinent. But the rest of the story seemed to be good enough: at the end, her audience applauded her to the rafters ('Don't avoid a cliché if it feels right,' she had advised them) and Mrs Adcock's vote of thanks was effusive.

'And now if anyone's got any questions, I'm sure Tessa will be happy to answer them. Try to keep your question brief.'

Four or five hands went up.

'Charlie,' said Mrs Adcock pointing to a gangly youth with an elaborately skewed tie.

'I was just wondering...' started the boy. His neighbour nudged him and there was some stifled horseplay. Regaining his composure the boy went on: 'Which of your books has, like, earned the most? And how much did it make?'

'Well,' said Tessa, 'I think the next one's going to make the most money. After that—*The Escape*, probably, though I can't remember the exact figure. But I wouldn't advise anyone starting on a writing career to think about financial returns. Much better to write because you enjoy writing.'

'An excellent answer,' opined Mrs Adcock. Then pointing to a girl in the front row: 'Bella.' Author of the response to Shevchenko, thought Tessa.

'Thanks for your talk, that was really interesting,' said the girl, neat and blonde and blinking. She looked down at a piece of paper, looked up again. 'I'd like to ask you about where you get your inspiration from and whether works like the Norse epics or the Kalevala have had an influence on your writing.'

'The Kalevala?' said Tessa. 'It's Finnish, isn't it. I haven't read it, I'm afraid. I think I read some Norse myths as a girl—Thor and Loki and people. . . I don't know where my ideas come from, to tell you the truth. It's a mystery. I think you'll find other writers saying the same thing. That's not very helpful, is it?'

Bella Freeman returned a puzzled smile and blinked a couple of times.

'Fatima,' put in Mrs Adcock and an Asian girl with a headscarf stood up and cleared her throat. In a quiet voice she said, 'Can I ask if you've got any children, miss?'

Tessa looked up at the ceiling, the faraway ceiling, and thought to herself *I should have expected this question.*

'Children…' she said musingly. *They'll think I've forgotten. Crazy old woman can't remember if she's got any children. It's slipped her mind, like the year she was born or where she left her house keys.*

'It's like this, Fatima,' she said at last. 'Twenty years ago or thereabouts I gave birth to a little boy. But…' She stopped. There was silence in the hall.

'Oh, I'm sorry, miss,' said the girl.

*

When Conrad arrived at the door of the Blenheim Suite holding a copy of *Hard Times* Pete was nowhere to be seen. Conrad consulted his watch: 2.34 p.m. He can't have come and gone, can he? *A 2.30 rendezvous is a 2.30 rendezvous* Conrad heard Pete's voice saying. (Pursed lips, shake of the head.) On the other hand maybe he'd been delayed. Conrad had gone straight for the lift, avoiding reception; perhaps even now Pete was struggling to free himself from the clutches of some dawdling buffer asking about the opening times of museums or whether the hotel offered a dry cleaning service.

The doorknob turned. Conrad moved quickly away and for want of anything better buried himself in the Dickens.

'What the fuck are you doing?' hissed Pete through the crack in the doorway. He opened the door to let Conrad in.

'Here's that book I was telling you about,' said Conrad as the door closed behind him. Pete took it and pocketed it. 'Top marks for verisimilitude,' remarked Conrad.

He looked around him. The white bolero jacket from yesterday evening was thrown over the back of a chair; a coffee cup sat in its saucer on a glass-topped table. Against one wall stood a mahogany desk upon which was an open laptop.

'Bingo,' murmured Conrad. He walked over to the desk, took the memory stick and his phone out of his trouser pockets and placed them next to the computer. Seating himself in front of the desk he raised the laptop to inspect its base. There was the serial number. He took a picture of it with his phone then inverted and opened the laptop and to Pete's irritation began humming. In went the memory stick, up came a list of recently opened documents: *bank, ben, house, medical, plans, tas-kar(1), taskar(2), vince.*

'Anything there?' asked Pete.

'I'd say so. We can open them all up later. I imagine the taskar documents will provide some interesting material.'

It took a couple of minutes to copy the documents. Pete stood behind Conrad and peered over his shoulder. Conrad could sense his nervousness in the shallow breathing and the white-knuckled grip of his hand on the back of the chair.

'Mission accomplished,' he said at last, removing the memory stick from the laptop and getting up from his seat.

At that moment there was a knock at the door. The two men froze, staring at each other. The knock was repeated. Pete's mouth was working, opening and closing;

Conrad thought of goldfish. Finally there was a third knock, followed by a female voice: 'Pete—are you in there?' and at once Pete had bounded over to the door and pulled it open. It was Tina.

'You said you'd just be five minutes, it's quarter to now and I have to...'

Her eyes fell on Conrad, perched on an arm of the sofa and observing her coolly.

'Why are you...' began Tina. She looked from Conrad to Pete and back again.

'Conrad caught up with me to lend me this book,' said Pete, pulling *Hard Times* from his pocket and holding it up for her inspection.

'Yeah, I saw Pete getting into the lift so jumped in with him,' explained Conrad. 'We'd been discussing Dickens a few days ago and I said if he read anything by him it should be *Hard Times* since in *Hard Times* you get a level of psychological realism which you simply don't find in...'

'Have you finished whatever you're doing, Pete?' interrupted Tina. 'Cos I have to be somewhere at three.'

'Sure, sure,' said Pete, 'I've left the message for Ms Wainwright, we can go now... Thanks for covering for me, Tina, and I'm sorry I took longer than I—than...'

'Whatever,' said Tina turning to go. 'It's my yoga class, I have to be there at three. I don't like to be late.' She was down the steps and had turned the corner into the corridor and they could hear her receding voice explaining why it was important that she should catch the bus in time to get to her class in Blackbird Leys, the teacher

was very insistent they should start on time, some people she could name were unpunctual but she… Finally
and in the distance came the *ping* of the lift arriving to
take Tina away, followed by the sound of the lift doors
closing.

'Yoga,' drawled Conrad. Then turning to Pete: 'Why
did you tell her you'd only be five minutes? That was
pretty stupid.'

'Let's get out of here,' replied Pete. 'I need to get back
to reception. Have you got the memory stick?'

'No, I threw it out of the window, didn't you see me?'

Conrad followed his companion out of the Blenheim Suite and stood by while Pete locked the door.
They took the lift separately, Pete first. Later as Conrad
walked to Meg's he felt the memory stick in his pocket,
turning it around in his fingers, stroking it secretly. Two
thousand pounds starting price. Roll up, roll up, Mervin
of the Mirror, Stevie of the Sun, who's going to be the
lucky recipient of this 24-carat scoop, we ask?

*

Meg rented a room in a shared house in Jericho. It was
an attic room, accessed by a retractable ladder and boast-
ing an excellent view of the heavens through its single
skylight. Hot in summer, cold in winter, patronised by
clothes moths but cosy and characterfully furnished:
the rugs, shawls, lacquered tables, guitar in the corner,
collection of seashells, candle in a bottle and disused
hookah all spoke of Meg, of her hippy leanings and her

tendency to forage. A beanbag and a three-legged stool provided the only seating.

Stretched out on the double futon, one ankle resting on the other, Conrad lay smoking a joint. Meg sat cross-legged on the floor beside him. Out of a speaker on a shelf came the voices of Beggars in Clover, a floaty soprano entwined with a gravelly baritone: *Babe, I'm gonna leave you...*

'Why's she gonna leave him?'

'I think it's a he,' said Meg.

'Why's he gonna leave her, then? Or perhaps he's gonna leave him. Who knows what the genders are— probably it's an it. It's gonna leave it. Maybe it's the same it, it's gonna leave itself.'

'A soliloquy.'

'Exactly. Poor little it, about to be deserted by itself. Left all alone. So alone, so completely and utterly alone, it won't even be there any more! Wow...'

He stared up at the pitched ceiling, smoke rising from his spliff.

'It's a he leaving a her, actually,' said Meg. 'He's got itchy feet.'

Conrad took a drag. 'Like Siegfried.'

Babe, I got to ramble, my feet start going down and I got to follow...

'Or Faust,' he added. 'He wants to have more experiences, cross more lines. Going where his feet go, going down... Stop it!'

She had stretched out a hand to his socked feet and was tickling the top one.

'Just seeing if you've got itchy feet.'

'I'm not ticklish,' he informed her. 'And if I get itchy feet I'll let you know.'

'I'm sure you will,' she said withdrawing her hand. 'I bet you're surrounded by admirers at college—must be tempting.'

'Pah. Too young, too innocent. You know I prefer older women.' She held out a hand and he passed her the spliff. 'Nineteen-year-old girls are like raw chicken. I prefer my meat cooked.'

'Hot and firm, you mean.'

'Exactly,' he said retrieving the joint. 'And succulent.'

'Salty?'

'Don't be dirty minded. She's got a nice voice,' he said jumping topic, 'but in the end the music's too shallow, too—benign. Even if they're singing about heartbreak. There's no real darkness.'

'You want something properly miserable?'

'No,' he said carefully, 'not miserable. But in great music you hear madness, disease. Fever and the threat of disintegration.'

'Why would you want to hear those things?'

'Because they're real. Everything else is cosy make-believe. Pink frills and stupid silhouettes against a stupid sunset.'

Meg stood up. 'I'm going to make some tea,' she said walking over to an electric kettle. Plump, barefoot, wearing jeans and a t-shirt, her cropped hair currently purple, Meg moved unhastily between kettle and tap, mugs and cupboard. Conrad watched her with satisfaction.

Eight years his senior, she must have felt she was lucky to have him. Sometimes when they stood together in front of the bathroom mirror he'd point to the tiny lines that were beginning to appear around her eyes and say 'Crone'; then when she pushed him away, add delightedly, 'But I like it! I like that you're a crone.' It would have been better still if she'd been in her thirties or forties. A middle-aged woman: complicated, good in bed—above all grateful.

She brought the tea over, lapsang for him, camomile for her. Beggars in Clover were on to another song—*Ah, why do you weep, my fair young maid, weep it for your golden store?*

Meg settled beside him and they held hands.

Or do you weep for your house carpenter who never you shall see any more?...

'Have you seen Tessa Wainwright yet?' she asked after a while.

'Yeah, she dined in the restaurant last night.'

'What's she like?'

'Writes crappy fiction.'

'I mean what does she look like?'

He shrugged. 'Just another middle-aged woman.' He closed his eyes and thought to himself: wearing a white bolero jacket and dark glasses. And a blue dress.

'Must be funny being that famous,' said Meg.

'What d'you mean?'

'Everyone's interested in you, everyone wants a piece of you—you become public property in a way. It must be hard to hang on to your privacy.'

'It's the deal you make. If you aim for fame...'

'...you become fair game.'

'Very poetic.'

'But it's not true. A human being can't become fair game. And nobody makes that "deal". That "deal" is an invention of journalists, it's the excuse they make to themselves for being nosey shits.'

Conrad sat up and began rolling another joint. 'Seems to me the author and the journalist are in the same boat. They're both going after money and limelight.'

'They might or might not be. Even if they are, it doesn't mean that one of them can treat the other as—as just a source of revenue. As some sort of milch cow. A human being is a human being.'

'Well, that's certainly true,' murmured Conrad lighting his spliff. 'You've really put your finger on it there, Meg.'

'But Con, surely you agree,' she said, exasperated; 'just because someone writes a successful novel doesn't mean they can be preyed on. Does it?'

He looked at her. 'Yes. It does. And she will be preyed on. And there's nothing she can do about it. And the earth will continue turning on its axis.' He took a drag on the spliff. 'Get over it.'

Meg's face was crumpling. Time of the month, thought Conrad.

'Look, sweetheart, there are more things in heaven and earth than are dreamt of in your soft-hearted puritanical philosophy, and it's even possible that you personally will benefit from wicked intrusions made upon the privacy of Tessa Wainwright.'

'What do you mean?' she sniffed.

'Have a toke,' he said offering her the joint.

'But what do you mean?' she repeated.

'Nothing much.' He lay back on the futon. 'Just something to do with the receptionist at the Marlborough. Guy called Pete. He seems to have his fingers in a number of pies. I wouldn't be surprised if—well, we shall see. It's all up in the air.'

'Sometimes you don't make any sense.'

'I know,' he said.

*

Tessa entered South Park by the entrance on Morrell Avenue and struck out across the huge sloping lawn that leads uphill towards distant trees and the invisible horizon, her thoughts on Charlie and Bella and Fatima and the conundrum of unparenthood. All those children, those teenagers, had reminded her of what she knew already: that she was an unparent, that she had been unparented—or had unparented herself—at the moment she had taken the road into solitude and begun to put an ever-increasing distance between herself and Ben. When had that moment been? Should she date it from the point at which Alex was granted custody? Or earlier, when somebody was doing things through her, acting through her body, using her hands and fingers, the incubus, the Svengali? Or earlier still, on day three, when the black cloud descended? *Post-natal depression* they called it, a condition affecting more than 10% of mothers, not to be confused with 'baby blues', certainly not something to feel guilty about Mrs Wainwright, sorry, Miss Wainwright, even if you do feel you can't love him (or anyone else) and even if you do sometimes feel suicidal. These things will pass, they will surely pass. They did, but too late.

She had had all these thoughts a hundred times before. They led nowhere, were a waste of time, waste of tears. And anyway. Anyway what? Anyway this: the past is going to be atoned for, it will be covered over and buried, dispensed with altogether and forgotten, when Ben and I meet again. For then we will embrace and kiss one another; he will tell me about himself, his life, who he is and where he's going. And this will all happen in a few days' time, on Friday afternoon.

She was near the top of the hill, with Morrell Avenue to her right, South Park stretching away on her left. A few hundred yards off was a children's play area in which she could make out a single male figure pushing a toddler on a swing. As she approached them, Morrell Avenue turned into Warneford Lane and she realised that if she turned her head to the right she would see the walls of the Warneford Hospital in which she had once spent a few drugged-up days and nights getting the incubus exorcised. Ben had been about ten days old.

Don't think about it, focus on what's in front of you, that man pushing his daughter on a swing, that dog-walker in the distance. Tall trees, summer foliage. Listen to the birdsong. And here comes an ambulance, and it's turning into the gates of the Warneford, delivering someone up to the doctors.

Tessa broke into a run, veering away from the road, skirting the play area and leaving it behind her. Ahead of her on the grass lay a young couple. *Dallying*, she thought, homing in on the archaic word, isn't that what young couples do? Dallying or worse. She slowed down to a trot, then a walk. Summer dalliance, autumn pregnancy. Ben had been born in March. Okay, heart, you can stop beating so hard, the danger is over now. She smiled a friendly smile at the young couple and the girl smiled back. The world is a benign place if you only have a mind to enjoy it. That's the sort of thing dead Alex would have said.

Will we talk about his father? Of course, why not? He'll want to know things. I'll want to know things. Whatever his faults, Alex is a key figure in both our lives. He looms.

She stood still, took some good deep breaths, felt the sun on her face. That Fatima seemed a sweet girl, I hope I didn't alarm her. God knows what rumour will have started up. *What's all this about a stillbirth?* she could hear Vince saying. Maybe I'll have to tell him the truth one of these days, she thought, he won't much like it but it could be for the best. It'd mean he was in a position to deny what's actually deniable for one thing.

The thought of Vince produced a pang of guilt. I must get back to the hotel, get back to work. Four more chapters to write and Taskar's story will be complete; his quest will be over. My editor at HarperCollins will be rubbing her hands. Soon queues of fans will form out-side bookshops in the early morning.

She turned her steps back downhill towards town.

*

Conrad poured himself a whisky and turned up the volume. Siegfried's Death and Funeral Music, from Act Three of *Götterdämmerung*: music to hammer the soul, hammer the incandescent soul into shape. The hero, treacherously slain, is borne upon his shield away into the mists. Conrad sliced the air with his free hand in time to the march's cataclysmic tread, with his other hand brought the tumbler to his lips. Beside him on the sofa sat his laptop in readiness.

It was late. Nearly midnight. The evening shift had been more tiring than usual, with several demanding diners and a new chef in the kitchen, apparently bipolar as well as tipsy. TW hadn't made an appearance. Conrad was mildly disappointed; he would have liked to have observed someone upon whose personal space he had, unknown to her, so casually trespassed. He imagined her innocent eyes smiling at him—smiling at the very man who was violating her and who stood to gain from the violation. He would have smiled back of course, all eager servility. A shame she hadn't turned up.

Now he was preparing to do some research on fantasy literature. The memory stick was poised on the arm of the sofa. A naked light bulb hung from the centre of the ceiling—one day he would get a shade for it—and an ashtray was at his feet. The living room and kitchen of his flat were ensuite and the smell of bacon hung around him in the air; he could have grabbed some food at the hotel, that was a perk of the job, but the atmosphere around the new chef had decided him against that and he'd made do with beans, bacon and half a Scotch bonnet. His mouth still burnt pleasantly. Scotch bonnet followed by Scotch whisky, Caledonian incendiarism. Chillies were a drug, he reflected, intense and consciousness-expanding, even mildly psychoactive. Yet available in Tesco's.

He took a sip of whisky. This was what they called deferred gratification. He was putting off opening the Wainwright files, putting off the delicious discovery which would enable him not only to pay off a debt to a rather unpleasant Reading trader but also to invest in some fairly serious bingeing on his own account. Might get Meg a present, too. What would she like? A box seat at the opera, ha ha.

Eventually he put the whisky down next to the ashtray and drew the computer towards him. All right, here we go—give up your secrets, little memory stick, give us the gen. A moment later the list popped up on screen: *bank, ben, house, medical, plans, taskar(1), taskar(2), vince*. He was on the point of clicking on *taskar(1)* when it occurred to him it might be nice to start elsewhere. One mustn't rush these things. Call it foreplay if you will, beating about the bush a bit, having a reccy of the old girl's hinterland. Who knows what you might find? *bank* would reveal just how stinking rich she was, he supposed. Might also contain some potentially useful passwords. *medical* would cast light on any illnesses or procedures she might have suffered or undergone. *house* sounded as if it would be boring. I'll take a look at *bank*, he thought, then at the last moment, he wasn't sure why, he dragged the cursor down a line and clicked.

Twenty minutes later he was on the phone to Pete.

IV

PETE HADN'T TAKEN KINDLY TO being phoned after midnight, alleging that Conrad had broken into a beautiful dream to which he would never now return and demanding to know what sort of emergency could possibly justify this intrusion.

'And what's that racket in the background?'

'The entrance of the gods into Valhalla from *Rheingold*,' Conrad replied. He soon realised that Pete was not in a sufficiently receptive state so organised with him to meet up the next day, when he would reveal to his friend both the contents of a document named *ben* and his own notions as to how they should proceed. Grumpily Pete had agreed. Now the two of them were closeted in Pete's office, a black coffee apiece, and Conrad was explaining matters. It was mid-morning and hotel traffic was low; guests were out and about, no one was likely to be checking in and Pete had closed the door against the world.

'So not only is she having an affair with Alex Delaney, Minister of the Crown and a married man, but she goes and gets pregnant by him. The result: a boy baby called Ben, loveliest little item in the world apparently, at least from the perspective of an older and a wiser Wainwright.'

'I wonder why she didn't have an abortion.'

'Beats me. But I often wonder that about other people's parents. The nub of our story, however, lies in what happens immediately after the birth. Three days in and she falls into a deep depression.'

'Poor kid.'

'Yeah. And while in said depression, guess what she does?'

'I don't know—finds God and becomes a Mormon?'

'Much better than that.' Conrad grinned. 'She tries to kill him.'

'Kill who?'

'Little Ben, of course. Gets a pillow and shoves it on his face, tries to smother the life out of him and would have succeeded if a passing nurse hadn't noticed what was going on and come to the rescue. The young mother, would-be infanticide and future world-famous novelist, is taken in hand needless to say, while the errant father is none too pleased and subsequently gets custody of the child, his good wife standing by her man and welcoming the little critter into the bosom of the family.'

Pete clicked his tongue and shook his head. 'What a sorry story. Why d'you think she wrote it all down?'

Conrad shrugged. 'A sort of diary—or getting it off her chest—whatever. The point is we know about it now.'

He leaned back in his armchair and did what Pete had never before seen him do: he winked.

'What are you on about?' There was incredulity in Pete's voice.

'Well...If we sell the plot of the book to the papers we get a lump sum, a one-off payment, non-repeatable. Whereas if we contact Miss Wainwright and inform her that we are in possession of certain biographical details which, were they to become public, might have a negative impact on her reputation as a writer many if not most of whose fans are children...'

'Bloody hell, Conrad, are you suggesting blackmailing her?'

Pete stared down at him, the fingers of his left hand twitching.

'Take it easy, old man, and do try not to shout, people might be within earshot.' Conrad reached for his coffee. 'As I was saying, it's a choice between a one-off payment and something more like an income. Potentially.' He took a sip. 'From someone who can easily afford it, by the way.'

'You can't be serious.'

Conrad frowned. 'Actually it's you who can't be serious, Pete, you and everyone else who thinks that life is a game of Happy Families. Life is an individual consciousness that lasts from time A to time B. It's a series of experiences which the Subject has the power to render pleasant or painful. That's serious, that's the bottom line.'

'What about other people's experiences?'

'Not my business. I'm sure the feeling is mutual. Now are you on board or not?'

Pete turned his gaze for a second towards the photo of the Queen as if consulting a higher power, then said: 'We had a perfectly good plan. A bit dodgy but not against the law as far as I know. Blackmail is definitely against the law.'

'The law!' said Conrad, his mouth twisted. 'Bogey-man of slaves. I break the law all the time, don't feel any the worse for it. What you and your kind get up to used to be against the law, that didn't make it evil, or d'you think it did?'

Pete ignored the jibe. 'If you get caught you go to jail. I don't want to go to jail. Simple as that.'

Conrad sighed. 'You're wetter than I thought. Well, it's your decision. I'm not going to beg you on my knees. I'm sure I can manage a thing like this on my own.' He stood up. 'Just a word of advice, though. If at some point I were to receive a visit from the police as a result of some sort of tip-off, I would naturally have to mention the part played by the kind person who let me into the Blenheim Suite and stood by while I transferred all those documents. Tina would be able to identify him.'

He made for the door. Pete didn't try to stop him.

*

Conrad sat on a bench in Florence Park, that network of paths, avenues, rills and flowerbeds that a rich councillor once donated to the city in memory of his sister Flo. A footpath ran parallel to the bench a few yards in front of him along which people of various ages, sizes and costumes walked, jogged or illicitly cycled. Every now and then one of them, usually of an older vintage, would wish him good day or the equivalent. Conrad ignored them. He was mulling. Pete really was hopeless—spineless and hopeless and altogether useless. Or rather he had outlived his usefulness, so that his effective resignation from the project was probably something to be grateful for; any proceeds arising out of it could now justly be viewed as the property of the sole remaining project director, regardless of how those proceeds were obtained.

It was important to state this latter principle insofar as Conrad was beginning to see the advantages of adopting both plan A and plan B: both the dodgy and the illegal, in Pete's terminology. True, plan A had originally involved Pete, and any payment coming from the *Mirror* or whichever rag bought the story would originally have been shared between the two of them. But it was clear Pete couldn't be trusted; he was nervy and subject to random moral scruples, and to keep him in the loop in any way would be dangerous. Moreover, Conrad had the memory stick and what was on it. Didn't they say possession was nine tenths of the law?

If plan A failed plan B might still succeed and vice versa. There was also the fact that the execution of plan A could be used to enhance plan B's chances of success: if TW saw that he (and who, she'd wonder, is this *he*?) was capable of getting the denouement of *The Quest* into the papers, she might decide he was capable of doing the same thing for her deranged attempt to kill her own son. All things considered he might as well keep plan A on the boil. It followed that he should get back in touch with Mervin Carroll asap. Problem was, he hadn't yet got round to inspecting the *taskar* documents. The excitement of encountering a true and sordid story had eclipsed the intention to investigate a fictional and no doubt heart-warming one. But he had the PC's serial number and that was enough to be getting on with. Carroll could go away and ascertain Conrad's bona fides and by the time they talked again Conrad would have at least a rough idea of the manner in which the much-loved tetralogy of the century was finally to cross, panting and exhausted, the finishing line.

He got out his phone and dialled. As he did so a small child approached him, a boy of four or five wearing a denim onesie. The boy planted himself a few feet away and stared. His mother, one hand on a pushchair in which another child lolled and kicked her feet, was engaged in conversation with a woman in a tracksuit and seemed oblivious of her son's doings. The little fellow continued to stare. Conrad was beginning to find his presence irksome. When Mervin Carroll came on the line Conrad twisted his body 90 degrees so as to get the brat out of his field of vision and said, 'Mr Carroll? It's Mr Jones here.'

'Who?'

'Mr Jones—we talked a few days ago. Tessa Wainwright. Volume four of *The Quest.*'

The denim onesie had sidled into view. Conrad twisted back 180 degrees.

'Ah yes. You said you wanted to sell me some information. Obtained from a personal computer.'

'Of which I now have the serial number, so if you'd like to...'

'Could you just hold the line for a moment?'

Muffled voices, a pause, voices again, a click. Carroll came back on the phone. 'Fire away,' he said.

Conrad hadn't liked that click. He decided to play it cool.

'Mr Carroll, I wonder if it wouldn't be best for us to meet in person so as to discuss things tête à tête? I prefer not to convey valuable information via telephone.'

'What's your asking price?'

'As I say, I would prefer...' He felt a hot breath on the back of his neck and wheeled round. The little brat had clambered up onto the bench beside him—the grinning face with its freckles and snotty upper lip was just inches away from his own. Jumping up from the bench Conrad yelled, 'Get the fuck away from me!' The boy began to wail.

'What's going on?' asked Carroll.

'Nothing, nothing, just a... I'm in a park and there was a dog...' Conrad was walking swiftly away from the distressed child. Looking over his shoulder he saw the mother and pushchair moving in.

'I'm at your disposal,' he went on. 'Just name a place and...'

'I'll be frank with you, Mr Jones,' Carroll interrupted. 'My newspaper doesn't wish to have any dealings with people engaged in criminal activity. You appear to be offering to sell stolen goods. We've contacted the police about this and they say...'

Conrad hung up.

'What have you been doing to my son?'

The voice came from behind him. Conrad turned round knowing what to expect. He felt an ineffable weariness. Still wielding the pushchair and now accompanied by her wronged child, snivelling and increasingly snotty, the mother hen faced him, eyes ablaze.

'I said what have you been doing to my son?'

'Madam,' said Conrad, 'that creature, which you claim as the fruit of your evidently overactive womb, ought to be on a leash. Alternatively might I suggest that you sell him for medical experimentation.'

'You... you...'

'Now piss off or I'll expose myself.'

With bulging eyes the horrified woman watched as Conrad undid the belt of his trousers. A moment later she was hastening away with her brood. Conrad was left to ponder matters alone. He walked slowly in the direction of the park gate. So much for plan A.

*

At the crossroads stood an ageing man clad in a loincloth and holding a wooden staff. Taskar had espied the man from afar and had kept his eyes fixed on the motionless figure as they approached him along the road. Lemula too could not avert her gaze from the mysterious vision.

'What manner of man is this, thinkst thou?' she asked her companion.

'I know not, my lady,' replied Taskar, 'but he appears old and unarmed: no threat can he pose to us, methinks.'

When they were within earshot of the man Taskar called out, 'Greetings, sirrah. We are two wayfarers in this inhospitable land, desirous of arriving at some habitation where food and lodging may be cheaply had. Knowest thou of any such?'

Close as they now were to the greybeard, Lemula and Taskar both saw the hooded eyes of one lacking the power of sight. Whispered Lemula: 'He is blind.'

'Yes, but hears well,' said the old man. 'I heard your question and will answer it. Three ways lie before you.' With his staff he pointed to his right, to his left, and finally to the road which lay behind him. 'These are the way of danger, the way of comfort, and lastly...' He planted his staff upon the ground. 'The way of death. But which road is which you must decide for yourselves.'

*

The traffic on Beaumont Street was slow-moving owing to major roadworks on Worcester Street. Large yellow signs predicted delays for the next three months. Might as well be in London, thought Vince as he stood looking across the road at the front of the Ashmolean Museum.

They'd arranged to meet for tea at the Randolph Hotel, venerable landmark and tourist magnet. A pretentious ironwork porch pushed out from the entrance onto the wide pavement and it was to one side of this that Vince had stationed himself, not so close as to be taken for one of the hotel flunkeys—which was fairly unlikely given the gaudy costumes they wore, but one couldn't be too careful. Occasionally he turned his gaze to right and to left, not knowing from which direction she'd be coming—probably from the right—but otherwise his pose was static, feet planted a little apart, hands folded together in front of his crotch. He could be on guard.

Tessa was a quarter of an hour late but there was nothing surprising in that. If she'd been held up by a creative spurt, all well and good. The more creative spurts she had the better. Not for the first time Vince wondered whether her visit to the UK had really been in the interest of stimulating writerly juices as she'd seemed to imply. It was a long way to come just for that. And why Oxford, given the unfortunate associations?

Vince's musings were cut short by the appearance of a taxi. It drew up in front of the hotel and through its window he saw Tessa in dark glasses waving and smiling. He moved forward to help her from the car.

'Vince,' she said alighting on the pavement, 'I'm so sorry I'm late, I've been to Blenheim Palace'—paying the driver—'and lost track of time. What a place! I'd never been before.'

'Some connection with Winston Churchill, isn't there?'

'That's right, he was born there. I thought that since they've put me in something called the Blenheim Suite I might as well check out the original.'

They were inside the Randolph now, Vince guiding her towards the tea rooms across patterned carpets and beneath chandeliers. The hum of conversation which Tessa had heard as soon as she was in the building eventually engulfed her as she entered a large high-ceilinged room; here people sat in twos and threes facing one another across white tablecloths, discrete bubbles of humanity between which waiters roamed like circumspect beasts of prey. The whole scene was dominated by a gilt-framed mirror hanging on one wall. Vince and Tessa wound their way through the chattering crowd to an empty table.

'Did you do the house and gardens?' Vince said as they sat down.

'Just the grounds. The weather was so nice and I'd been cooped up all morning. But you can see the outside of the house and the outside is probably just as good as the inside.'

'Cooped up in your hotel room, d'you mean?'

'Yes, Vince,' she said putting her dark glasses on the table, 'and in answer to your next question yes, I was working on the book. Tessa has been a good girl.'

Vince gave a crooked smile and started trying to attract the attention of a waiter. Tessa looked around her. This was certainly more opulent than the Marlborough. But she'd begun to feel at home at the Marlborough, even to enjoy her periodic sightings of Bernie bustling about or that rangy receptionist disappearing into his lair. The place had character and she was glad Vince had booked her in there. Maybe she would write a novel about it one day.

'And how was Hillgrove Academy?' asked Vince.

'Oh, it was fine. They seemed to like my talk. One girl wanted to know if I'd been influenced by the Kalevala.'

'The what?'

'Kalevala. The Finnish national epic.'

'And were you? Did it?'

'Not that I know of.'

'Well, I have another appointment for you, my dear Tessa, which I hope you'll enjoy just as much. A book-signing at Blackwell's on Monday. Don't sprain your wrist between now and then, it'll have plenty to do.'

Tessa was only half listening. Her gaze rested on nothing in particular and with one hand she was slowly folding and unfolding her napkin. 'Vince,' she said at last, 'do you form opinions about your clients' books? I mean, do you form opinions about whether they're any good, whether they're actually worth the paper they're printed on?'

He looked at her askance. 'What questions you ask. I'm a literary agent, not a critic. It's not my job to form personal opinions.'

'But you must have your likes and dislikes. For example, did you like reading *The Boy Without a Name*? Or *The Way of Danger*?'

She was smiling. A challenge, she thought. Or an invitation.

Vince said, 'Before I went into this business I didn't read much except newspapers. The Telegraph and the Mail for preference. I used to read a lot when I was at school though. Your books would have appealed to me as a teenager; I probably would have devoured them, I probably would have been one of your keenest fans.'

'And now?'

'Now is irrelevant. It's when I read your books with the eyes of a teenager that I know they're the real thing. Absolutely the real McCoy. That's my trick, my way into a book: try on different eyes, see how it looks. When I was in the force I used to do something similar. People called it intuition.' He stroked his moustache. 'Can get you quite far.'

'I'm sure it can,' said Tessa. 'Vince, you never tell me about your time as a policeman. I'd be interested to hear about it. You must have some good stories to tell.'

'That's for another occasion.' He leant forward. 'Now: this book-signing event. They've stocked a hundred of each of the three volumes...'

A buzzing sound came from Tessa's bag, slung over the corner of an adjacent chair. Tessa reached for her phone—it was a text message. The waiter had arrived and Vince ordered a cream tea for two. Turning back to Tessa he saw her pass her hand across her eyes and give a quick shake of the head before returning the phone to her bag.

'Everything all right?'

The real reason for her visit to the UK, he thought. Right there.

'A friend's unable to see me tomorrow, that's all. He wants to rearrange. It's a little disappointing but nothing...' She shook her head mutely.

'Close friend?'

'Very close. We go back a long way.'

Vince considered. Some doors you just have to push. 'You know it's generally easier for me to do my job if I have your complete confidence. Now why don't you tell me who that text was from?'

He sounded like a policeman.

*

Meg was waiting for a call. To fill in time she made herself another camomile tea. *Nothing to worry about* the man had said. *It's a very standard procedure. Your mother should be up and about within a few days.* Now they were keeping her in. Apparently a 'complication' had arisen. They were to ring Meg with an update this afternoon but even if Mum was okay she should maybe go to see her in hospital, get the bus to Bristol and be there within a couple of hours, it would be better than fretting here in Oxford. Should she wait for the call or just set off? Pouring the hot water into a mug covered with poppies Meg recalled the last time she had been in that hospital, seated beside a bed with her mother seated opposite her, her mother puffy-faced, clenching a handkerchief with both hands and unable to process what was happening. Dad was dying, that was what was happening. Meg had felt oddly detached, whether because she hadn't really got on with her father or because she was naturally stoical she couldn't work out. He was an old man in any case, much older than Mum.

What was an aneurysm anyway?

She sat down on the beanbag and looked at her phone, scrolling through old messages, the mug of camomile on the floor next to her. Conrad had sent her a weird text earlier that day, something about egalitarianism and violation. He was probably stoned when he wrote it. In that brain of his swirled schemes and notions of which she knew nothing. This was something she had learned to live with, classifying it as a masculine desire for privacy, the sort of urge which in middle-aged men manifests itself in building a shed at the bottom of the garden and retiring into it for hours at a stretch. *Up to no good* was a thought she wouldn't entertain. To entertain it would be ungenerous and a love that wasn't generous wasn't really love.

Love. The heavy monosyllable. And do I love him? she asked herself. Let me count the ways. I'm happy when he's nice to me, sad when he's not. I think about him a lot. I miss him when he's gone for any length of time. When he touches me I go weak at the knees. I hate it when he looks at other women. Other men seem pallid by comparison.

I love him all right. I'm a hopeless case.

'What do you see in him?' some of her friends used to ask. 'What do you see in that twenty-year-old egoist? Doesn't he treat you with contempt? And that novel, isn't that just a fraud, a big hoax? He's a slacker, that's what he is, an idler, a parasite. A nobody who thinks he's a somebody.'

She'd stopped seeing those particular friends. She needed support from her friends, not sabotage. Don't sabotage my hopes! she exclaimed inwardly. They were feeble enough as it was.

Her phone was ringing.

'Hello?'

Meg shifted off the beanbag, knelt on the floor with the phone to her ear, looked up at the skylight, listened.

'I see...stable...For how long?... mm...And will she... okay. Okay.'

She nodded invisibly to her invisible interlocutor.

'Okay, thanks. Goodbye.'

No immediate cause for concern. Doing well. Keep her in a few more days, just as a precautionary measure. You had to trust them. They were the experts after all. Bristol could wait; they'd certainly ring her if there was any deterioration and it was only a couple of hours away on the bus. Yes, Bristol could wait.

Meg sank back into her beanbag and sipped her tea. She heard the sound of the front door banging shut: Elise must be home early from work. I could go downstairs for a chat with my housemate, she thought, as a relief from this tension. But it would look weird—Elise moved in two months ago and we've barely exchanged a word, why would I suddenly want to talk to her? Suspicious behaviour, against the norms. None of the occupants of this house talks much to the others, it's a house of free-floating females, a bit like a Trappistine nunnery except for the fact that the nuns in a community are bound together by a common purpose, even if they don't talk about it. Did fair Rosamund talk much with the other sisters at Godstow? she wondered. As the king's former mistress she'd have quite a lot to talk about and presumably no lack of an audience. Whispered conversations in the cloisters, breathless confidences between the chapel and the refectory. *He was good to me, oh yes he loved me all right—it was Eleanor's jealousy that put paid to our happiness, God rot her. Why couldn't she have stayed in Aquitaine? Or got herself killed on a crusade.*

Meg imagined herself saying to Elise 'He's good to me, oh yes he loves me all right' and Elise nodding sympathetically.

*

'Hello, Vince?'

'Tessa?'

'Yes. Look, something awful has happened. You need to know about it and you need to know about a lot of things I haven't told you before, I never got round to it, I should have, I should have, but—and just this afternoon when you...'

'Tessa, Tessa—calm down will you? Talk slowly and distinctly. Otherwise I can't follow what you're saying.'

'All right, yes... Well. I could have told you this afternoon but I didn't. I batted it away.'

'When I asked you who that text was from?'

'Yes.'

'And who was it from?'

'Vince, I have to lead up to this, I have to give you the background. My affair with Alex Delaney. In the nineties, you remember? The MP.'

'I remember.'

'He was a married man, lived in London and...'

'Yes yes, I remember all that. What about him?'

'I had a baby. He got me pregnant and I had a baby.'

From the other end of the line came a silence, a hard cold silence, the silence she had always feared. Tessa pressed her knuckles to her forehead and carried on.

'Then I got post-natal depression.' She waited for a response, some noise, but there was nothing. 'It was as if I became another person, Vince. I wasn't myself, the things I did weren't my own actions...'

He interrupted her: 'What did you do?'

Tears were running down her cheeks. Next to the envelope on the desk was a box of tissues and she groped for it, pulled out a tissue.

'What did you do?' repeated Vince.

She blew her nose. 'I was like a sleepwalker, Vince. You know sometimes a sleepwalker opens a window and steps out onto the window sill and people have to get her back inside without calling to her, without waking her up...'

'Tessa.' She could hear the impatience in his voice. 'You need to tell me what you did.'

'I tried to smother him.'

There. It was out. The bullet, the shard—gouged out and held up by bloodsoaked fingers, visible to all. A different sort of silence followed in the wake of the statement, calm and deliberative, or that's how she heard it. Vince was going to take charge. He would shoulder her burden. Tessa took a deep breath.

'Ben—the boy—was brought up by his father and stepmother. Alex died last year and Ben got in touch with me. We're going to meet for the first time in twenty-three years, here in Oxford.'

'The text message was from him?'

'Yes.'

'And what is the awful thing that has happened?'

'When I came back to my hotel room about half an hour ago, there was an envelope pushed under the bottom of the door with a note in it demanding money.'

'Money?'

'Whoever it is seems to have got hold of the story. Alex and Ben. And me, me trying to...' She stopped.

'Oh Christ,' said Vince.

'I'm sorry,' said Tessa.

Silence again. Then 'How much?' said Vince.

'Ten thousand.'

He sighed. 'It could be worse. The problem is, he might come back for more. What form of payment?'

'There are instructions in the note. Cryptocurrency, basically.' She pulled the note out of the envelope and read it to him.

'Right,' he said when she'd finished. 'So we have a number of options. We could go to the police, in which case the whole story will come out into the open one way or another...'

'No! No, I don't want that. It would...'

'I'm glad you think so. I'm of the same mind. Another option would be to stall, but there's not much point in that given that we can't go on stalling for ever. I think we'll have to cough up.'

'And if he comes back for more?'

'We'll cross that bridge when we come to it. But it may never get as far as that. Do you have any idea how someone might have come by this information? Have you told many people?'

'None. No one knows except Alex—well, he's dead—Ben's stepmum, and the doctors and lawyers.'

'Who dealt with the matter twenty-three years ago. Seems unlikely. So could anyone have got hold of documents? Papers, letters?'

'The only document I can think of is one on my computer—I wrote it all down years ago...'

'And never deleted it, of course.'

'Of course not.'

Vince made a noise with his throat. 'Chickens coming home to roost... Perhaps it's surprising it's taken this long. You're sure there are no other sources? No close friends you've confided in, no priests or psychoanalysts?'

'No. And Vince, it has to be someone who's read the document on my laptop. It has to be.'

'Why?'

'Once or twice I refer to Alex as Mr Turnbull—that was the name he used to give at hotels where we were staying... At the end of the blackmail note whoever it is writes *I look forward to doing business with you, Miss Wain-wright—or should I say Mrs Turnbull.'*

She could hear the smile in Vince's voice when he replied.

'Hubris. It always lets them down.'

V

ONCE YOU'RE OUT OF LONDON with the road ahead of you and a deal behind you it's a case of letting the machine do what she's meant to do, tearing up the asphalt, weaving between the other vehicles while you keep a sharp eye out for cop cars behind or ahead... *Festina lente* basically or, if you prefer, flying like an alert bat out of hell. To be stopped by the police would certainly be annoying, especially with this cargo, even if it is stashed in a bespoke chamber under the seat. Of course if they pull you over for speeding they'll assume the cause is just the usual overflow of animal spirits common among leatherclad petrolheads. Moreover any fine imposed will be well within one's means. So a brush with the constabulary would hardly be the end of the world. Worth avoiding even so.

'Well within one's means.' How pleasant to be able to use that expression! The first instalment had come through very swiftly, not that TW would be thinking of it as an instalment. Yet. In a few weeks she would, or whatever length of time it took him to get through £10k.

It was something like an income, as he'd explained to Pete the Hopeless, an income to supplement the scrapings to be got from waiting on tables in a second-rate hotel in the absence of any decent parental assistance.

Conrad overtook a white van with a roar, earning himself an angry honk. Satisfactory. The Triumph Scrambler was on good form, responsive as a woman, urgent as a greyhound. He wasn't one to lavish love on the thing, however, not the sort of person to solicitously polish it or address it by a name; it was a means to an end, that was all. Just a motorbike. It joined the long list of tools, human and mechanical.

He glanced at the petrol gauge. Better fill up at the next service station, he thought. Might pay a discreet visit to the gents while I'm at it.

'Come into some money, have we?' Nick had asked him. 'Mr Big Spender.' He'd bought three or four times his usual amount, a pick 'n' mix bag of coke, hash, mandy, tina and skag, with some complimentary shrooms thrown in as a garnish. Some of it he'd sell on of course, but most of it was for personal use. Nick (not his real name) offered high quality merchandise and his prices reflected that fact, but (a) Conrad could afford it and (b) it was worth the additional expenditure to know you weren't going to be snorting talcum powder or smoking soil. 'Only the best for a man of taste,' Nick complimented him, and he reeled off as was his custom the names of some of his loyal customers in the worlds of music, media and fashion. Conrad had heard the names before and neither knew nor cared whether

Nick was fabricating. But he didn't mind being called a man of taste. If the cap fits etc.

Turn-off for services in two-thirds of a mile. He slipped into the left-hand lane behind a red mini. The countdown signs by the edge of the road eased him, three—two—one, into the requisite state of calm and in a moment he found himself gliding onto the forecourt of a petrol station. He came to a standstill and set about filling up the machine. It was like feeding your horse. Oats and mash have been replaced by petroleum. And whereas the rider might have broken his journey with a tankard of ale, we moderns are wont to enjoy sharper, more intense forms of refreshment.

Conrad hung up the pump, replaced the petrol cap and walked over to the main building. There was no queue and within less than a minute he had paid for the petrol and been given directions to the toilets. Once ensconced in a cubicle he drew a sachet from one of his jacket pockets and conducted a tasting session, what the French call a dégustation, kneeling on the tiled floor and utilising the lid of the toilet as a surface. Although not strictly necessary such quality control is always advised.

KAZAAM. Nick, my man! Conrad returned the empty sachet to his pocket and sniffed vigorously. Oh yes... ten out of ten, ten out of fucking ten. And there's a whole lot more where that came from. Then it was: wipe nose with bog paper, flush down toilet (verisimilitude), proceed on journey grinning happily.

Almost as soon as he was back on the M40 Conrad saw a police car in the distance, sitting in the left-hand lane. As he gained on it he decided it was hugging the speed limit, setting itself up as a role model for other vehicles. *Go any faster than this and you're breaking the law.* All around it cars and lorries dawdled respectfully, some of them inching past the police car with agonising deference. Everyone was moving at more or less the same speed, maintaining distances, staying in their lanes—like a bunch of schoolgirls in a deportment class, thought Conrad as the coke buzzed around his body. The urge to step on it, to overtake the lot of them at 100 mph, was almost irresistible. But that would be folly. The legal limit for cocaine in your system if you're a motorist is 10 micrograms per litre of blood. He was probably several hundred times over the limit.

He joined the dawdlers, coasting along in the wake of the cop car and suppressing thoughts of acceleration. Patience, patience. But what if the arsehole's going all the way to Oxford? That would be too much, it's simply not possible when you've got the bit between your teeth; I'm on a *motorbike*, for Christ's sake. The coke was kicking in hard.

He looked beyond the police car and traced a path through the traffic, with some overtaking here and some undertaking there, all the time putting distance and objects between himself and the cop—easy as spitting. In his mirror he'd see the blue light start up, other cars making way for it as the cop put his foot down, but each time he looked in the mirror the blue light would be smaller and before too long it would have disappeared altogether. The vision was startling in its reality. So why wait?

Just as he was about to accelerate the police car's near-side indicator started flashing. Conrad hadn't noticed the earlier sign for a turn-off. The cop was evidently going to exit left, leave the motorway and go about his dirty business elsewhere to the relief and rejoicing of all right-minded motorists. Conrad waited till the slip road appeared then let rip. The police car was sailing off, too late for a change of mind, their paths were diverging irrevocably and Conrad could only hope that the cop observed this flouting of authority with rage in his eyes. Flaunt the flouting and flagrantly fly. On the speedo he read ninety, a hundred—110 mph... He was driving mainly in the fast lane but when necessity or impulse dictated would veer into the middle lane and occasionally, for laughs, into the slow lane where one might career up behind some timid old biddy to give her the fright of her life before twisting past her at the last minute and all this in a blissful coke-crazed high, yelling like a fiend, a fiend with a lot of luck in the bank, more luck than he knows what to do with, did you see how my luck drew the cop car down that slip road? And before then how it dropped a document called *ben* into my hands, how it pushed Pete out of the picture, how it persuaded Tessa to be so obliging, to give herself up so willingly to her violator? I have a guardian angel, let me tell you, he's working full time for me, showering me with luck, endless luck –

Conrad saw an open diagonal like in a chess game and with a gleeful roar of acceleration he crossed the width of the motorway from the fast lane over to the slow lane narrowly missing the front of a black 4x4 and causing a car pulling a trailer with HORSES written on it to shudder and careen. He bounced back from the slow lane into the middle lane, dropped his speed a bit and looked into his mirror. The black 4x4 had changed lanes, it was dancing about drunkenly amid the traffic and the horsebox was toppling over in slow motion, over into the path of an oncoming lorry which hit it full on just as the 4x4 collided with the red mini of twenty minutes ago. Other cars could be seen veering off the motorway into the central barrier. The whole dreamlike scene was receding into the distance and just before he took his eyes off it Conrad saw a beautiful ball of fire erupting.

*

Pete was having a chat with Tina when the man entered the hotel. He wore a hat and dark glasses and stood looking around the lobby, his gaze lifted upwards as if he were examining the light fixtures. Finally he approached reception.

'Good afternoon, sir,' said Pete, 'may I help you?'

Looking at him over the tops of his glasses the man said, 'I'd like to make an enquiry about a room.' He was tall and bulky with a pockmarked face and a gingery moustache. His pink shirt was open at the collar and he wore mustard-coloured corduroy trousers. 'I'm thinking of booking something special for my wedding anniversary next month,' he explained.

'I'm sure we can find you something very suitable, sir,' Pete said in his most unctuous voice and reached under the counter for a brochure which he laid before the gentleman and thoughtfully opened for him. 'Here you can see the range of double rooms we offer. For a special occasion I think I would recommend our luxury penthouse suite'—he turned some pages and pointed at a series of enticing photographs, 'with marvellous views over Oxford, ensuite bath and shower...'

'Looks good. Yes.' The man scanned the photos quickly, checked a few other rooms in the brochure, returned to the penthouse suite and said, 'Am I right that some famous author is staying here at present? Tessa Cartwright or something—I read it in the local paper the other day.'

'You're quite right, sir,' beamed Pete. 'Tessa Wainwright is indeed one of our guests.'

Smiling in return the man looked at Pete, then at Tina, then back at Pete again. 'I suppose the receptionist at a hotel like this must see quite a few notable people coming and going. Must be an interesting job. D'you share it between you?'

Tina giggled.

'Well, sir,' said Pete, 'Tina here works in the kitchen, actually. I am the main receptionist.'

'Day and night?'

'Oh no, we have a night porter. I'd have to be a lot fitter than I am to do a twenty-four hour stint. A thermos of coffee would hardly answer, I fear!' He laughed amiably. Be entertaining, soften up prospective guests.

'Sometimes I cover for him,' put in Tina, 'so you could say we do share the job between us.' She directed a teasing glance at Pete.

'Like when?' he demanded.

'Like when you took that note up to Miss Wainwright's room and were away for quarter of an hour.' She turned to the gentleman: 'I nearly missed my yoga lesson.'

Pete appeared flustered. 'I don't remember that,' he muttered.

'Don't they ever give you the afternoon off?' enquired the man.

'It's a full time job, sir. Now would you like me to reserve you a room?' He had adopted his brisk manner. 'It's best to book in advance to avoid disappointment; we do get booked up quite quickly at this time of year, and...'

'I think,' interrupted the man, 'I'll need to consult with my wife first. But you've been very helpful, very helpful. Both of you. Would you mind if I had a quick look round so I can report back to the missus? She has arthritis so it's good to check for stairs and things.'

'Please feel free, sir,' answered Pete. 'You'll find that all our disabled access is excellent.'

The man drifted off. After he'd gone Pete went into his office and poured himself a drink. He hadn't been sleeping well lately and his nerves were on edge. Conrad. That was the problem. The two of them had been in the habit of meeting up, having a talk, having a drink, all very pleasant, then this scheme of Conrad's intruded itself. It intruded itself then it metamorphosed into something different, a nasty dangerous affair, hard-hearted and greedy, and the end result was that they were avoiding each other, were keeping their distance from one another. Or Conrad was. Pete felt hurt and anxious. He settled into the green armchair, Conrad's customary throne, and drank a draught of regret, amber and fiery.

Tina's voice reached him from the hotel lobby, a chirruping bird discussing the day's news with another—*I said, she said, she didn't? she certainly did!* With variations. He was annoyed with her. It was hard enough—no, not hard so much as tedious—to maintain his façade of oily propriety with guests and prospective guests without being undermined by Tina's inappropriate contributions. What must Mr Pink-Shirt have thought, hearing of the receptionist's habit of wandering off and leaving a dishwasher and onion-slicer in charge? Well, it probably didn't matter. Mrs Pink-Shirt would have the final say in any case.

Pete downed his whisky and addressed a belated 'Cheers' to the photograph of the Queen. Then he got out his phone and dialled Tony's number.

*

Blackwell's bookshop was busier than usual. Those wishing to shop or browse in the normal way had to negotiate a straggling queue which began in Broad St, negotiated the steps up into the shop and wound its way to a large table placed at the far end on the ground floor. Behind this table sat the world-famous author Tessa Wainwright. The queue consisted predominantly of teenagers and children with or without their parents, though there was a good smattering of fantasy-oriented adults, mainly male. So far about eighty books had been signed and purchased. Some had brought their own copies for signing but the publishers had instructed Tessa to show herself eager to sign only 'fresh copies', a policy she was half-heartedly following. A few people wanted all three volumes signed. 'You'll have to come back for the fourth,' she joked, her wrist aching.

At 6 pm she was due a short break. 'Tea?' one of the friendly hovering staff asked her when the time came. 'Yes please,' said Tessa putting her pen down. The person at the front of the queue, a long-haired youth in a sleeveless top, backed away tactfully. Tessa turned to her phone. A text had come in from Vince asking her to call him. She waited till her tea had arrived then dialled his number.

'How's it going?'

'We're in half time,' she replied. 'I'm just having a cup of tea.'

'And how many books have you signed?'

'Oh, I don't know—dozens. *To X, best wishes Tessa Wainwright* a hundred times, like a school punishment. Some of them have got pretty odd names, they have to spell them for me. Did you know there was such a name as X—O—E—Y?'

'It's a misspelling of Zoe.'

'Right.'

'Tessa, I've been making some enquiries at the Marlborough.'

He means about the blackmailer, she thought. I'd almost forgotten.

'We're not going to have any luck with CCTV,' he went on. 'Although the lobby has a couple of cameras there aren't any in the corridors so I doubt if there's one outside your room. Still, I might have a lead. It depends on the answer to a question I'm going to ask you.'

'Ask me it then.'

'Apart from the blackmail note, have you received any other notes or letters while you've been there? Delivered straight to your room, I mean?'

'Brought by someone to my door?'

'Or just left there by someone—on your desk, maybe.'

'No, nothing.'

'Are you quite sure? No notes, letters, envelopes, anything like that?'

'No, absolutely nothing. Why should I have?'

'Why should you indeed. No reason at all is the answer. It means we have a suspect.'

'Really? Who?'

'At the moment it's only a strong hunch, my dear Tessa, so I think I'd better not point the finger just yet. Let me do a little more spadework. But while we're on the phone shall we make a date to meet up again soon? Are you free tomorrow at all?'

'Tomorrow morning I'm having coffee with an old schoolfriend but the afternoon and evening are free.'

'What time's your coffee date?'

'Eleven o'clock, I think—why?'

'Just curious. How about dinner then?'

'Lovely. Name a place.'

'Have you ever tried the Cherwell Boat House?'

She had tried the Cherwell Boat House, yes. When Alex took her three months pregnant and they'd had that terrible row. She'd wept, he'd taken her back to his flat, they'd made love. A familiar ritual. But this was no reason for vetoing Vince's suggestion; on the contrary, it was another opportunity for staring down the past.

'Great idea,' she said. 'We could have a table outside and watch the ducks sailing by.'

Her tea break over, Tessa resumed her pen. At her smile of encouragement the long-haired youth stepped forward. 'I love your books,' he said, 'could you sign a copy of *The Way of Danger* for me?'

'Of course, is that your favourite?'

The boy nodded.

'And what's your name so I can address it to you?'

He told her.

'Maybe you could spell that?'

*

It was late. Nearly midnight. Conrad poured himself another whisky and staggered back to the sofa with the *Liebestod* surging from two speakers that sat on the floor facing him. The *Liebestod*, Isolde's hymn to the great orgasm of death. To come is to go and to go is to come. It took Wagner's genius to see that and to embody it in music so ravishing you might actually die of it. Thing is, there's something erotic about death *per se*, it doesn't have to be your own; the idea of someone dying just does give one a thrill, a shiver of pleasure, can't be denied. One moment they're alive, trundling along in their 4x4 on their way to a family lunch or a child's graduation ceremony, the next moment they're dead. Bang. End of story. And then that ball of flame, like a second climax. . .

I have tasted of the fruit of the tree.

He stretched out luxuriously, the music washing over him. Here's to Coke and Mandy and Skunk and Booze, your hostesses for this evening, good-time girls dancing naked around the fire of my brain. What a delicious coven. And let's not forget that other bevy of cuties, the ones who were strutting their stuff on the M40 this afternoon, Norns or Furies or whatever you want to call them, the blades of their scissors going like a can-can dancer's legs, snip snip snip—what a show! And didn't you just love the stage business? A *horsebox*, for crying out loud! A fit of laughter engulfed him, coughing and hiccupping, the tears starting in his eyes. Whisky spilt from his tumbler onto his knees and he put the glass down on the floor with a shaking hand. With the abrupt change of mood characteristic of these episodes he grew still and in a grave voice told the room 'I'm going to write an email.' Somehow or other he got to his laptop. Placing it on a chair he knelt in front of it and held his head in his hands for a minute or two. Then he dictated as follows:

> *Dear Father, this is to inform you that I don't need your money. You can keep it, you stingy bastard. I have enough and more. I'm standing on my own two feet as you always told me to do, making my own way in the world. I don't need your money and I don't need your love, not that that was ever really on offer was it, not for a black sheep like me, oh no, and anyway who do you love but yourself, you miserable shit? Certainly not my mother, certainly not her. Treating her like dirt all those years. She should never have married you and I should never have been born, those are the facts. You probably agree. Well, I thought I'd be in touch. I hope you rot in hell.*

Conrad stared at the blank screen breathing heavily. Finally he added a postscript: *Tell mummy I love her.*

He closed the lid of the laptop and stood up.

'More,' he said, 'I need more. Haven't tried any of the skag yet. Bit of Mr Needle.'

He walked into the middle of the room and gazed at the sofa. There didn't seem to be anything on it except a cushion. His eyes moved to the nearby table: whisky bottle, packet of rizlas, a chunk of hash, a few pills...No skag. In fact nothing much. Nor on the floor nor anywhere else. Where the fuck is my stash? he thought.

Dimly he remembered pulling a few items from under the seat of his motorbike and pocketing them. Why hadn't he removed the lot? Too much stuff, that's why. Should have brought a bag down from the flat and emptied the whole trove. Do it now, then.

He went over to a drawer in the kitchen and took out an old Tesco's bag from among a pile. Then he crossed the flat to the front door, turning the Wagner off en route, and left, leaving the door on the latch. A few paces along an unlit corridor took him to the stairs. It was four flights down—the lift rarely worked—and twice in his hurry he stumbled, grabbing the handrail the second time and feeling his stomach lurch unpleasantly. The smell of urine on concrete didn't help. At least he was unlikely to meet anyone else at this time of night.

The fresh air once he was out of the building blew some, but only some, of the swirls of fog from his brain and he made his way with fairly even steps to the carpark round the back of the block of flats. A single wall-mounted LED illuminated the tarmac and the parked cars. Conrad couldn't immediately remember where he'd left his bike and he was having trouble interpreting the jumble of shadows and forms that surrounded him. Gradually the scene began to fall into some sort of order. Someone had parked their bike more or less underneath the LED but it wasn't his: it was the wrong shape and had a metallic seat. The reflected light hurt his eyes and he turned away. Moving towards the centre of the carpark from where he would obtain a more panoramic view of things, he turned his head this way and that and was eventually rewarded by the sight of the Triumph Scrambler directly ahead of him. It was floating a few feet from the ground and had a blue-green aura. A gentle humming emanated from it. Conrad felt a mixture of love and awe and fell to his knees. A moment later he vomited onto the black tarmac.

'The world is...made...of vomit,' he managed to articulate between breaths. Then with a huge effort he got to his feet, turned around and made for the wall-mounted LED beneath which he now remembered leaving his bike. Again he spotted the metallic seat, apparently in the process of sliding off the bike—but as he got nearer it resolved itself into the seat's concave underside, sitting on its hinges and open to view. The stash chamber, the secret stash chamber...He had forgotten to close it. And standing above it he saw that it was empty. Somebody had stolen his stash.

*

Pete was in his office reading a newspaper. The usual stuff: parliamentary scandals, floods in Somerset, a pile-up on the M40 leaving three dead. Meanwhile in Oxford the sun was shining and it was a pleasant 24° C. Tessa Wainwright had wished him a cheerful 'Good morning' as she left the hotel wearing a lilac blouse and cream-coloured slacks. Bernie had made an appearance, asked a few questions and moved on. A couple were sitting in the lobby surrounded by luggage as they waited for a taxi to the train station. Just another morning at the Marlborough Hotel. He turned the page and was examining a photograph of a celebrity wedding when the bell rang at reception. It was Mr Pink-Shirt from yesterday, now wearing a yellow shirt and bow tie in addition to the hat and dark glasses.

'Good morning, sir,' said Pete coming out of his office.

'Good morning to you,' the man replied. 'I've come back about that room. Having discussed the matter with my wife. . . ' He glanced at the waiting couple. 'She's keen on the one with the four-poster bed, what's it called? We looked at it online.'

'The Victoria Suite?'

'Yes, that's the one. So not the Penthouse Suite. The Victoria Suite.'

'Of course, sir, I think that should be available.' Pete began tapping on the keys of a computer.

'Would it be all right for me to have a look at it first? I'd be very grateful if you could give me a tour, so to speak. Just to be absolutely sure.'

A fussy one, thought Pete. 'Naturally, sir,' he smiled, and he took down one from among a row of keys on the wall behind him. 'Follow me, please.'

They walked out of the lobby and had got as far as the lift when the man said, 'D'you know, I wouldn't mind having a look at the Penthouse Suite as well. I have a feeling that my wife might be persuadable if I could say I'd actually seen it. Don't see why we shouldn't push the boat out.'

'Absolutely, sir,' said Pete. He suppressed a spasm of irritation. A minute later he was back with the key to the Penthouse Suite. The lift arrived and the two men stepped into it. In the lobby the wife said to her husband, 'This taxi's taking ages—we'll miss our train.'

'It doesn't go for another three quarters of an hour,' the husband replied. 'Plenty of time.'

'It makes me nervous. If he's this late already he might never come at all.'

'It's probably just the traffic.'

'They're meant to take that into account, aren't they. Don't say you'll be ten minutes if it's going to take you longer. If they say "He'll be there in ten minutes" he should be there in ten minutes.'

The husband didn't reply. Meanwhile in the scullery Tina was discussing the latest episode of a new reality TV show with Maria. Maria had recently arrived from Brazil. Her views were even stronger than Tina's. They agreed on the absurdity of the show's premise: suburban couples were to endure the rigours of life in an igloo for a month, killing seals for sustenance and having sex in their sleeping bags.

'The film crew's there with them,' said Tina, 'and they can leave any time they want. It's not for real, is it.'

'It's schoopid,' declared Maria, 'so schoopid. Why they not film Eskimos, like? Like Innuit people? Then we see the life in the igloo.'

Tina was standing with her back to the window. Maria faced her holding a mop. There was a lull in the conversation during which they heard a distant shout and exactly two seconds later Tina saw a shadow flicker over Maria and her mop and heard a near-instantaneous thud behind her. Maria began screaming. The mop fell to the floor with a clatter. Maria's left hand was over her mouth, her right hand pointing past Tina at the window. Her screams soon brought other people onto the scene and amid the confusion that followed Tina heard someone shouting 'Out the back', at which point there was a general movement towards the door which opened onto the passage at the rear of the hotel where the wheelie bins were kept and where Conrad Merrivale often parked his motorbike. She joined the exodus, stumbled down the stone steps into the passage and not knowing what to look for gazed wildly about her until someone's pointing finger directed her to the body. It lay sprawled on the concrete, face down, one knee jutting out in an ungainly fashion, a trickle of blood oozing from the head. 'Pete,' she gasped.

Maria's screams had stopped abruptly, perhaps she'd fainted. Another noise replaced them, the growling of an engine. At the end of the passage a motorbike had appeared—its growling cut out and the rider dismounted.

'Can you lot move out of the way,' he called, 'I need to park my bike.'

*

When the police and ambulance arrived the couple in the lobby were just on the point of leaving, their taxi having arrived a few minutes earlier, but their departure was prevented by *fiat* of the grey-haired police officer who stood in the middle of the lobby issuing orders and occasionally asking questions. His underlings had rounded up the hotel staff plus any guests that happened to be wandering about so that the lobby was beginning to feel crowded when through it there passed a stretcher borne by two paramedics on which was a dark green blanket moulded into tell-tale hills and valleys. The crowd drew back like the Red Sea and Tina turned away and hid her crying face in her hands. As Pete disappeared for the last time through the doors of the Marlborough Hotel a hush descended on the company. A hiccup of grief escaped from the bearlike figure of Bernie as he leant against a pillar. 'Somebody's going to have to tell Tony,' whispered one of the kitchen staff to his friend. 'I know,' said the other.

There followed a tedious hour or two of interrogation, taking of names and addresses, sending of a forensic team up to the relevant floor and putting in place the signs and symbols of a designated crime scene. Conrad, having given his personal details and told them of his relatively late arrival, milled around in order to pick up whatever scraps of information he could from people's conversations. The only balcony from which a person could fall on that side of the building belonged to the Penthouse Suite. Nobody seemed to know what Pete could have been doing up in the Penthouse Suite. Subsequent questioning of the married couple was to reveal that he had left the lobby with a gentleman who had specifically asked *not* to see the Penthouse Suite but rather the Victoria Suite; so perhaps Pete had simply decided to have a look at the Penthouse Suite himself and then had leant too far over the balcony... The gentleman interested in the Victoria Suite was nowhere to be found. Bearded and wearing a blue shirt the wife attested, her husband adding that he would have said clean-shaven and jacketed. The CCTV cameras in the lobby would decide the issue. The police noted the man's existence and his evident status as a key witness but anticipated difficulties when it came to laying their hands on him.

Later that day Pete's death was a topic of conversation between Tessa and Vince as they dined on the terrace of the Cherwell Boat House. Tessa had returned to the hotel from her mini-reunion (Sally from schooldays, now working in Human Resources) to find policemen guarding the entrance and disorder and anxiety within. She learnt the truth from Bernie in as euphemistic a form as he could give it. A policewoman asked her a few polite questions, later texting her family that she'd just interviewed Tessa Wainwright ('looks young for her age'), and Tessa had gone up to her room to be alone. She had spent the afternoon tinkering distractedly with *The Homecoming*.

'Do you think he killed himself?' she asked Vince.

'Very likely. It's a more common method that you might suppose. Fairly foolproof and you don't have to get hold of any drugs or weapons. Moreover,' he went on, leaning back in his chair, 'I suspect he may have had psychological problems.'

'Really? How do you know?'

'I had a little chat with him yesterday and he was very twitchy, very odd in his behaviour. I've come across those manifestations before in my time as a policeman. Classic symptoms of psychosis, I'd have said.'

'Was he your suspect? The person you think sent the blackmail note?'

Vince smiled his crooked smile. 'No, that's someone else, one of the cleaning staff. Still—' He cracked open a pistachio nut and popped it in his mouth; 'if the black-mail stops, you never know, Pete Rowlinson might have been behind it. It's true that blackmailers are often psy-chologically disturbed individuals.'

Tessa looked down at the River Cherwell on which a punt was plying a zigzag course to the accompani-ment of shrieks of laughter from its passengers. Ducks and swans swimming in the vicinity observed the pro-ceedings disdainfully. On the other bank the foliage of trees glowed in the light of the setting sun. Tessa said, 'I suppose if you spoke to him yesterday you should get in touch with the police.'

'You're quite right, I should do that.' Vince stroked his moustache. 'Indeed I should. Now would you like to or-der some food?'

VI

TASKAR AWOKE FROM TROUBLED DREAMS to find himself alone in the glade in which the two travellers had passed the night, now ringing with the chorus of morning birdsong. He threw off his blanket and was about to call out when Princess Lemula appeared carrying a pitcher of water and a basket.

'This I have filled from a nearby stream,' she said, placing the pitcher upon the sward, 'and this basket will supply us with a meagre breakfast. Our fire of yestereve may be easily rekindled, methinks.'

'You have picked mushrooms before, my lady?' enquired Taskar, observing the contents of the basket.

'Many a time,' smiled Lemula as she began to feed the fire with new twigs and leaves. 'My parents taught me when...'

'Your parents—' interrupted Taskar. 'My lady, thou must know...' He halted.

'What sayest thou?' asked Lemula, her gaze upon him.

Taskar continued: 'When I found thee living among the Hoshi, rememb'rest thou my telling thee of the commission I had been placed under?'

'I do. You have been commanded by the king and queen of a faraway land to find me and bring me to them.'

'The king and queen you have referred to are your parents. When yet a baby you were abducted from them by a disloyal knave and sold in slavery to the Hoshi. This is God's truth, o Princess.'

'In slavery? But never as a slave was I treated. The Hoshi have no slaves—they are a free and peaceful people. I was told indeed that I was a foundling... But sir,' she said looking him full in the face. 'If all this be true—if it be as you say—tell me: who art thou?'

*

Depressing. Depressing and somehow nauseating. That was Conrad's verdict on Pete's funeral. As he walked away from the crematorium he recalled again the sight of the person referred to as Tony, chief mourner it appeared, front and centre throughout and crying almost continuously, wearing an ill-fitting suit and scarcely able to get through a single line of that awful poem. Why do they have to read poems? Can't they just consign the body to the flames and be done with it? So it seems that Pete had a boyfriend. Never mentioned him, not once, perhaps he was embarrassed, perhaps despite being obviously gay he was in the closet, though I thought that sort died out years ago. An extinct species, like transvestites and male primary school teachers.

Well might Tony cry, the guy was only forty-something, in good health and of sound mind. So why the hell did he kill himself? Or was it an accident? Did he slip on a banana skin? Perhaps he got depressed. Perhaps the froideur that had descended between us had chilled his soul; he might have harboured a secret passion after all, Tony or no Tony. Unrequited love can be fatal, so the poets tell us.

Conrad stood at a pedestrian crossing and waited for the lights to change. A black 4x4 drove past with a dog's head sticking out of one of the rear windows, tongue lolling. A ball of flame was kindled in Conrad's memory, sickly-sweet image... morning-after smell of stale cigarette smoke and vomit, caked blood on hot tarmac. An epiphany, however intense, may be followed by a fur-tongued loose-bowelled hangover from hell, something like an expense of spirit in a waste of shame but without the shame, since when did shame do anyone any good? You needn't kid yourself there, just need to engineer some more epiphanies, there should be no shortage these days. Annoying to have lost that stash but we have the wherewithal to replace it.

He was walking south, towards Jericho. To see Meg. Sometimes that was what he needed, he didn't mind confessing it to himself—to see Meg, to have the comfort of her physical presence and to receive her little favours, her burnt offerings. The prospect was soothing and he was someone who could do with a bit of soothing. I have a lot on my mind, he thought, and a lot's been happening. For example a close acquaintance has just killed himself. Threw himself off a fifth-floor balcony and bashed his skull in. No wonder I need a bit of TLC right now.

A quarter of an hour later he was ringing the doorbell of a house in a Victorian terrace devoid of front gardens, like most of the terraces in Jericho. Stepping back into the road he looked up at the skylight in which nothing was visible but the reflection of the sky, just as nothing but the sky itself could be seen in it when you were inside Meg's attic. A skylight is not a window: it reveals no movement, no evidence of life, except perhaps at night when a light is turned on and a faint shadow passes across a portion of the ceiling. Curtains are unnecessary. The anonymity of the skylight appealed to Conrad. That's how a person should be, he thought.

The door opened. It was Elise, dressed for jogging and chewing gum.

'Hi, Con. Meg's just gone to the Co-op.' She looked at him, jaws moving, lips a centimetre apart.

'Can I come in?' he said.

She opened the door wordlessly and stood aside as he entered.

'I'll just go up to her room,' he informed her.

'Whatever,' replied Elise and went out, slamming the door behind her.

'Articulate girl,' murmured Conrad as he mounted the stairs.

It was warm in the attic and Conrad was tempted to open the skylight but inertia got the better of him and he threw himself onto the beanbag after removing his jacket. It was a linen jacket, the only smart piece of clothing he possessed and his nod to propriety at Pete's funeral along with a navy blue tie he found in the back of a drawer, probably a gift from some uncle or aunt. He still wore his old jeans and something in a side pocket was digging into his hip annoyingly as he shifted around on the beanbag. Thrusting his leg out he forced a hand into the pocket and pulled out the offending object. It was the memory stick.

A smile crossed his face as at a remembered joke. Little cask of red-hot information, source of illicit possibilities. He leant over towards a pile of paperbacks and placed the memory stick on top for safe keeping, then sank back into the beanbag and closed his eyes.

He was still in this attitude when Meg appeared, rising up through the trapdoor like a stage mermaid. She hoicked a shopping bag ahead of her onto the floor then completed her entry with a graceful jump.

'Greetings, earthling,' said Conrad opening one eye.

'Hello, Con. Did Elise let you in?' Meg carried the bag into the kitchen area and began unpacking the shopping, these in the fridge, that in the cupboard, those in the pending pile.

'She did. A bovine character, unless she was very deep in thought.'

'I don't really know her,' said Meg putting a packet of toothpaste on a shelf. She turned her head and smiled. 'But it's good to see you.'

'You too. I've just come from a funeral.'

'Really?' Meg stopped what she was doing and turned to face him. 'You never told me. Who's died?'

'Just a guy from work. Receptionist at the hotel. A bunch of us went, the manager corralled us into it, had the idea the hotel should be represented.'

'That was a nice thought.'

'Mm.'

'How did he die?'

'Threw himself off the balcony of the Penthouse Suite.'

Meg's hand went to her mouth. 'God, how awful!'

'At least it was quick. No lingering hospital death.'

Dust to dust, he thought, ashes to ashes.

No: strictly speaking, fire to ashes.

*

The weather had been like this, hot and rather humid. They had lunched at the Perch, visited the little church at Binsey with its holy well of St Frideswide, returned hand in hand down the country road and struck out across Port Meadow just as she was now doing. Alex was in jovial mood, stimulated by the beer and the sunshine, talking humorously of the personalities and peccadilloes of Westminster. She was herself one of those peccadilloes, Tessa noted, and unknown to him she was about to grow from a peccadillo into something bigger, an embarrassment, perhaps even a millstone. Let him talk, she told herself, let us enjoy these unfraught moments in the summer of our love, we will have plenty to be serious about in the months to come. But it couldn't be put off for ever. Eventually she had to tell him *Alex, I'm pregnant.* Those three words, rehearsed in advance, announcing a miracle or a curse, which finally she summoned up the courage to speak out—they winded him, they popped the balloon of his boyish good humour and in that instant their relationship keeled over and died. It was enough to see the look on his face to realise that. Poor weakling, poor coward. Only a man after all.

And had it been a miracle or a curse? It was easy to answer that question now. For one thing, life is always a miracle. Love is the other great miracle and if she had lost one sort she had gained in its place a better and a deeper sort. No curse, then, whatever the world and Vincent Parker might think. To his credit Alex must have come to see that also for he had loved Ben with a father's love, a fact which surely brought the two of them together again, reinstated their relationship on a different plane as you might say. The only enigma in the picture was Miranda—Mrs Delaney, stepmother to Ben, the woman to whom Alex had entrusted the care of his son when the boy's mother turned out to be a homicidal lunatic. Tessa had never met her, never so much as heard from her. She dimly recalled an old photograph Alex had once shown her of a woman in glasses, quite pretty, sitting in a deckchair in front of a bush. And Ben, what would Ben's feelings have been towards that woman? Ben probably loved her as a mother... I should feel grateful towards her, thought Tessa, of course I should. But in the end a person has only one mother. Ben knows that. After all that's why he got in touch, wasn't it.

Did he know why he'd been given a substitute mother?—why his real mother had been deemed unfit to care for him? What exactly had Alex—or Miranda—told him? Such questions tormented her. *A nervous breakdown, post-natal depression, unable to function...* these diagnoses she could live with. *Mummy was unbalanced* would elicit compassion, or at worst mild disgust, but *Mummy tried to kill you* would sink into his soul and stay there, it would be like a lump of something radioactive, forever lethal, impossible to cancel. She felt fairly confident that Alex wouldn't have burdened his son with such knowledge, both out of protectiveness and because he wasn't, whatever his other faults, a vindictive man. But his wife? The wronged wife, lumbered against her will with another woman's brat? Surely if she loved the boy at all she would spare him that? Tessa must hope that the woman did love her son, that the substitute mother was to him indeed as a mother. If so, she would be grateful.

She was walking parallel to the river, the sun almost directly above her. Other walkers were about, a group was picnicking on the grass not far off, a man and a woman were passing a frisbee back and forth between them. It was a lazy summer's day on Port Meadow. *Alex is dead*, she thought. *It is strange.*

Ahead of her on a bench a young man with a goatee was talking into his phone. His face seemed vaguely familiar. He was looking at the ground and tapping one foot rhythmically; occasionally he nodded. As she approached she heard him say, 'Okay, see you this evening,' after which he hung up. Tessa was trying unsuccessfully to remember where she had seen him before. At the Cherwell Boat House, perhaps?

The youth stretched his arms along the back of the bench and looked about him, his gaze falling on Tessa's face just as she drew level. She smiled at him and was surprised to see a jolt go through his whole body as if he'd been electrocuted.

*

On her return to the Marlborough she encountered her first paparazzi. Three journalists and two photographers lay in wait for her in the lobby, unfazed by Bernie's disapproval, which anyway must have been tempered by the thought that the world-famous author had finally been tracked down staying in his hotel. It was the natural consequence of Pete's death: the police could hardly be expected to keep the identity of this particular guest a secret from the world. If she wanted to regain her anonymity Tessa would have to move hotel.

'Miss Wainwright, I wonder if you'd care to tell us what's brought you to Oxford, and whether you'll be. . .'

'Is the fourth volume near completion yet, Miss Wainwright?'

The cameras clicked. Tessa found herself encircled. Looking between two of the journalists she saw behind reception a portly man in his sixties, Pete's replacement. The man put a hand to his mouth and coughed discreetly, then attended to something on his computer screen.

'I'm sorry about this, madam,' said Bernie over the shoulder of one of the cameramen. 'I expressly told these persons that it was your wish not to...'

'That's all right,' smiled Tessa, 'since they're here now I might as well answer their questions.' Vince would certainly have advised as much. A haughty Tessa Wainwright declining an interview would make bad copy. 'One at a time, please.'

Tessa had sufficient experience to be able to give vague and general answers to intrusive questions, supply particulars on unimportant matters and season the whole with disarming good humour. But she was unprepared for the question addressed to her by a representative of the London Evening Standard. Out of the blue the woman asked her: 'After the recent tragic death of an employee of this hotel, do you feel your own safety to be at all compromised?'

Fortunately Bernie was out of earshot. Tessa replied, 'I think it was suicide.'

The woman objected, 'The police are treating it as suspicious.'

'Are they?' said Tessa. 'I understood the man was psychologically unstable.' *I shouldn't have said that*, she thought. The journalists were writing. 'Though really I know nothing about the case,' she added feebly. 'Anyway, I don't feel any less safe. This hotel is a wonderful place to stay. The staff are lovely...' *Except the person who's blackmailing me. He's not so lovely.*

'And is Taskar going to marry Princess Lemula?' enquired another journalist.

Tessa laughed. 'What do you think?'

'I think he is.'

'No way!' put in one of the cameramen. 'He's her brother.'

'What are you talking about?'

'Absolutely...'

A quarter of an hour later she was back in her room. The interview, or interviews, had seemed to satisfy the members of the press. Once her whereabouts were published she could probably expect to receive more attention from the wider world, whether from fans or from the merely curious. In itself this didn't bother her. There was only one event in her diary from which she desired to exclude prying eyes and it was certainly going to be a task to guarantee its privacy, a task now to be made marginally more difficult. She was reluctant to ask for Vince's help in this, both because of his disapproval of her past and because her reunion with Ben must involve nobody else. It was to be an event as intimate as birth itself, if not more so, and she would organise it and execute it on her own.

She ran a bath. As the water roared from the taps her thoughts went back to the walk she'd taken in Port Meadow that afternoon and to the boy she'd seen sitting on a bench, arms stretched along its back, gazing about him and at peace with the world. It came back to her where she'd seen him before—working in the hotel. Waiting on her and serving her, a smile on his face and merriment in his eyes.

*

Conrad parked his machine alongside another one and well away from the wall-mounted LED. He was better prepared on this occasion, having armed himself with a plastic bag before he set off on his round trip to London. Nick had been much amused at the tale of the missing stash, consoling him with such remarks as 'You're not the first one' and 'At least you didn't park outside a police station'. 'Lucky my supply lines are good,' he added.

'It's not going to happen again,' said Conrad.

'Don't mind if it does,' said Nick, 'so long as you pay for it. Keep spending like this and I'll have to start giving you discounts.' And he laughed that laugh of his, the upper lip drawn back to reveal rodent teeth.

Conrad had a fairly good idea which occupant of the block of flats was most likely to have helped himself to such a windfall. None of the tenants was officiously law-abiding and a few were of the opposite tendency. Taking into account factors like opportunity and character it hadn't taken him long to home in on the most likely candidate. In the nature of things it was a hypothesis he couldn't test: all he had to go on by way of confirmation was the smirk on the guy's face. But there was nothing he could do about it and no point in crying over spilt milk.

Relying more on touch than on sight Conrad transferred his fresh stash to the plastic bag one item at a time. Nick used cardboard boxes for larger orders; some of these rattled when shaken, others merely whispered suggestively. A rhythmic rustling came from the bag as items were dropped into it. Anyone standing at a window in the block of flats might guess that a fox or squirrel was moving around in the vegetation beyond the car park, nocturnal fauna going about its clandestine business. In the distance the sound of the ring road was a steady sigh, ceaseless traffic through the sleepless night.

Gingerly Conrad closed the chamber and with a click the motorbike seat was back in place. He turned and walked to the rear entrance of the block of flats and let himself in with a swipe card. Four flights up and he was back in his flat. Out came the cardboard boxes, their contents to be spilt over the living room table, a whisky bottle and tumbler presently joining them, while Conrad selected *Parsifal* for the night's soundtrack, the plangent trumpet melody of the prelude snaking upwards as the first spliff of the evening sent forth its plume. Triple X skunk. This will do your head in, Nick had promised.

Conrad kicked his boots off and reclined on the sofa, eyes half closed, one arm hanging over the end. He was thinking of Tessa Wainwright. A few days ago she had dined in the hotel and he'd actually had the chance to be her waiter for the evening. She'd ordered the Dover sole followed by tiramisu and a decaf coffee. A glossy brochure called *Things to do in Oxford* sat by her elbow, probably plucked from among the complimentary items that were strewn about the Blenheim Suite, and from time to time she would turn a page of it and glance at a photo or a bit of text. On one occasion her finger went to the brochure's index and slid down the page to some entry, whereupon she picked the whole thing up and flicked her way to... he had craned his neck but was too far off to see what. Later she said, in the voice which had already surprised him as being lower than he'd expected, that 'tiramisu' was Italian for 'pick me up', to which he replied—but he couldn't now remember what he'd replied. At the end of the meal she'd paid more than was specified as the service charge on the bill: a tip, in short. *She* had given *him* a tip, a bonus—for his pains. It was exquisite.

He took a puff on his joint and downed some whisky. Then he got to his feet, skipped over to the table and popped an ecstasy pill just as the great Dresden Amen was being announced by the orchestra, Wagner's Christian leitmotif emerging from the pagan mists in a halo of golden sound. *God is dead*, thought Conrad, *long live God*. Aloud he intoned: *Amen*.

So what happens when we die, Merrivale?

Ask Pete, he'd know. Ask that pile of ashes, grey with a few bits still glowing, wisps of smoke rising out of it—ask that what happens when we die. Address your question to that smouldering heap and listen for the answer, and if you don't hear anything, if the heap stays silent despite all your pleading and interrogation, well maybe that *is* the answer. After we die it's [ ]. And the meaning of life is [ ]. Wasn't there some philosopher of the ancient world who realised the futility of saying anything at all (including 'It's futile to say anything at all') and so ended up sitting still and waggling one finger in answer to all enquiries? That's wisdom, that's the whole thing summed up once and for all: just... (He stood in the middle of the room swaying slightly and held out a hand, index finger scratching the air.) I came into the world and at some point I will go out of it and in between those two events there'll be a series of experiences, pleasant, painful or neutral. It isn't a journey, there's no Grail at the end of it—whatever the holy fool Parsifal thinks—and I'm not on a quest. I'm not the hero of a fantasy novel fighting off baddies and protecting princesses. Nor am I a node in a matrix of love. I'm *this* (he thumped his chest), what goes on goes on *here* (he slapped his skull), and the meaning of life is (more air-scratching). Everything else is shite. Everything and everyone.

He found that he was sitting on the floor with one arm wrapped around a table leg. The room rocked gently. 'Maybe not Tessa Wainwright', he murmured.

'You think she's an exception?'

Conrad looked up. The query had come from a man in a yellow jumpsuit sitting on the sofa. A grave smile played about his lips and he held a pipe in his left hand. In his nearly circular face the eyes, one green and one brown, twinkled and blinked.

'Who are you?' asked Conrad. 'And what the fuck are you doing in my flat?' He tried to form the intention of getting up but it led nowhere.

'You'd left your door open—I hope you don't mind,' said the man. 'I heard Wagner so I thought I'd come in. There's a fellow spirit, thought I. We're probably birds of a feather, I said to myself.'

'But who are you?' demanded Conrad.

'I live in the flat above you.' The man was poking in the bowl of his pipe with a matchstick. 'A neighbour.' He puffed on the pipe a few times and exhaled some smoke into the room that smelt of apples.

'A neighbour,' repeated Conrad dully.

'Yes. But I'd like to hear more on the subject you raised just now. You were saying, I think, that whereas the generality of humankind are to be regarded as—as...what was your expression? It was a very lively one, whatever it was.'

'Shite,' said Conrad.

'Exactly,' beamed the man. 'Shite. Everything and everyone is shite. A statement of remarkable pungency. Perceptive too, if I may say so. And yet—' He puffed some more on his pipe. 'And yet you wished to make an exception. You suggested that the generalisation you had just uttered failed in one instance, implying that the particular person you had in mind enjoys a special—nay, a unique status, separating her from the common run of humanity and putting her, so to speak, in a class of her own. Am I right?'

Conrad mumbled something inaudible. The room had stopped rocking but it seemed to have got darker, the lights were surely a notch dimmer. Electrics need sorting, he thought vaguely then coughed hard. His chest hurt.

'The woman in question,' continued the man, re-lighting his cigar, 'would appear to be a *ludus naturae*, a freak of nature. An anomaly. And yet she is merely the well-known author of a number of second-rate books belonging to the fantasy genre, delightful only to the middle- or low-brow reader. Is it really to be believed—' he leant forward as if to emphasise his point, 'that this mediocre person should constitute in herself an exception to what is in effect a law of nature?'

Conrad again attempted to shift his body, to move his limbs with a view to (perhaps) raising himself, but all he found he could do was scratch the carpet with one finger. Speech however had not deserted him.

'She gave me a tip,' he asserted.

'You mean she paid a little extra into the hotel coffers. That won't be coming your way, will it. That's Bernie's tip, not yours.' The man laughed—a falsetto roulade ending in a grunt. Removing his dark glasses he licked his grinning lips and croaked, 'Squeeze her, Conrad. Get your second instalment. What's hers is yours.'

Conrad nodded. It made sense. On the other hand he still had a fair bit of money from the first instalment. He didn't exactly need any more just yet even though the theft of stash #1 had required him to spend more than he would have liked.

'I –' he began.

'You're going to say you've got enough for the time being. But that's not the point. That woman is loaded, she's sitting on a ton of money, and you've simply found a way of siphoning some off. It's the reward for ingenuity. Plus...' The man's eyes were gleaming. 'It's fun, right? It's making her do things she doesn't want to do. Forcing her against her will, twisting her arm, squeezing her throat—harder, then a little harder... pushing into her...' He sniggered obscenely. 'Gets you aroused, doesn't it, Conrad? Are you getting hard? 'Course you are.'

And in fact an erotic tingling was spreading through Conrad's body, he began to moan, hugged himself and closed his eyes –

He was sitting on one of the kitchen chairs. Time seemed to have passed, he didn't know how much but his visitor had also moved, he was sitting across from Conrad on the other side of the table on which were spread pills, sachets, chunks of hash, a syringe and a whisky bottle. The man reached over for the bottle and half filled the tumbler that was standing in front of him. 'Cheers!' Conrad picked up his own and they clinked glasses. 'To your success,' proposed the visitor. He tilted his head back, took a swig and brought the tumbler down again with a bang, smacking his lips. A thin hand rose to undo the top button of his shirt, at the same time loosening the paisley necktie with a couple of sharp yanks.

The light in the room was strange; outlines of objects were sharply defined but at the same time their sizes and locations appeared fluid and changeable, so that a clock or a bowl that had seemed to be yards off was a moment later within easy reach. Meanwhile that same clock's ticking was the sole sound in the flat—the music of *Parsifal* had long since come to an end and the open kitchen window yielded only a vast silence. Outside the four walls of the flat the world might have ceased to exist.

Conrad spoke with a voice that surprised him by its distinctness: 'What is your name? You haven't yet introduced yourself.'

'You can call me Mr Hall.'

'Is that what other people call you?'

'I have a number of aliases.'

'And what is your line of work? Do you have a job?'

'I have a very long list of jobs—as long as your arm if I may so put it. Or longer. I'm a sort of general facilitator.'

'I'm afraid I'm none the wiser.'

Mr Hall bent his head apologetically. 'My present concern is to help you. I have a feeling you need encouragement, Conrad. You're a very special human being—you know that as well as I do—and although, as you rightly say, life is not a journey or a quest, nevertheless a person of your calibre does in a sense have a destiny to fulfil, a certain path that they must tread.'

Conrad poured himself some coke from a sachet and began cutting it. For a while Mr Hall watched him in silence, then he continued:

'In all such cases the problem is other people. Your friend Pete eventually showed himself to be more of a liability than a help, an obstacle rather than a comrade in arms, as it were, and I fear that his stupidity may yet come back to haunt you. But that is another topic. Again and again you will find that other human beings, either deliberately or accidentally, throw themselves like spanners into the works of a machine that would otherwise run perfectly smoothly. In this way they of course make themselves vulnerable to whatever measures or sanctions might be necessary, and it is for you to execute those measures or impose those sanctions with the same unflinching sense of purpose in every case.'

Conrad snorted a line and dropped the rolled-up banknote onto the table.

'In *every* case,' emphasised Mr Hall.

'I saw her in Port Meadow,' said Conrad irrelevantly. 'She just appeared in front of me. Out of nowhere.'

Mr Hall smiled. 'Beware of illusions, Conrad.'

'Aren't you one?'

'Certainly not. The test of an illusion is whether it guides you right or wrong. A mirage in a desert beckons the thirsty traveller to his untimely death—an oasis saves him. Follow me and you will arrive where you need to arrive, you will encompass what belongs to you. But you must avoid the tempting paths to either side that lead nowhere.'

He sucked on his pipe, gazed up at the ceiling and blew out three perfect smoke rings which hovered and disappeared.

'A woman's smiles and a woman's tears are mirages in the desert.'

'You sound like a bad nineteenth century poet,' said Conrad.

'If the truth is tawdry the expression of it will be equally tawdry,' replied Mr Hall and he put his feet up onto the table one after the other, the second resting on the first. Shiny patent leather boots reflected the light from the candles which Conrad only now noticed lined up on the mantelpiece on the other side of the room. The flame of the end candle was guttering annoyingly and he managed to extinguish it with a well-aimed breath. Mr Hall clapped silently by way of congratulation then went on:

'Tomorrow night would be a good time to issue a second demand. On this occasion you should use the stairs rather than the lift, I think. Do it in the wee hours when the lady will be fast asleep dreaming of whatever she dreams about. Murdering babies, perhaps.'

Suddenly he was on his feet reaching for his hat and coat. Conrad regarded him bleary-eyed, one hand round the whisky bottle.

'So good to have made your acquaintance,' said Mr Hall smiling sweetly beneath his toothbrush moustache. 'Thank you so much for your hospitality this evening. May your ventures prosper. I hope, I expect, we shall meet again.'

Conrad poured himself some whisky. When he looked up again his visitor was gone, leaving only a lingering smell of apples.

VII

The King he said, 'O mistress mine,
Queen of my heart, what's mine is thine,
*   My love, my dear.'*
A ring he gave her of silver and gold.
When this to Eleanor was told
Unto her lord she hied and said,
'Thou shalt not share my marriage bed,
*   My love, my dear.'*
King Henry's face was ashen grey. . .

Meg sat cross-legged on the floor cradling her guitar and singing. Her voice was a light pure soprano, childlike in timbre. Two or three simple chords underpinned the unfolding story, minor major minor. It was a new song, still undergoing polishing but nearly ready; Meg hoped to sing it at the Hedgehog soon. Maybe Conrad would come along to hear her.

She put aside the guitar and got up. It was several days since she'd seen or heard from Conrad and she was resisting the urge to phone him, knowing that neediness is a turn-off and suspecting that he might have disappeared for a while to do some writing. Whether his hours at the hotel were flexible or he just absented himself was a question to which she didn't know the answer. Both might be true, of course.

Humming snatches of newly minted melody she made herself a cup of orange blossom tea and thought vaguely of the coming week. On Wednesdays she worked in a health food store in east Oxford, on Thursdays she gave a few hours of guitar lessons. Apart from these sources she relied on her savings and on her mother's generosity. It was as well the rent was so low, something to be explained by reference to the unworldliness of an aging landlady as much as to the condition of the rooms.

As she sat down mug in hand Meg noticed a small grey oblong sitting on a pile of paperbacks a few feet away. She sipped her tea, incurious, her mind still half occupied with schedules and finances. One of her guitar students was leaving at the end of the month; she might need to advertise on Daily Info. Or she could ask Ann if she had any students going spare. What was that thing? She reached over and picked it up—it was a memory stick. She couldn't remember using a memory stick recently, let alone leaving it on top of that pile of books. Frowning, she held it up between thumb and forefinger as if to interrogate it. Then it occurred to her: it must be Conrad's, one of the numerous stray items he left about, signs that he sort of lived here, symbols of incipient domesticity (if only). Packets of rizlas, loose change, a pen, some keys, all marks of his presence or equally of his absence, depending on one's mood at the time. However, a memory stick was more than this, it was a door which if opened would reveal... But what would it reveal? Meg blushed at the thought of investigating. It would be like reading someone else's diary. Except that it seemed unlikely Conrad would transfer his private and intimate thoughts from a PC to a memory stick. A memory stick is for backing up material and for enabling you to continue working on it on other computers—oddly old-fashioned given the existence of the Cloud, but then sometimes Conrad was old-fashioned, it was a way of keeping out of step with the herd.

The novel. Of course! He'd probably copied what he'd so far written of it onto this stick, its first few chapters perhaps, or a plan, a synopsis, scenes and sketches—she had no idea how he wrote. Would it be wrong of her to take a peek at the work in progress? He'd be angry if he knew, very angry, of that she was aware. But he need never know.

For a minute or two Meg vacillated. Finally she persuaded herself with the argument that if she knew what sort of thing Conrad was writing she might one day be in a position to help him find a publisher for it. Conceivably. She went over to a low table on which her own laptop sat and settled down in front of it, the memory stick in her hand. Soon she was viewing a list of document names: *bank, ben, house, medical, plans, taskar(1), taskar(2), vince*. Which one was the novel, or which ones? The two biggest documents were *taskar(1)* and *taskar(2)*. The word *taskar* rang a faint bell; could Conrad have let slip the title of his book during one of their conversations? Or maybe the name of its hero? She was about to click on *taskar(1)* when her phone rang.

A nurse from the hospital was speaking down the line. For a moment Meg froze with alarm. But it was good news—her mother was well enough to go home. The doctors are very pleased with her, she's up and about, would like a word with her daughter, here she is now, hold on a second... there was a sound of fumbling then:

'Margaret?'

'Hello, mum, how are you doing? They say you can go home.'

'Yes, the doctor thinks I've made an excellent recovery. I just need to take it easy for a few days, he said. A nice man, I think he's Scottish...'

She sounds tired, thought Meg.

'Mum, I'll come down and stay with you for a couple of days. You'll want someone in the house.'

'Darling, you don't need to...'

'Don't be silly—I'll catch the next coach, there'll be one this afternoon. Tell them I'll take you home myself. Don't go anywhere, mum, I can be there within a few hours.'

They chatted for a little longer then Meg hung up. But she didn't leave immediately. She resumed what she'd been doing before the phone rang. Three paragraphs of *taskar(1)* were enough to jog her memory: Taskar, as she knew from posts on social media and conversations in the pub, was the hero of Tessa Wainwright's *The Quest*. Was Conrad writing a spoof? But it was too straight to be a parody—indeed, it could be the real thing. The genuine article.

That thought occupied Meg for much of the journey from Oxford to Bristol.

*

The parish church of St Giles gives its name to the great tree-lined thoroughfare in Oxford at the north end of which it stands. In its grounds is a war memorial topped with a cross. Stone steps surround the base and a flowerbed is laid out before it. Some distance in front of it there are two municipal benches looking south down St Giles. Seated on one of these was Vince Parker. In the distance he could see the Randolph Hotel on the corner of Beaumont Street; over to its left was the decorative Gothic spire of another memorial, the one which commemorates the Protestant martyrs Cranmer, Latimer and Ridley. Ensconced in his niche Thomas Cranmer returned Vince's gaze across the expanse of tarmac and traffic. Vehicles driving north peeled off into the two streams of Woodstock Road and Banbury Road flowing to either side of Vince where he sat.

But for the lack of an easel he could almost be a painter eying up Oxford's great boulevard. In fact he had an appointment with Tina Roberts. Ringing reception earlier in the day and asking to speak to her, he had in response to 'Who shall I say is calling?' answered simply 'Police'. When Tina came on the phone he reminded her of the gentleman who'd been enquiring about a room for his wedding anniversary a while back, just before Pete Rowlinson's unfortunate accident. That had been him, he explained—Arthur Mayhew, undercover detective working for Thames Valley Police. There was a criminal investigation underway relating to a person or persons working or staying at the Marlborough Hotel and he very much hoped she would be able to supply some information, in particular as regarded staff members, of whom she must have considerable first-hand knowledge. Her curiosity piqued, Tina readily agreed to meet him.

Vince had himself been phoned first thing that morning by Tessa, distraught and on the verge of tears.

'I've had another note pushed under my door, Vince.'

'What?'

'Another note demanding money. Ten thousand pounds. I can't keep paying at this rate, can I?'

Back to the drawing board, he thought. Bad luck. We all make mistakes.

'When was it delivered?'

'Some time after midnight. I was asleep in bed. It just said *Second instalment now due, Mrs Turnbull. Same amount before the end of this week.*'

Vince was silent.

'D'you think it's your suspect, Vince? One of the cleaners, didn't you say?'

So now he was counting on Tina Roberts for some enlightenment. It was she who had mentioned the note which Pete Rowlinson took up to Tessa's room, his extended absence from reception nearly causing her to be late for her yoga session. Could she have been fabricating? His intuition said no. His intuition also told him that there might be things she knew which it would be valuable to be told. She was that sort of person.

A couple in their sixties, both wearing shorts and dark glasses, sauntered past. The man clutched his smartphone in readiness for something or other, the woman swung a bottle of water by its neck between her index and middle fingers. American tourists, presumably. One of them addressed the other in French and Vince felt a pang of irritation. His powers had better not be deserting him. That business with Rowlinson had been a blunder, no doubt about it, one that he would very much like not to have committed. It reminded him of an unfortunate episode in his police career involving a suspect who turned out (too late) to have had a perfectly good alibi. Some serious hushing up had been required on that occasion. 'Your problem, Parker,' he remembered the superintendent saying, 'is jumping to conclusions. A little less rushing in where angels fear to tread and you'd make a half-decent copper.' He knew the ways of his erstwhile colleagues well enough not to be much bothered in the present instance by the thought of a criminal investigation: the trail would start to go cold, the detective on the case was probably looking forward to his retirement and a verdict of suicide would soon strike everybody as the obvious choice, whatever the coroner said. Even so he preferred not to make mistakes.

Well, that's all water under the bridge, he thought. The past is the past; what's important is planning the next steps. I'll get my man yet and God help him.

He caught sight of Tina Roberts walking briskly up past the Lamb and Flag, a slight figure in a white coat with a tote bag slung over her shoulder. Soon she would be coming over by the pedestrian crossing on Banbury Road. He turned in his seat to watch her. Good to assess your witness before they have a chance to assess you. A moment later she was approaching him, myopic-looking eyes blinking in the sun and a nervous smile on her face. When he stood up to greet her they both found that her nose was roughly at a level with the top button of his waistcoat.

'Good afternoon, Miss Roberts,' Vince said looking down at her. 'Thank you for sparing the time. It's much appreciated.'

They sat down on the bench and Vince cleared his throat as a preamble while Tina deposited her bag on the ground and tried to adopt the stiff-backed posture of an obedient citizen.

'Naturally I can't divulge all the details of the investigation to which I referred on the phone,' began Vince, 'but in a nutshell one of the guests at the Marlborough Hotel has had her bank account hacked by someone we believe to be associated with the hotel and it's possible that the individual in question is targeting other people in the same way. At first it looked as if Mr Rowlinson might be the criminal but that hypothesis has been abandoned in light of subsequent events.'

Tina nodded to show her comprehension.

'Miss Roberts, do you mind repeating to me what you told me on the day I visited the hotel, concerning Pete Rowlinson's conveyance of a written message to one of the guests?' Vince asked this to check Tina's memory and narrative consistency, and in case any other details might emerge. In this he was to be amply rewarded.

'The note to Tessa Wainwright, you mean?' said Tina, picking up the thread at once. 'Yes, well, Pete said he had to take this message to Miss Wainwright that had come through for her and would I stand in for him while he was gone...'

'Stand in for him at reception?'

'That's right. So after quarter of an hour I go up to fetch him—he was meant to be only five minutes and I had my yoga class to get to, the instructor doesn't like us to be late, you know—and I find him in the Blenheim Suite with Conrad Merrivale.'

'With who?'

'Conrad Merrivale, he works in the kitchen. Or rather he's one of the waiters, comes in three or four days a week.'

'What was he doing there?'

'He had some story about wanting to lend Pete a book, said he'd followed him up to the Blenheim Suite to hand it over. Something to do with psychological something or other. I remember its name—*Hard Times*.'

'Can you describe this man?'

Tina pulled a face. 'He's a creep. Ponytail and a stupid little beard. Studies at the university, or so he says, takes drugs, I s'pose lots of them do...'

'Drugs? What sort of drugs?'

'Pot mainly, I think, but I'm pretty sure he does the hard stuff as well. I think he deals too—saw him round the back of the hotel once with one of the maintenance men, huddled in a corner and swapping something for cash. I'd say that was probably drugs, wouldn't you?'

'I wouldn't like to venture an opinion, Miss Roberts,' said Vince judiciously. 'You could very well be correct. Do you happen to know when this Merrivale fellow comes in for work? It might be a good idea for me to interview him, given what you've told me.'

'He'll be in this evening.'

'Will he now,' said Vince, and he resolved to dine that evening with Tessa.

Their interview was soon over. Vince thanked Tina warmly for her co-operation and assistance; Tina headed towards the city centre to do some shopping. As she made her way down St Giles she reflected on Arthur Mayhew's considerable bulk—doubtless he was as strong as an ox what with those broad shoulders and huge hands. In uniform he must cut quite a figure, as imposing as... But it was without his uniform that she fell to imagining him, massive and powerful and pressing the hot breath out of her.

*

Bloody computers, I hate them, thought Conrad. You're in the middle of working on something, all is going smoothly, when for no reason at all the screen freezes and half an hour's toil looks as if it'll have been in vain, a few hundred carefully chosen words down the plughole. Fuck it, frankly.

For once Conrad had been working on something to do with his degree, writing an extended essay which had to be submitted half way through next term. The overall theme was a comparison of DH Lawrence's treatment of sex with James Joyce's. In the middle of a paragraph on *Sons and Lovers* his laptop had gone on strike, the cursor sliding impotently over the text like a long-legged fly on the surface of a pond. It was the Word programme that had seized up; other programmes seemed to be working. For his age group Conrad was remarkably computer-illiterate and on occasions like this he generally sought out a friend or if necessary an IT assistant. He would have to do that now. But there were certain documents that would need deleting before the laptop could be entrusted to anybody else.

He went to the File Explorer page and located the Wainwright documents. Not suitable for innocent eyes, these. Since they were preserved on a memory stick there was nothing to prevent him deleting them and that is what he now did. He then spent some time phoning around till he found someone available to fix the problem—in the end he got hold of an outfit on the Cowley Road called PC Vets. The cost would be nugatory, especially considering the boost that one of his bank accounts would shortly be getting (the one in the name of John McKendrick). He smiled at the thought and at the still fresh memory of paying a nocturnal visit to Tessa Wainwright's hotel room, secretive as a lover. Pimpernel the postboy.

To think that all her riches came from writing fantasy fiction. Eat your hearts out, Lawrence and Joyce. Really he should read some more of *taskar(2)*; reading *taskar(1)* had entertained him more than he'd expected and it would certainly come as a bit of light relief from *Lady Chatterley*. As soon as he got his computer back he'd do that. Just re-transfer the documents from the memory stick and Bob's your uncle.

His thoughts stopped in their tracks. The memory stick. Where was it? He was sitting at his living room table, the open laptop in front of him with some odds and ends around it—a couple of books, a pencil, ashtray, breadcrumbs, a used knife. No memory stick. Vaguely he turned his head from side to side as if looking for it but what he needed to do was go back in time to whenever it was he'd last had it in his possession. If he'd lost the thing that made his claim to dangerous knowledge shakier; he hadn't memorised the text of *ben* and if push came to shove TW might just throw any allegations back in his face, or the face of the relevant media outlet. She might even sue for libel. Push might not come to shove, indeed it was to be hoped that it wouldn't, but it was stupid robbing a bank with a gun that wasn't loaded.

Rack your brains, Conrad. I've been carrying it around with me, haven't I. It was in my jeans pocket. He patted his pockets just in case, to no effect. An image came of himself in Meg's attic wrenching the memory stick from the right-hand pocket, leg extended. He was sitting on the beanbag. Yes, that's it...he'd taken it out and put it somewhere for safe keeping, then forgotten all about it. It was the day of Pete's funeral. The remedy was straight-forward. Go round to Meg's this evening to retrieve the thing.

He found his phone and dialled her number. Even as it rang the thought occurred to him that he mustn't tell her about the stick—just invite himself round. (She'd ac-cept.) If he mentioned the stick curiosity might after all get the better of her.

'Hello, Con.'

'Hi, Meg. How are things?'

'Actually, Con, this isn't a great time—I'm with my mum in the hospital. I can't talk for long.'

She sounded somehow cool, distant. Maybe her mother's seriously ill, thought Conrad, maybe she's try-ing hard to hold it together.

'Oh—sorry. I was hoping to come round to your place tonight, that's all. Haven't seen you for a bit.'

'No...It's been a while. But I'm in Bristol right now, I won't be back for a few days.' Pause. 'I'll call you, okay?'

'Sure...okay. I hope everything's all right.'

Definitely on the cool side. Not the sort of lovey-dove manner to which one has become accustomed. The shadow of a frown crossed his face. Still, whatever—that didn't matter, what mattered was that she'd be out that evening when he called round and got Elise or whoever to let him in. It's easier searching a room if you don't have to do it under the occupant's gaze.

*

The second blackmail demand poisoned Tessa's feelings about staying at the Marlborough. It was fairly clear now that someone who worked at the hotel was doing this to her. Whoever it was had pushed that second envelope under her door while she slept only a few feet away; they had crept down the carpeted corridor that led to the Blenheim Suite, listened at the door for any noises of activity, smiled to themselves and left the insolent and outrageous message for her to find in the morning when she had showered and dressed and was on the point of going down for breakfast. There lay the envelope looking up at her, its blank face signalling evil as eloquently as a sadist's sneer. She had opened it with a sick feeling in the pit of her stomach, knowing in advance what it would be. *Second instalment now due, Mrs Turnbull.*

The result was that she could no longer regard her room as a cosy haven, a private refuge in which to work and rest. Her space had been violated. She would obviously have to move to a different hotel. After ringing Vince with the news of the demand she had left the Marlborough and breakfasted in a nearby café, then gone for a long walk. This to some extent had calmed her nerves. They were further calmed by Vince's phone call in the early afternoon in which he told her he was now confident of the blackmailer's identity and just needed to establish one or two extra facts before moving in for the kill. His plan was to scare the person off thoroughly, to emphasise if not to exaggerate the legal penalties of blackmail and to offer a deal: 'You can keep the first ten thousand but any more demands and you'll be nicked. The story you want to put about will be denied as false, the lurid fantasy of a diseased mind, and you'll be done for libel in addition to blackmail. My advice, sonny (she imagined Vince saying) is to quit while the going's good.'

Tessa accepted Vince's plan as the best option, even though a chance remained of the blackmailer's publicising what he knew about Ben. It was, she hoped, only a small chance. In any case, weekly payments of £10k would simply bankrupt her—Vince's advice was to ignore the second demand and she was as usual happy to go along with what he suggested.

'We can talk about it some more over dinner.'

'Of course, Vince. Where?'

'At the Marlborough if that's all right with you. I need to come in anyway. Want to get a closer look at our suspect.'

Despite vague misgivings Tessa had agreed. In the interim she bought a copy of the Oxford Mail, on page two of which she saw her own face staring out at her above the 'interview' she had given a couple of days ago in the hotel lobby.

> Fans of The Quest *had a unique chance to meet its author, Tessa Wainwright, last Monday when she*

*chatted and signed books at Blackwell's Bookshop.
Sam Gardiner of the Mail caught up with her at the
Marlborough Hotel where she has been staying to
ask her about her trip to Oxford.*

*Tessa Wainwright (46) last visited the city
when she was in her twenties, she told him. 'I love
Oxford. It's always been very close to my heart. I'm
so glad to be here again.' And what did she think
Taskar and Lemula would have made of it? 'Oh,
they'd love it too,' she laughs. 'It's a place full of
adventure'...*

Carrying the newspaper with her Tessa went down to
the restaurant shortly before eight. It was busy so she
asked for a table in the corner where it would be possible to converse in relative privacy and hadn't been
seated there long when the young man who'd waited on
her recently and whom she'd seen on a bench in Port
Meadow glided into her presence and said, 'Good evening, madam. Can I get you something to drink?'

A gentle voice, attentive gaze—Tessa felt a warmth in
his demeanour and smiled back at him.

'A glass of white wine, please.'

'We have several white wines, madam.' He leant over
her to indicate the wine list on the reverse of her menu
and she registered a breath of patchouli. 'The Chilean
chardonnay is very popular, or you could have this
South African chenin blanc, that's one of my own favourites...I believe you ordered the pinot grigio a few
nights ago.'

'Did I? What a good memory you have.'

He inclined his head modestly.

'Well, let it be the chenin blanc this time, then,' said Tessa.

'A small or a large glass?'

'Make it a small one,' she replied, at the same moment perceiving Vince's motionless figure standing a little way off. His eyes were on the two of them and he appeared to be waiting for something to happen.

'Certainly, madam.'

The young man turned to go and Vince's glance slid to one side. Tessa followed it and saw at the door of the kitchen a woman nod her head once. Then like a statue coming to life Vince shifted and moved, crossing the floor and arriving at her table.

'My dear Tessa,' he said, 'I hope you haven't been waiting long.' He pulled out a chair and lowered his heavy frame into it.

'Do you know that girl?' asked Tessa. Vince looked round to where the woman had been standing. She had gone now but even so he answered, 'I consulted her earlier today. She had some useful information to offer concerning our problem.'

Our problem. A problem shared is a problem halved. Vince had the matter in hand. It was good to know but she had a queasy feeling about unscheduled possibilities and shadowy procedures.

He'd noticed the copy of the Oxford Mail at her elbow. 'Reading material,' he remarked redundantly.

'Yes, it's today's,' she said opening it up. 'Look—there's me.'

She handed the paper to him at page two and he began to read.

'They've shaved two years off my age but apart from that it's accurate. Though it does make me come across as a bit of an airhead; that always seems to happen, I don't know why.' For some reason her voice had begun trembling.

Her chenin blanc arrived. Vince looked up from his paper. Smiling politely the waiter asked, 'Would you care for something to drink, sir?'

In a clipped voice Vince answered, 'Just tap water, thank you.'

The young man nodded and went off.

'Vince,' said Tessa. 'The person you suspect of leaving those notes—is he nearby? Is he in this room? Why was that girl nodding to you like that? Please tell me, Vince, I need to know. Being in this hotel has become very stressful for me since this morning, I really don't know if...'

'Tessa,' he interrupted, 'you mustn't worry yourself like this. Everything's going to be all right—I'm on top of it, I promise you. The best thing you can do is to focus on your writing. I will sort out the other matter.'

The other matter, alias *our problem*. All right, all right. Vince will deal with it, Vince the ex-policeman. Focus on *The Quest* and on Ben. She drank some wine. Clear your head of worries and think about the completion of your novel and your reunion with your son.

As if he had read her thoughts Vince asked, 'When's your meeting with Ben?'

'On Thursday. I'm meeting him here between two and three.' She managed to smile. 'Thanks for asking.'

*

The dinner was a pleasant one although Tessa's mood remained on edge. The ponytailed waiter was efficient and courteous but there was none of the friendly loquacity that he'd displayed on her arrival—that seemed to have evaporated with the advent of Vince. Tessa had three more glasses of wine, progressing from chenin blanc to cabernet sauvignon. Vince as always stuck to water. Over dessert (profiteroles x 2) he repeated what he'd said earlier: that she shouldn't worry about a thing, should instead put all her energies into finishing *The Homecoming* and seeing her boy and that he, Vince, would take care of everything. It would be a case of giving a petty criminal the equivalent of a clip round the earhole, after which everyone would be able to sleep easy.

At around 10.15 Tessa said she was tired and would go to bed. 'You don't have to go, Vince, you're still drinking your tea.' (He'd ordered a mint tea.) 'I'll see you tomorrow or the day after, I expect. Please let me know of any developments.'

'Of course.'

He watched her get up and leave, walking with careful steps, her gaze bent down and avoiding people's eyes. I hope she gets some sleep, he thought.

The restaurant was emptying out now. Eventually the three waiters on duty were just hanging around, two of them chatting in a desultory way while the third, his quarry, stood apart, hands behind his back, eyes half closed. Vince examined the face: he had talked to Tessa about a petty criminal but the expression on that face was not that of a petty criminal, it was at once merrier and bleaker than the face of any criminal he'd ever met—sardonic, nihilistic. Just a fancy little reptile, Vince said to himself. Should be easy to squash.

He was the last customer to leave. Having paid the bill fifteen minutes earlier he finally got to his feet at the point when the odd light was being switched off as a gentle hint to diners, made his way through the lobby and went out of the building and round to the side. A passage leading off took you to the hotel's back entrance; it was in this passage that Pete Rowlinson had met his end. It was also in this passage that Conrad Merrivale kept his motorbike, according to Tina Roberts. Sure enough there it was, leaning against the wall and partially obscuring two large wheelie bins that stood beyond it—a Triumph Scrambler if Vince wasn't mistaken.

He stationed himself within the shadows at this end of the passage to observe proceedings. His car was nearby. He'd had to park it on double yellows but in the unlikely event of his getting a fine he could always pay himself out of the Wainwright coffers. This whole mission was for her sake, after all. Once he'd verified that Merrivale was getting on his bike he'd return to the car. At a discreet distance he would then follow the young man to his home address, having established which he would be in a position to make use of the information the following day when Merrivale was out.

He didn't have to wait long. Out of the door and down the steps came Merrivale wearing leathers and carrying his helmet. A moon was in the sky and light came from the window of the hotel scullery; Vince could follow every movement of his prey, the donning of the helmet, the zipping up of the jacket. Satisfied, he slid away and twenty seconds later was in his car on the other side of the street from the Marlborough's main entrance, fingers of one hand drumming on the steering wheel. Merrivale appeared a moment later pushing his bike. A car drove past, music thumping. The biker stood awhile as if in thought then without haste got astride his machine. Vince reached for the ignition.

Their journey was a sedate one, carrying them from the Banbury Road across to Woodstock Rd, down Observatory St to Walton St and from thence via Richmond Rd to the labyrinth of streets constituting the district of Jericho. Vince kept his distance, once allowing another car to come between them but never letting the bike out of his sight. Eventually he saw Merrivale pulling up outside a house in Wharf St. He drove past as the rider was getting off his bike, noting the house number: twenty-seven. Parking a little further down, Vince got out of his car and walked back towards the house. Merrivale was just entering. The Triumph Scrambler stood close by. On Vince's side of the street an alley led away somewhere and in the mouth of this alley the ex-policeman took up his position. From here he had a clear view of the house, a two-storey terraced property—three-storey if you counted the loft—Victorian, red brick, unpretentious. Let to tenants, no doubt. Through the curtains of the ground floor window a light was shining as it had been when he'd driven past but the first floor was dark. Then as he watched Vince noticed for the first time a skylight in the roof. He noticed it because a light had come on in the attic and a faint shadow could be seen passing over the ceiling within, the shadow of a human body moving about. The shadow of Conrad Merrivale.

VIII

MRS OWENS WAS TAKEN HOME in a taxi organised by her daughter Meg. During the taxi ride their conversation persuaded Meg that her mother was almost fully recovered from the aneurysm that had landed her in hospital and twenty-four hours later she felt her conscience clear when she decided to go back to Oxford in the evening. Although she loved her mother, staying with her for any length of time was always a test of Meg's patience and good will. Moreover, there was a conversation she needed to have with Conrad. It would, she hoped, clear the air; in the meantime it hung over her oppressively so that she was distracted and irritable. Even her mother noticed.

Mrs Owens wanted to see her daughter off at the bus station but Meg vetoed the suggestion as firmly as she was able. 'You should take it easy for a few more days, mum,' she said. 'Doctor's orders. I'll ring you tomorrow to see how you are.' They kissed at the front door of the house Meg had grown up in and then she was off.

Back at 27 Wharf St that evening she met Elise in the hallway with wet hair and wrapped in a large pink towel. 'Hi, Meg. Conrad called round last night, he said he'd left something in your room which he wanted to collect. I let him go up, hope that was okay.'

'Did he say what it was?'

'No, but he must have found it—the front door banged not long after. Conrad always bangs it, doesn't he?'

'Mm.'

'How's your mum?'

'Oh, she's fine, thanks. Much better.'

Meg climbed the stairs with a heavy weight inside her. Why hadn't Con told her? Maybe it was something trivial he'd left, not worth bothering her about. But she couldn't help thinking of the memory stick, with what seemed to be a chunk of Tessa Wainwright's novel on it. Tessa Wainwright who was staying at the hotel Conrad worked at.

Easing open the trap door into the attic Meg pushed her bag through ahead of her then climbed up after it. The room appeared much as she'd left it. Her eyes went to the pile of paperbacks that stood under an old standard lamp with a red shade. It should be sitting on that pile and—her heart sank—there it wasn't. He'd come for the memory stick after all. Oh well, she thought, it does belong to him, it's not as if he was stealing. She began making herself a cup of tea. As she waited for the kettle to boil and in order to force her mind onto pleasanter things she sang softly to herself: *A ring he gave her of silver and gold. When this to Eleanor was told...* She was pleased with the song. They'd like it at the Hedgehog. 'Very Meg,' Callum would say, 'very mediaeval.' Callum played the Northumbrian pipes and was a widower in his sixties, full of zest, wiry and balding. He had a habit of putting his arm round your shoulders but she didn't mind that, it was more fatherly than anything else. Sometimes he sang if anybody would accompany him and his voice was mellow and tender, it surprised you when you first heard it. If he were there on Saturday they could do some songs together.

Instinctively she glanced over to where her guitar was propped up in a corner of the room. Something looked different in that part of the attic. A few feet from the guitar stood a low table, Moroccan in design; it appeared somehow different, its lacquered top seemed oddly uncluttered. Something's meant to be sitting on it, she thought. An object isn't there which is usually there. A missing object.

My laptop.

*

bank, ben, house, medical, plans, taskar(1), taskar(2), vince. He resisted the impulse to open the document that bore his name. Indeed, he hardly needed to open any document, the list itself spoke its origins clearly enough. Property of Tessa Wainwright, no doubt about it. He would take a quick forensic look at ben to ascertain its contents, determine the degree of gory detail gone into in connection with the post-natal episode, and search for occurrences of 'Turnbull'. That should suffice. It was unlikely he'd need to bother Tessa with any queries.

He clicked on *ben* and ten minutes later closed it, a moue of distaste on his pockmarked face. You had to feel sorry for the girl but even so—what a way to mess up your life. His own brief marriage had been childless and he didn't look back on it with any feelings of nostalgia or regret: no thwarted ideals either of romance or of parenthood cluttered up his psyche, thank God. As a consequence it was hard for him to regard the writhings of more sentimental types without a certain disdain. But there was another component to his response, one that he scarcely liked to admit to himself. The fact was that he felt aggrieved that Tessa had kept him in the dark for so many years. He had served her faithfully all this time, been by her side professionally and, yes, personally, and yet she had seen fit to exclude him, keep him at arm's length, withholding from him this vital fact about her even as she called him friend. Well, she had had to spill the beans to him eventually. She had realised her mistake, had come to him in distress and maybe now felt a little ashamed of her past secrecy. Whether or not that was the case, he certainly wasn't the sort to forget that Tessa was his charge, the woman it was his job to look after and protect. Nothing could change that. And now he had his man. He most certainly had his man.

A peremptory solution would ordinarily have had a strong prima facie appeal but it had to be said that he'd recently lost some of his appetite for that sort of approach. He now thought it likely that both Merrivale and Rowlinson had been behind the blackmail but he might be wrong, Rowlinson's innocence couldn't be ruled out. Whatever the truth about that, one person (Tina) definitely knew of his motive for hostility to the hotel waiter while another (Tessa) might well have inferred it. A peremptory solution could easily have the effect of drawing suspicion upon Vincent Parker. Hence it would have to be more or less as he'd outlined to Tessa: put the fear of God into the little runt.

Vince was sitting in his room in the B & B on Iffley Rd that he'd checked into for the duration of Tessa's Oxford visit. The laptop he had brought away with him from Wharf St sat open on the desk in front of him. The operation of obtaining it had gone as smoothly as he could have wished. Having determined from Tina that Merrivale would be on duty again that evening he had simply visited the house at around six o'clock and, the Triumph Scrambler being nowhere in evidence, had presented himself to the nice black girl who answered the door as a representative of a pest control company. He flashed a card in her face as confirmation—an old library card in fact—and explained that his company had been phoned by the owner of the property in connection with an infestation in the loft.

'Oh my god! Infestation of what?' Adaego had asked.

'Pharaoh ants, miss. A serious pest. We'll need to inspect the loft. Do you know if the occupant is at home?'

Adaego, conditioned by society both to respect people's undeclared gender identities and to protect the anonymity of vulnerable females, opted for the third person plural pronoun and replied, 'No, they're out. Don't know when they'll be back.' The dust thus inadvertently thrown in Vince's eyes he made his way up to Meg's attic, a black briefcase of 'inspection equipment' in his hand, and swiftly found the PC he was looking for. This he loaded into the briefcase. That the attic's furnishings should have displayed a—to Vince's mind—distinctly feminine taste only confirmed the degeneracy of the individual concerned. Not that Vince had had the time to look around him much.

Going downstairs again he sought out Adaego in the kitchen to tell her that he'd made his inspection and would be sending a report, with quotation for the necessary works, to the owner of the property.

'Whatever,' replied Adaego smiling, as she put a potato into the microwave.

He had let himself out of the house at precisely 6.35. He didn't know it but this was at just the time Meg's coach was pulling out of the central bus station in Bristol. It was now 7.15. At his meeting with Tina Roberts the two of them had exchanged phone numbers and he decided to give her a ring.

'Hello, Tina?' (He sensed that she would like it if they were on first name terms.)

'Is that Mr Mayhew?'

'Do call me Arthur.'

A simpering noise.

'You've been very helpful so far, Tina, and I wonder if I could prevail on you once again to lend me your assistance.'

'Of course—Arthur.'

'Perhaps it seems strange to you that I didn't take the opportunity of interviewing Mr Merrivale last night?'

'I did wonder.'

'Well, I don't mean to name-drop but Tessa Wainwright's an old friend of mine and I spotted her at one of the tables. Merrivale was actually her waiter, I suppose you noticed that. I knew she was staying at the hotel so it came as no surprise to see her, but having bumped into her like that I had to go and say hello. Ended up with me having dinner with her. But I might try to catch Merrivale after he clocks off tonight—if he'll be there, that is.'

'Yes, he's in tonight.'

'There, you've answered my first question!' He permitted himself a friendly laugh. All in a good cause. Tina reciprocated. 'My second question is less a question, more a request. You mentioned that this Merrivale partakes of illegal substances, possibly even does some dealing. If you could keep a lookout for any of that sort of activity, gather any information about his drug habits etc. etc., I'd be grateful if you'd let me know, Tina. In the event of his being charged in connection with the other matter, that kind of additional background could assist the police case materially.'

'Oh yes, I can see that,' said Tina. 'I'll definitely keep my eyes peeled, Arthur. Eyes and ears. Maybe I'll see you again this evening?' she added hopefully.

'It's quite possible, Tina. It'll depend on how I decide to broach the issue with Mr Merrivale. Sometimes the element of surprise is the crucial thing.'

*

Bernie was disconsolate. For reasons he could only guess at (and his guesses were mainly wide of the mark) Tessa Wainwright had decided to transfer her custom to another hotel. She wouldn't even tell him which hotel. It was a terrible blow. Still, the world-famous author had spent a whole fortnight at the Marlborough. To those curious about her departure he indicated that this had always been her plan, that she wished to experience some of the variety which Oxford has to offer—a natural enough motive in a novelist, you had to admit.

As he stood at the entrance of the Marlborough to see her off Bernie caught the words she uttered to the taxi driver: 'The Zenith Hotel, please.' The *Zenith*? That two-star establishment? Bernie felt almost indignant. 'Maybe she's writing *Down and Out in Paris and Oxford*,' he said to himself. His mood improved a little with the consciousness of having produced a witty thought. It improved further as he reminded himself that the newspapers had reported her as being a guest of the Marlborough, not of the Zenith. As far as the reading public was concerned she was still here. Going back inside and passing reception Bernie wondered, not for the first time, whether Pete's suicide had spooked her. Impossible to say.

Meanwhile Tessa was conveyed safely to the comfort of the Zenith Hotel, somewhere in Summertown. Here she would be a forty minutes' walk away from the city centre; more importantly—she hoped—she'd be out of reach of her blackmailer. Even given the decision to ignore any further demands, the idea of his continuing to harass her was loathsome. Creeping up to her room in the middle of the night and leaving those envelopes... what sort of a person does that? A sick one.

Shaking her head to banish the thought of him (though who knew?—maybe it was a her) Tessa unpacked her things. She had spoken to the manager on her way up telling him of her desire for complete privacy and anonymity. He had been entirely amenable. Now as she hung up dresses in the wardrobe and arranged toiletries in the bathroom she found herself relaxing, the tension of the last thirty-six hours lifting. Dinner at the Zenith went on till ten o'clock and she would get in a couple of hours working on *The Homecoming* before that. Back to wholesome health-giving routine.

As she set up her laptop on the coffee table—not the best height but there was no desk—her phone rang. It was Vince.

'Tessa, I thought I should get in touch to see how you are. You seemed rather fragile last night over dinner. Understandably so, of course.'

'I've moved hotel, Vince. I'm staying at the Zenith.'

If Vince was annoyed at this unilateral decision he didn't show it. 'Ah. Yes. To put some distance between you and the blackmailer. A sound idea. And are you comfortable in your new abode?'

'Perfectly.'

'I assume you've told young Ben. You wouldn't want him turning up at the Marlborough and. . . '

'Yes, I texted him this afternoon. He knows where to come.'

'And the book, my dear Tessa? I hope all this unpleasantness hasn't disrupted the flow of your creativity.'

'I was just settling down to do some work on it when you phoned.'

'I mustn't disturb you any further in that case. Just to let you know that my investigations have been bearing fruit; I very much doubt if you'll be receiving any more bother after today.'

Tessa felt lucky. How many literary agents have prior experience working in the police? He was one in a million was dear old Vince. Her good and faithful servant.

'Thank you, Vince, thank you for all you've been doing. It means a lot to me.'

'Please don't mention it. It's what I'm paid for, isn't it. And it's good to have something to keep the old grey cells ticking over.' He chuckled. 'A bit like playing chess with an unseen opponent.'

*

The bipolar chef hadn't lasted long. His replacement was a woman, the first woman chef to have run the kitchen at the Marlborough Hotel and another feather in Bernie's cap. 'Here at the Marlborough we pride ourselves on an ethos of diversity and inclusivity,' he would sometimes pronounce when the occasion seemed to demand it. Conrad couldn't care less. So long as things were managed efficiently and nobody pestered him he'd have been happy if the chef were a horse. Inge had been in post for four evenings and all was going smoothly so far.

'Makes a nice change,' Tina said. 'Don't you think, Conrad?' She'd been firing pointless questions at him quite a lot recently. He just shrugged. Tina stared at him for a second then went back into the kitchen.

The restaurant was going to get busy: they were expecting a party of twelve later on, conference delegates of some description. In readiness three tables had been pushed together to make one. There was a smattering of hotel guests but TW wasn't among them. As he was wondering idly whether she would appear, a lone diner on table five caught his eye and beckoned. Conrad recognised the man at once and felt a nauseating mixture of anger and surprise. The idiot was grinning openly, much as he must have done when he lifted the stash from Conrad's motorbike and walked off with it. He beckoned again. There was no ignoring him.

'It's Mr Motorbike, isn't it,' said the man when Conrad arrived at his table. 'Didn't know you worked here.'

'What can I do for you?' said Conrad quietly.

'Do for me? Do for me?' The man began laughing. 'That's lovely, that is. Do for me!' He had a beer and now he drank from it. Crewcut, shallow forehead, bad teeth, misshapen nose. A regular *Untermensch*, though Conrad. What do you expect.

'Between you and me,' the man went on, lowering his voice confidentially, 'I was staggered. Gobsmacked.

At the street value, I mean. That was a four-figure sum, that was. Waiters must earn a fuck of a lot of money!' He guffawed and slapped the table with a hairy hand. Conrad remained silent. 'Good quality stuff too, from what I could see.' Suddenly the man's face assumed a serious expression. 'Which is why I contacted the police.'

He held Conrad's gaze for a few seconds then turned away to look around the restaurant. 'Nice place, this,' he murmured. 'Somebody recommended it. I'm just waiting for my girlfriend. Nice evening out, you know, dinner for two, all the trappings.'

'So you're all right then?' said Conrad finally. 'You don't need anything?'

'No, bugger off,' replied the other and he drank some more of his beer. Conrad withdrew.

He knew better than to take what that ape had said about contacting the police seriously. It was his idea of a joke and given that he was an ape it wasn't much of an idea. A little later when Conrad looked over to table five he saw that the ape had been joined by his girlfriend, a tartily dressed hunk of flesh with bits of metal in her face. What a sweet couple. To be passed over in silence.

It wasn't long before the conference delegates began trickling in from whatever lecture or seminar they'd been attending, men mainly but with a handful of younger females. Conrad made himself useful, bringing menus, taking charge of the odd coat, chatting personally and directing people's attention to today's specials, listed on a blackboard behind the bar. From the conversation of the delegates he picked up that it was a philosophy conference they had come from, relating somehow to issues in Artificial Intelligence. Several times he caught the word 'post-humanism'. A man in his thirties who had seated himself at the midpoint of one of the rectangle's long sides was holding forth on the topic of inter-species obligation. As far as preliminary orders went, the company desired beer or tap water. Alcohol must go to their heads, thought Conrad on his way to the bar.

Twenty minutes later the party was in full swing, a well-behaved full swing, and Conrad was doling out the mainly vegetarian starters. From this group of diners he received none of those cooing, groping attentions that had been lavished on him by the hen night girls two weeks ago; to these people he was invisible, a mechanism that supplied their wants while they carried on the important business of talking. He didn't care which sort of treatment he got, fulsome or negligent. It was all in a day's work and in any case his mind was elsewhere, he was feeling nervy and distracted. Partly it was because of what that oaf had said, which he knew was only intended to disconcert him but even so... There was also the text he'd received from Meg just before his shift started. *Need to talk to you, Mx*, was all it said. Talk to him about what? What subject was so weighty she couldn't give a hint of it in a text message? Was she thinking of leaving him? Was she pregnant? This sort of mystery-mongering was unlike her. He'd give her a ring after work but if she wanted a tête-à-tête it'd have to wait till tomorrow.

The evening dribbled away. Once Tina nabbed him while he was in the kitchen to tell him what she was up to over the weekend—Alton Towers with her nan, apparently—and to ask him whether he had any plans himself. It occurred to him to wonder whether she was developing a crush; this was the third time in one evening she'd addressed him on a matter of no importance. 'I don't know yet,' he'd replied, to her evident dissatisfaction. Meanwhile the ape and his girlfriend had finished their meal and departed, no doubt off for some mutual zoophilia. The philosophers carried on to the bitter end, larynxes outdistancing mandibles by several circuits, until finally only a rump of the original party remained, three men including the mid-table oracle, the latter still banging on about inter-species obligation would you believe. And all evening no Tessa Wainwright. Conrad felt a tad wistful.

At 11.15 he got away, and after changing out of his uniform and checking his phone for any further texts—there were none—he made his way out of the building via the scullery. As usual he went through the back door, down the stone steps and into the passage where his bike awaited him. Standing beside it he put on his helmet and fastened his jacket. As on the previous evening the moon was out. I'll ring or text Meg when I get home, he said to himself. If she's going to be so mysterious she'll have to wait a bit. And then I'm going to hit the sack to sleep the sleep of the just, ha ha.

He wheeled the Triumph Scrambler down the passage. Ahead of him by the corner of the hotel grew a large hedge whose shadow engulfed anyone passing near it. Conrad was thinking about taskar(2) and whether he might read some of it before going to bed when he reached the hedge and steered his bike to the right, heading towards the street. The building was on his right, the bike between him and the building. As he walked he heard the sound of footsteps coming from up ahead. He stopped to peer into the semi-darkness but couldn't make anyone out. The footsteps had also stopped. When he carried on they started up again, keeping time with his, faint but deliberate, getting neither louder nor softer. This was weird. Again he came to a standstill and stared ahead of him and this time the footsteps continued. Turning his head a couple of degrees Conrad realised that the sound wasn't coming from in front of him at all but from behind—in front and behind can get mixed up especially if you're wearing a crash helmet but the point was the steps were getting faster and louder and that meant that... Taking his right hand off the handlebar he turned awkwardly to face whoever it was but he was too slow and the next moment an arm was round his throat dragging him backwards, his left hand was wrenched from the bike and a leg began kicking his own legs from underneath him. Losing his balance he flailed out and felt his arm strike something or someone and the shove that came back at him made him partly regain his balance so that after staggering a couple of steps like a drunkard he was able to right himself, just about, at which point the other chap charged him. Conrad caught a glimpse of a face before finding himself sprawling on the ground with a knee digging into his chest and two capable hands undoing the strap of his helmet. In a moment the helmet had been wrenched off and chucked away to one side. A large hand gripped his face, thumb and fingers squeezing his cheeks painfully.

Who? What the fuck? What does he want? Is he trying to kill me? Confused thoughts raced through his head. Was it a dissatisfied customer? Had some of Nick's drugs been cut, damn him? Maybe it was a case of mistaken identity, a jealous boyfriend on the verge of beating up the wrong person? Or was he about to be anally raped?

With all his strength Conrad pushed at the weight that was on him but it didn't budge so he brought his fist round to the side of the massive head, making contact satisfactorily and causing the hand to release him and the knee to give way a little. A scuffle ensued and the two men separated, each getting to his feet, Conrad less swiftly. The other man lunged. Conrad managed to duck and dodge to the side and from this new vantage point delivered a hefty kick to the shin but it just seemed to bounce off and now the other was at him again. He realised he was being manoeuvred back into the shadow of the hedge and soon he was having to work half-blindly, swiping the air as often as not, grunting and cursing while the other made no noise, not even a hum or a murmur. Whoever it was was being cool and systematic, he seemed almost to be taking his time about the whole thing, his movements had a dreadful calm inevitability to them and with a sense of panic Conrad could feel his own energy waning and the power draining out of his limbs. A punch in the stomach laid him out. In a second the other man was on top of him again, the knee pushed even more firmly into his chest, two iron hands holding Conrad's arms against the ground. A black silhouette of a head with the moon behind it came up close to his face and from it a voice spoke.

'Tessa Wainwright doesn't like what you've been doing, Conrad. She'd rather you stopped. Not to beat about the bush: if she gets one more blackmail note I'll break your neck. Understand?'

'Who are you?' croaked Conrad.

'I'm a friend of Miss Wainwright's. I take her welfare very seriously and I don't appreciate it when worms like you come along and make her life difficult. It makes me'—he released Conrad's arm for a moment so as to ram his temple with the heel of his hand—'angry. Very (another ram) angry.' Conrad groaned. 'So do I have your undertaking not to bother Miss Wainwright again?' the man concluded.

'How...do you...know any of this?' Conrad managed to say.

'I've seen what's on your computer, sonny Jim. That's how.'

'My computer?'

'Yes, your computer. It's currently in my possession and I'm minded not to return it to you for the foreseeable future. Transferring data like that counts as theft, by the way. Blackmail, theft...ooh, and while we're on the subject of your criminal activities perhaps we should mention the little matter of class A drugs. Possession, dealing, that sort of thing. Doesn't go down well in a court of law, not well at all.'

Conrad spoke slowly. 'My computer's in my flat. I don't know what you're talking about.'

The man chuckled. 'In your flat, is it? Maybe you've got more than one. I wouldn't know. Maybe you've got several of them carefully secreted around that attic of yours. Maybe one of them's stuffed in that stupid bean-bag. But I've got one of them, sonny Jim, and that's all I need.'

Conrad was beginning to see a path out of this. And for once, against all the odds, the truth was on his side.

'Where do you think I live?'

'You live in Wharf St. Don't try and get funny with me, Merrivale.'

'I live in flat 19, Belview Tower. You've got the wrong person.'

'Oh yes? So what were you doing in 27 Wharf St last night? Visiting your girlfriend?'

Conrad paused. He needed to play this carefully. 'I know someone who lives there. I was dropping something off—a book.'

'*Hard Times*, was it?'

This completely floored Conrad. How the hell...? Pete was dead. But he died after the first blackmail demand was made. Could this guy have...? Then it came back to him. *If you read anything by Dickens it should be* Hard Times *since in* Hard Times *you get a level of psychological realism which you simply don't find in his other books.*

Delivered as a smokescreen to the untimely intruder standing on the threshold of the Blenheim Suite, looking at the pair of them with pointy little eyes. Tina.

'Ask anyone,' he said. 'Ask anyone in the hotel where I live. They'll tell you it's Belview Tower. As I said—you've got the wrong person.'

For the first time a note of doubt entered the man's voice. 'It's an easy matter to confirm. Wherever you live, you're involved in this, Merrivale, I know that. You better take to heart what I said to you about those blackmail demands; until further notice the buck stops with you and it's your neck I'll be breaking. Got it?'

Conrad said nothing. The man pushed himself up and in so doing delivered a parting dig with his knee to Conrad's ribs. Then he turned and melted into the darkness. Conrad heard his steps receding hastily down the side of the hotel. His head and chest hurt horribly and when he tried to move he found he was shaking all over. Inside him a desire to give way to tears was pushing upwards but he managed to squash it. It had been like this on his first day at secondary school, exactly like this. With an effort he got to his feet and started searching for his helmet. The Triumph Scrambler had fallen neatly against the building and it stood propped and ready for use as if unconcerned at all that had passed a few feet behind it. He soon found his helmet, undamaged if a little scuffed. In the distance a car engine started up... The car drove off into the night and Conrad returned to his motorbike. He grasped the handlebars and only at this point did the hot tears well up and begin to flow. Sobbing like a schoolboy he pushed the bike along towards the street.

*

With a moist cloth the Princess dabbed Taskar's beaded brow as he lay groaning upon the grass. She had staunched the wound he sustained to his thigh from the stone-tipped arrow. This now lay thrown to one side. Who could have fired it? Again she glanced towards the darkness of the trees from whence it had come flying but half an hour since. Dusk was falling and they had been ready to pitch camp for the night but her heart misgave her at the thought of enemies or brigands so close at hand.

Taskar's parched lips opened and in an almost inaudible whisper he said, 'My lady, I fear for my life. Worse—I fear for thine. We are in an evil place.'

'All will be well, sir,' replied Lemula in an effort to calm him. 'We have your bow and the arrows you fashioned yesterday, and if you cannot use them I can. If what you say is the truth I am of royal blood: courage must therefore flow in these veins.'

Taskar smiled feebly then of a sudden groaned anew as a spasm of pain swept over him. He reached for her hand and clasped it.

Under her breath she murmured, 'Oh Taskar, Taskar.'

IX

TINA ROBERTS LIVED IN A semi-detached house in Kidlington which her parents had bought for her. Her friends thought her lucky but she would roll her eyes and say 'Kidlington!' as if that were sufficient comment. Only a large city could earn her approval as a place to live—Oxford itself was a borderline case, London being the paradigm. Metropolitan meant sophisticated, provincial meant boring. She dreamt of the capital but for the time being would have to be content with this little town to the north of Oxford, hardly a separate entity, from which she took the bus every day into work, a journey of just fifteen minutes.

She was on the verge of leaving her house to catch that same bus when she had a call from Arthur Mayhew. She threw her housekeys onto a chair and pulled her phone from her bag.

'Hello, Tina?'

Tina sat down on the arm of the chair. 'Arthur...'

'I'm sorry to disturb you so early in the morning. I hope it's not inconvenient?'

'Oh no—not at all. I was just... it's fine. Please, go on.' She slid off the arm and into the chair.

'It's about Merrivale. I managed to speak to him last night but he's a slippery customer and inclined to with- hold information. One thing it'll be necessary for us to confirm is his home address. On that question he was uncooperative so I was wondering whether you might know what it was?'

'His home address? You mean where he lives?'

'Exactly.'

'I'm afraid I don't, Arthur, but I'm sure I could find out.' *Ask Bernie*, she said to herself.

'I'd be grateful if you could do that for me. And there's something else it would be useful to get some informa- tion on. Certain details of the case suggest that Merriv- ale may have an accomplice, somebody quite close to him—possibly a girlfriend or boyfriend. Do you happen to know of any such person? He might have mentioned them, or have been seen with them—perhaps brought them into the hotel...'

'Conrad has a girlfriend, that I do know. Pete told me about her—said she was a singer-songwriter.'

'A singer-songwriter...' Arthur seemed to be digesting this. 'And would you know the young lady's name by any chance?'

Tina thought hard. If Pete had known he would cer- tainly have told her. But no name came.

'Sorry, Arthur.'

'No need to apologise at all. But if you do happen to find out could you let me know?'

'Of course.'

Tina got to the Marlborough a little later than usual but the fact went unremarked and she performed her duties in the kitchen—scrambling eggs and frying mushrooms—with her customary efficiency. She would seek out Bernie as soon as her breakfast shift was over. Finding out the name of Conrad's girlfriend could prove trickier; a point-blank question would arouse his suspicions but she couldn't at present think of any other method. In her imagination she pitted the two men against each other, Arthur's imposing presence versus Conrad's shiftiness, stern questions meeting with sly evasions. She could just see Arthur, firm but fair, his eyes fixed on Conrad's, calmly seeking the cooperation of that self-satisfied pothead and having to let the little weasel out of his grasp when he could have terrorised him simply by bringing a clenched fist up to his snivelling face. Lost in this pleasing reverie and gazing at a panful of mushrooms Tina didn't notice that someone had entered the kitchen and was approaching her. The person stopped by her side.

'Hard at work, Tina?'

She let out a shriek and dropped the spatula she'd been holding onto the tiled floor. A few heads turned in her direction.

'Bloody hell, Conrad! What are you doing here? It's a Wednesday.'

She picked up the spatula.

'Though I'd pop by.'

Tina didn't like the look on his face. She went quickly to the sink to wash the spatula then returned to her station where she continued tending to the mushrooms.

'You all right, Tina?' called out one of the kitchen staff, Alan, holding a flitch of bacon. She smiled back at him and nodded.

Conrad was dressed in his biking leathers. 'I think I met a friend of yours last night, Tina,' he said. 'Big chap. Seems to have something against me.'

'Oh really?' said Tina.

'Yeah. I can't think why. But he's got it into his head I've done something terribly wicked. Where would he have got that idea from, Tina?'

'You should have asked him.'

'He wasn't much in the mood for listening. He's more the yelling and ranting sort. A bit thick if you ask me.'

'Arthur's not...'

'Arthur, is it?' Conrad smiled. 'Nice old-fashioned name.' He moved a few inches closer. 'Well, I'd like you to tell your Arthur the following. Stealing computers is a crime. I've got more on him than he's got on me. And if I don't get what I asked for—he'll know what I mean—the shit is going to hit the fan big time, despite all his threats. The woman he's taken it upon himself to protect is going to be left high and dry and her knight in shining armour will have to leave the field of combat with his lance all flaccid and drooping. Can you tell him that, Tina?'

Throughout this speech Tina had kept her eyes on the mushrooms. She would have liked to pick up the metal frying pan and smash it into Conrad's face but she managed to remain calm, only saying, 'This isn't going to end well for you.'

'Ha!' Conrad's laugh was like a gunshot.

'What's going on here, please?' It was Inge, blonde round-faced Inge, come to break up the meeting. She took a dim view of distractions in the kitchen.

'Just going,' said Conrad.

'Please do,' said Inge and she watched him leave.

*

On his way past reception Conrad overheard the woman who was standing there say, 'Yes, the Blenheim Suite. I booked it yesterday.' He stopped to look at her as if doing so would bring enlightenment. Feeling his gaze upon her the woman turned in his direction at which Conrad smiled courteously and walked on, saying to himself *She can't get away that easily, oh no.* And yet it was as much disappointment that he felt as anything else. It was possible he'd never lay eyes on TW again. For some reason the thought was depressing to him and this depression of spirits, mingled with the anger generated by last night's encounter, was like the taste of bile in his mouth.

He had come away from that encounter physically humiliated and full of a tearful rage which in the course of a few hours became a focused and venomous hostility. No way would he let a thug like that get the better of him. The first surprise coming the thug's way would be getting a communication through Tina—Conrad felt sure she'd convey his message—and the second surprise would be discovering that his bully-boy tactics hadn't worked. *I'll break your neck.* Oh yeah, tough guy? What if I call your bluff? Let's face it, you're not as clever as you thought you were, mistaking where I live and stealing someone else's laptop. That's something you're going to find out pretty soon. Of course you're absolutely right, I am the blackmailer, but the problem is you can't prove it and your threats mean nothing to me. So you'd better go back to your mistress with your tail between your legs and tell her to pull her finger out asap.

He was walking towards where he'd left his bike a couple of streets away. The idea of parking it in the passage by the wheelie bins hadn't really agreed with him this morning and anyway he'd only been coming in to have a few words with Tina. He'd drive straight back to his flat, maybe do some work on Lawrence and Joyce, maybe go to bed. Last night he hadn't slept so well.

I'm meant to ring Meg, he thought. Mystery-mongering Meg. A feeling of puzzled resentment towards her was growing inside him. He realised both that she had examined what was on the memory stick and that the suspicions of TW's thug might end up falling on her the as owner of the laptop and resident of 27 Wharf St. The thug would probably infer that the two of them were conspiring, Conrad and Meg together. Should he warn her? He was inclined to think she was getting her comeuppance for nosing around in other people's, i.e. his, business. How much of the transferred data she had looked at was anyone's guess but the point was she

had found the memory stick lying around and had suc-
cumbed to the same temptation that got Pandora into
such trouble. On her own head be it.

By now he'd arrived at his bike and as he got on it
he thought: It's funny how people set themselves up—
Wainwright leaving her autobiography on view, Tina
meddling, Meg putting herself in the thug's line of fire.
They all deserve what they get. He revved the engine a
few times as if targeting all the suckers of the world then
set off home.

*

Why leave your hotel room if you don't have to? Tessa
didn't have to and found that she didn't much want to
either. The writing was going well, in fact she was on
a roll; away from the Marlborough and her tormentor
she was able to relax, concentrate and simply write. The
fact that her reunion with Ben was due to take place the
next day added a sort of joyous urgency to the task. In
twenty-four hours my life will change irrevocably, she
thought. So now: work.

The denouement was panning out nicely. Taskar and
Lemula, having been through many adventures and
fought off many dangers, finally arrive at their destination, the palace of King Vorbos and Queen Alumel.
Lemula is their long-lost daughter and Taskar—as any
moderately acute reader will have guessed—their son,
presumed dead but actually brought up by an old shepherd. (As a youth Taskar saved the queen from the rav-
ages of a wild boar during a royal hunt and for that service

was made one of her attendants.) Lemula and Taskar are therefore siblings. Only the old shepherd could possibly know this—or rather, only the old shepherd and his wife. When the news of Taskar's betrothal to Lemula reaches their ears... But that's something you'll have to wait till the end to find out, dear reader. Safe to say that none of the hypotheses aired on social media, or in the papers for that matter, nails the actual denouement, though a few come quite close. In fact only two people in the world know how *The Homecoming* ends, a man and a woman, just like the old shepherd and his wife. Those two people are Vince Parker and Tessa Wainwright. It is a closely guarded secret.

Kneeling in front of the coffee table Tessa tapped away at her laptop. The document called *taskar(2)* was growing: it was in its third trimester, the period of its gestation was approaching its end. In a short time from now a new book would be born, coming into the world to a fanfare of trumpets. The Quest would finally be over after all these years. Would she miss it? She didn't think so. Taskar was a figment, soon to be occluded by a living breathing human being, the fruit of her body not her mind.

Her shoulders ached. This coffee table was definitely too low, she had been crouching for hours. Time for another stretch break. Tessa got to her feet and leant backwards, pushing her arms out, then leant forwards, then backwards again. Antenatal exercises. Her body was not much less supple than when she had twisted and stretched it in preparation for Ben's birth twenty-three years ago. She hadn't, in the horrible phrase, *let herself go*. Nor for that matter had she lived without the comforts of bodily intimacy over the years, sharing her bed with now this man now that, even coming quite close to loving one of them, a schoolteacher called Marco, dark-eyed and lugubrious. At this distance those interactions seemed like ancient history—by contrast she could in certain moods imagine Alex walking through the door as if he'd only been gone an hour. He must have been the special one, she reflected, the one you don't forget. Like an early trauma.

By a natural association of ideas her thoughts turned to the faceless figure of her blackmailer, anonymous employee of the Marlborough Hotel and Vince's quarry. Don't worry about a thing Vince had said and on the whole she was managing to follow his advice. Best not to think about the person at all, and yet... That someone should be capable of doing this was a puzzle, it betokened an alien psychology about which she couldn't help being curious. To dig into the tenderest part of a stranger's past so as to pull something out that can be used to extort money from them—what kind of a being is able to encompass that? She'd asked herself the question many times. The obvious answers—someone selfish, callous, greedy and cruel—however true, were obvious, and beneath the level of the obvious she knew there must lie a more subterranean, labyrinthine and murky reality, one as specific as the flecks and hues of an individual iris that has been labelled 'blue'. The blackmailer's psyche, she felt, must have the same arbitrary-seeming complexity as the malign splash of a tumour or the outward spread of an uncontrolled infection, tendrils groping blindly—a complexity that, beholding itself in the mirror, sees a beautiful sophistication. This psyche would most likely remain hidden from her. Vince would puff and it would disappear like smoke. And after all, good riddance.

Tessa knelt down again in front of her open laptop to continue where she'd left off. As she did so it occurred to her that her blackmailer might have taken the opportunity to have a look at *taskar(2)*. The document opened with a rough plan of the second half of *The Homecoming*. If he'd read that outline he'd be the third person in the world to know how the saga ended, along with her and Vince. A select trio, bound together by shared knowledge. Of course they were that already—hence the blackmail, hence Vince's campaign of action. She had written the document *ben* because she had to, it wasn't something she regretted at all and yet she could see why Vince might question her wisdom in doing so. He would point out that what counts as wise is relative to what other people are capable of, in other words relative to how low they can sink. Perhaps that was true. If it was she was unwise. But so what?

*

The voice of the satnav in Vince's car was that of a thousand other disembodied helpmeets, those who instruct us in the ways of self-service supermarket checkouts or fob us off on the phone in the name of Customer

Services—calm, patient and female. It advised him to take the next turning on the left. Vince obeyed. He was a few minutes away from his destination, a block of flats in one of the seedier Oxford suburbs by the name of Belview Tower.

After her breakfast shift Tina had sought out Bernie, who as hotel manager had the addresses of all his staff, full time and part time, and told him she wanted to send Conrad a Thank You card for something he'd done for her and could Bernie please let her have Conrad's address? Bernie liked to think of his employees as the crew of a happy ship, team members bound by love and institutional loyalty, and in a case like this considerations of privacy would have struck him as irrelevant: one member of staff wanted to make a gesture of gratitude to another so why *shouldn't* he help her? He took Tina to his office and there consulted his lists. Under 'Merrivale' he found, along with a National Insurance number and date of original employment, the address 'Flat 19, Belview Tower'.

'Have you bought the card yet?' he asked. 'Because if you haven't there's an excellent card shop in Summertown I can recommend.'

'I've got one already, thanks,' replied Tina. Smiling she left him there and a minute later was on the phone to Arthur Mayhew. She told Arthur the address and he was suitably grateful. Tina also passed on Conrad's message that if he didn't get what he'd asked for the shit was going to hit the fan big time. 'And he said something about stealing computers being a crime,' she added. If she'd hoped for Arthur to cast some light on these obscure remarks she was to be disappointed; all he said in response, after a lengthy pause, was 'That little turd is playing with fire.'

At the next junction turn right. Vince stopped at the junction, let a lorry go past then turned right. He could see the block of flats now and switched off Ms Satnav just as she was saying *In one hundred metres*... There was a car park round the back of Belview Tower but Vince left his car some distance away on the main road, using a Pay and Display machine. Then he strolled back towards the block of flats, stood awhile in contemplation of the dirty grey edifice and made for the car park. It was the middle of the afternoon and not many vehicles were there but underneath a wall-mounted LED was the familiar sight of the Triumph Scrambler, resting on its prop and with its handlebars twisted at a jaunty angle. Vince registered the bike's presence and walked back round to the front of the building. Entering the lobby he saw on one side an array of postboxes and ahead of him the stairs. A bit further down there was a lift but he ignored it. Part of the purpose of this visit was to reconnoitre and that meant getting a general view of the place floor by floor, however unpleasing it was as an object of study. Besides, the lift probably didn't work.

Concrete with damp patches, an incomplete banister, cigarette butts, graffiti, foul smells. He'd experienced many such environments in his time, climbed many such staircases on his way to interview a suspect or a victim, or to intervene at some scene of domestic violence.

Sometimes on his own, sometimes with backup. Buildings like this one were liable to house human beings caught in webs of crime, wronging or wronged, people who needed the heavy-handed interference of the state to get a bit of respite from themselves or their neighbours. And here he was on the trail of just the sort of pest he'd so often encountered in places like this when he was in uniform—a parasite, a slob, a menace to humanity. His present modus operandi differed from the traditional policeman's in various ways, of course. That was one of the advantages of having retired from the force: you were your own master.

Each floor was accessed from the staircase via a fire door and when Vince pulled open the door on level four he at once heard muffled sounds of music coming from one of the flats. It was classical, that was all he could tell, some woman shrieking above an orchestra, very full on and romantic. Moving forwards he saw a light switch on the wall and flicked it without much hope of success. A light came on. Wonders will never cease. Given the absence of proper windows this made his job a lot easier: he could now see that the door from which the music emanated bore the number 19, brass numerals set into the wood. Number 20 was diagonally opposite. Along the corridor the walls were the greenish colour of mould, the chipped paint of the doors had once been white while the linoleum floor was a swirl of dirty greys.

So this is where the little sod lives, he thought. I suppose he thinks he's highbrow listening to music like that, if he is listening that is, as opposed to sprawling on a sofa in a drug-induced haze. Vince recalled the goatee and the heavy-lidded eyes, remembered the fear in the face as he gripped it hard, a sweaty fear bathed in moonlight. And that specimen thinks he can ignore my instructions? Vince smiled grimly and reached into his jacket. From an inner pocket he pulled out a blank envelope containing a note he had written earlier in the day. He could have left it in Merrivale's postbox in the ground floor lobby but preferred to indicate, by taping it to the door of his flat, that he'd paid a personal visit, just as Merrivale had been wont to do when delivering his own post to Tessa Wainwright at the Marlborough Hotel. He had already stuck the envelope to the door when he was visited by a happy inspiration. Drawing out his pen he added to the top right-hand corner of the envelope the words *BY HAND*. Then he went back the way he had come, down the malodorous staircase and out into the sunlight.

*

Returning home after his conference with Tina in the morning Conrad went straight to bed and slept through till one o'clock. On getting up he popped out for a quick lunch at a MacDonald's. Back in his flat he managed to put in a couple of hours writing about the dirty bits in *Ulysses*, as Pete might have called them. Later he dined on tinned tomato soup and a Co-op sandwich. A nap in his armchair followed; when he woke up it was dark outside. He did another stint of work and then it was happy hour: the whisky bottle was brought out, the first joint of the evening partaken of, a sachet of white powder produced. Time to put the feet up, old boy. Time to take a look at *taskar(2)*, why not? He'd been going to do that last night but had postponed the pleasure. The advent of the thug had put it out of his mind. It was partly to spite the thug that he now resumed his plan. Of course 'Arthur' wouldn't be aware of what he was up to so it was more a case of *despite* than *to spite*. I will peruse Tessa Wainwright's deathless prose despite Arthur and his awful injunctions, said Conrad to himself as he rolled a second spliff. And despite the fact that volume four of *The Quest* is certain to contain zilch by way of dirty bits, however thrown together Taskar and Lemula find themselves. There'll be no ululations of 'Yes' from Lemula, I'm betting. They're brother and sister after all, and what Wagner dares Wainwright must avoid, given the market.

He returned to his laptop. The screen still displayed his latest thoughts on Molly Bloom's libido. He dismissed the document from view and searched for the Wainwright files. Then he remembered that he hadn't restored them since getting his computer back from PC Vets; they'd need to be transferred from the memory stick. Again. Which meant finding the memory stick.

'Life is so complicated,' he muttered as he got up from his chair.

After a brief hunt he found the stick—it was on the floor of his bedroom—and was now back at his laptop. Up came the document names: *bank, ben, house, medical, plans, taskar(1), taskar(2), vince.* He read the list out loud as if it were an incantation or spell, one bringing eternal luck to the speaker. At the same time he rolled another spliff and reached for his lighter. Tchi, tchi. No flame. Try again. Tchi, tchi, tchi. Still no flame, the damn thing's out of fluid. Tchi (pointless). He threw the useless bit of plastic into a corner of the room and went over to a cupboard in the kitchen in which he kept matches, candles, blu tack, string and other oddments. No matches.

This was serious. If he'd had a gas hob he could have used that but all the kitchen fixtures were electric. He looked at his watch—ten fifteen. Not too late to ask a neighbour. Ahmed at flat 20 would have a lighter, he smoked forty a day, Ramadan must be a big deal for him. Within thirty seconds Conrad was knocking on Ahmed's door. The door was opened by a middle-aged Pakistani man with grey stubble and bleary eyes.

'Yes?'

'Sorry to disturb you, but have you got a spare lighter? Or some matches? My lighter's dead.'

Ahmed turned round and drifted away as if he couldn't be bothered talking to Conrad but returned a moment later with a lighter in his hand.

'Thanks, mate,' said Conrad taking it. Ahmed grunted and closed the door.

Conrad crossed the corridor back to his flat. It was nearly dark but not so dark that he didn't notice the rectangle, a lighter grey against the dim grey of his front door, more or less at head height. He reached out to touch the thing. It was an envelope. Pulling it off and going back into the illumination of his flat he read the

inscription *BY HAND*. Someone must have left it without knocking, cellotaped it to the door and departed
while Conrad worked, slept or ate within the flat, oblivious. His heart was beating hard as he ripped open the
envelope and pulled out the note.

> *I'm sorry to have doubted you, Mr Merrivale. Flat
> 19, Belview Tower is indeed your address. It's good
> to know where I can find you. Perhaps you should
> consider putting a chain on your front door, though
> frankly I don't think that'll help you much.*
>
> *I'll be paying a visit to your singer-songwriter
> girlfriend also—to get her version of events, you
> understand.*
>
> *Now let's see who blinks first, shall we?*

Conrad read the note through a second time then
crumpled it into a ball and threw it on the sofa. I'll think
about that later, he said to himself as he sat down in
front of his laptop and picked up the spliff he'd prepared.
Where was I, where was I? But his mood was spoilt. He
didn't fancy reading *taskar(2)* now. At least Ahmed's
lighter worked. He closed the laptop, poured himself a
large whisky and took a drag on the spliff. The image of
a huge head silhouetted against a brilliant moon came
before his mind, black, featureless.

X

TODAY IS THE DAY. IN less than an hour I shall meet my son for the first time in twenty-three years. He will walk through those doors, look around him for the much-photographed face, see me sitting here, approach smiling. I will stand up, we will embrace and kiss. Looking down at me he will say the single word 'Mother'. I will burst into tears.

The scene played itself over in Tessa's mind, familiar from repetition, and she leant back in her armchair, an unread newspaper on her lap and a cup of coffee at her elbow. An empty chair stood nearby in which Ben would be able to sink, tired from his journey but happy. Of course happy—how could he not be, how could the very tables and chairs, the plush carpet, the fake chandelier, the coffee machine, fail to join in the happiness of this moment? Even the sour-looking receptionist over there, she too would succumb to the irresistible and all-conquering happiness. Let all the world in every corner sing... At last the denouement had come, at last the longed-for reunion. Alleluia!

He'd said he'd be driving down to Oxford: from Manchester it was a trip of three and a bit hours, assuming no delays. Ben had some sort of IT job in Manchester, she'd find out all about it no doubt, as about everything else—did he have a girlfriend, was he renting, what were his hobbies and pastimes, where had he travelled? All in good time. She'd booked him a room at the Zenith for two nights, that was all he said he could spare. But she was already planning a trip to Italy. He'd have to put up with her generosity, as a millionaire she had every excuse, wouldn't take no for an answer in fact. In Italy she'd show him off to all her neighbours, they'd stroll into town together to dine at Gino's trattoria and people would whisper, 'Who is that handsome young man staying up at Il Tramonto? Her son? You don't say so!' Emilia would blush when introduced, Marco would scowl initially but come round over a bottle of chianti. Ben would be the toast of the town. As for the longer term and whether they'd carry on living in separate countries, such questions could be postponed for the time being. Everything and anything was possible.

A party was entering the hotel, seven or eight people, maybe booked in for lunch at the restaurant. There were an elderly couple, a woman in a yellow coat, a boy in a wheelchair, a man in a suit, two children... Perhaps not all one party; the old couple had moved towards the lift, they must be guests, while the boy in the wheelchair was stationary and the yellow coat and the suit had fallen into conversation. The two children, a girl and a boy, were staring at the fish in a modest aquarium over to one side. Tessa decided to check her phone for messages. There was one from HarperCollins alerting her to a recent piece in an American paper which compared her and JK Rowling's approaches to writing. To read this article in full one must subscribe etc. etc. Later, thought Tessa, or alternatively never.

'Tessa?'

She looked up. It was the boy in the wheelchair. Maybe he'd recognised her and was a fan, a bit over familiar using her first name like that but it had happened before, she didn't really mind.

'Hello, yes, I'm Tessa,' she smiled.

The boy, she now saw, was more of a young man, slight of build and with black curly hair and pale skin. The motorized wheelchair in which he sat held him like a cupped hand. For a few seconds he looked at her with an unreadable expression on his face, then a flicker of a frown crossed it and he spoke.

'Mum. It's Ben.'

Ben. Her son Ben. A thousand scripts, screenplays, prophecies and dreams were consigned immediately to oblivion. In their place the reality faced her, a crippled youth in a wheelchair sitting a few feet away from her. She caught her breath and heard within her an echoing *No*, but the echoes were already dying as the shout of *Yes* overlaid them, the *Yes* of an unconditional love.

'Ben. Ben. Ben.'

Her eyes filled with tears and in a moment she was kneeling on the floor next to him grasping his hands, stroking his hair—Alex's crinkly black hair—while the poor boy, embarrassed and confused, muttered 'Mum, please' and shifted around in his wheelchair. On the other side of the room the two children had stopped looking at the fish in the aquarium. Tessa pulled herself together.

'Ben... My God, you look like your father,' she said drinking in his face. 'Just like him. Oh Ben, dearest Ben— don't worry, I'll behave myself now, look I'm back sitting in my own chair, but tell me, how was your journey, how are you feeling? And Ben, where's your luggage? You're staying at the hotel, aren't you? Here, I mean?'

A tolerant smile appeared on Ben's face. 'Mum, stop fretting. My luggage is in my car, right outside the entrance. I'll have to move it at some point, the car that is.'

Tessa was on her feet. 'Let me get your luggage for you. If you give me your car keys I can...'

'Not necessary. I'll just book in at reception then ask them to bring it in for me. Why don't you sit still? I might have a coffee...' He nodded towards the coffee machine. 'Do you want one?'

Tessa gazed at him.

My son, my son. They have given me back my son. He was dead, and is alive again; he was lost, and is found.

And she began to weep.

*

They had lunch in a nearby café. After some initial shyness Ben opened up completely, telling her of his work, of his daily routine, a little even of his prospects. He had a ground floor flat with all the necessary adaptations

courtesy (in part) of the council, got around easily
enough, enjoyed Manchester nightlife, had plenty of
friends. Sooner or later however their talk was bound
to move backwards in time. Gingerly, delicately, Tessa
raised the question of his disability, fearful that by doing
so she would offend him and equally fearful that she'd
offend him if she didn't mention it. He had been in a car
driven by an older cousin when on holiday in France:
the cousin had turned left onto a main road and found
himself on the wrong side of it facing another oncoming
car. The head-on collision left Ben with a broken back
and his cousin with cuts and bruises. He spent several
weeks in a French hospital after which he had to start
his life over again, aged fourteen.

'Dad would never forgive him.'

'Your cousin?'

'Mm.'

'I don't think I would have either,' said Tessa. 'At
least. . .'

'There's no point dwelling on a thing like that. What
happened happened. Think of all the bad things that
don't happen.'

'That's a very philosophical attitude. I think you must
be very brave.' Tessa knew her words were banal. So often the best response is silence. But Ben didn't seem to
notice, he went on chatting, changing the subject now
and wanting to know all about her career as an author,
when it had started, how she'd managed to break into
the publishing world, who her agent was. . . He'd read

only *The Boy Without a Name* so far, which he said he'd enjoyed.

'I'm just putting the finishing touches to the last volume,' Tessa told him. There were other people in the café so she was careful not to go into too much detail. Vince has trained me well, she thought. Nevertheless she was able to give Ben a picture of the overall sweep of the saga and of the media hype surrounding its completion.

'Yeah, I had a sense it was a big literary event. I imagine you must be. . . I mean—' He looked at his hands.

'What? What were you going to say?'

He smiled awkwardly. 'You don't have to do anything else, right? You make a living as a writer. You don't have to work.'

'That's true,' she said. 'Or you could say that my work is pleasanter than most people's. Which it probably is.'

There was a pause. In the end Ben broke it by saying, 'Are you very rich?'

'Very,' said Tessa simply. It was good that he should know, natural that he should want to know. 'I have a villa in Italy. I hope you can come and visit me there.'

Ben's face shone. She had said the right thing, she hadn't put her foot in it. Thank God.

'That would be great. . . so long as. . .' He glanced at the wheelchair. At once Tessa remembered all the stone steps, some of them crumbling, that led up the slope to the door of the villa, not to mention the open wooden staircase that connected the two floors, the nineteenth century bathtub with its shower fixture, the narrow doorway into the loo. . . Her face fell.

'I could have the place adapted,' she ventured.

'There are always hotels. What's the nearest city?'

'Or just sell it—buy a new place, modern and up-to-date, fully accessible...'

He put his hand on hers. 'Stop fretting.'

Oh Alex, what a boy we have produced, how lovable, how sensible, the darling son we should have brought up together, except that... except. But look at him, won't you? Your eyes, your hair—my mouth perhaps. The way he smiles. You must have seen me smiling out at you during all those years.

'What happened when I was a baby, Mum?'

With dreamlike pointlessness a waitress appeared at their table to ask, 'Is everything all right here? Can I get you more of anything?' Tessa shook her head and the waitress evaporated—perhaps she had been an illusion. Ben's question hung in the air, hollow and black.

'When you were a baby? Didn't your dad tell you?' Her voice was small, she felt numb.

'Not really. He said you got depressed. But he didn't much like talking about it. I think it was painful for him.'

'I... I did get depressed. Post-natal depression. It was quite bad. Very bad, I mean.'

'But was that a reason to exclude you? To take custody away from you? Just because you were depressed?' Ben was frowning. 'Lots of people get depressed. You were my...' He shook his head.

'Ben darling, it was such a difficult time, the authorities got involved, you know—doctors and social workers and people—they had to, it was their job, and your father didn't, he really didn't. . . He wasn't to blame, really he wasn't!'

Ben looked at her. 'Then who was?'

Her lips were dry, she couldn't speak. Ice, sharp cold ice, was in her heart. Spreading.

Ben sighed and waved a hand as if dismissing someone. 'I guess nobody was to blame.' He smiled a wan smile. 'Like I said before, what happens happens. Is that the gist of it?'

She nodded. 'What happened happened.' The past is buried. No one shall dig it up. No one.

*

In a back garden with high walls somewhere in Islington the widow of Alex Delaney sat smoking a cigarette. Since Alex died Miranda's nicotine habit had intensified; it's better than turning to drink, she told herself, remembering the alcoholic haze of her father's last years. Cigarettes allow you to remain in control. Your dignity can survive intact, more or less.

The lawn needed doing and weeds were coming up between the paving stones of the patio. For the tenth time Miranda wondered about taking on a gardener. Some human company would be nice, male company to be exact, now that the only person she saw regularly was Chedlia her Tunisian cleaning lady. A year ago there had been two men in the house, her husband and her son, even if Ben was only around in the holidays, but now the husband was gone and the son seemed to be drifting away. He was reconnecting with his 'real' mother, real meaning biological meaning blind instinct and irresponsibility, rights without duties apparently, a woman exploiting her body, the old story. First she seduces a man with it, then she drags back the child she never cared for towards it, flesh claiming flesh. Some of the people she knew thought it odd that Miranda should love the human being who embodied Alex's infidelity but she did, she always had, she'd loved him as if he were her own child, and moreover she knew it was the scheming woman that had been to blame, that Alex was merely a weak and silly man momentarily dazzled by a youthful body. Flesh claiming flesh.

She stubbed out her cigarette and pulled another from the packet. It was understandable that a young man should want to know who his parents were. A person wants to know how they came into this world. Ben simply desired to learn the truth about himself; it didn't mean he was suddenly going to stop loving Miranda, she realised that. And she respected his desire. He *ought* to know the truth about himself. So why hadn't they told him? They had kept him in the dark till he was a teenager and even then they hadn't given him the full story. Alex wished to protect him from it, he thought the full story would hurt too much. 'It would traumatise the boy,' he used to say. Maybe. Maybe. But Ben was grown-up now. It wasn't for her or anyone else to decide what he could or couldn't know.

That day when he'd first appeared among them, a squirming baby with pudgy fists, impossible to resist— and Alex watching her with fearful eyes, *Will she reject him? Will she hate him?...* Odd to think of it now. Part of the impulse behind her decision to love, it was true, arose from the need to bind Alex closer to her, this new trio of love evidently being stronger and less fragile than their paltry duo had been. But as the years went by the child became more central to her existence than his father. The two males swapped places. Had it helped that she wasn't able to conceive a child herself? Unanswerable question.

A dog was barking in a neighbouring garden. Perhaps I should get a lodger, she thought vaguely. At any rate it would help with the bills—Alex hadn't exactly left his finances in perfect order. She wondered whether Ben's mother, the real one, would turn out to be a generous parent. A world-famous author could surely afford to be. As for whether Ben would be impressed by Tessa Wainwright's fame and wealth, she rather doubted it. He had too much pride. And anyway, what was the source of that fame and wealth? Writing pulp fiction.

He will have met her by now. Driving down from Manchester to Oxford he will have sought her out in her hotel and for all I know they are even now talking and laughing together. Perhaps Tessa has given him an expensive gift. With natural sensitivity she takes on board that he's in a wheelchair and treats him as an equal. They find they are on the same wavelength and have much to talk about. She exclaims at his likeness to his father. Mother and son delight in their long-delayed reunion.

Of course I should be hoping that's how it is, I should be hoping that all is sweetness and light between them.

Now Ben can have two mothers; he's lost a father, after all. Still, thought Miranda exhaling cigarette smoke into the summer air, one of those mothers did once try to smother the life out of him.

*

Meg sat on the grass with her back against the stone wall. The voices of some teenagers reached her from another section of the ruins, kids doubtless bunking off school to head to Godstow for an afternoon of frolics and fags. It was nicer having the place to yourself but she couldn't complain. Just zone out, she told herself. Zone out and take stock.

She picked a daisy and placed it on one knee, picked a second and placed it on the other knee. Two daisies gazing at one another across the abyss between her knees, for ever separate, never to be united. With a puff she sent them flying. Stupid daisies.

At some point she would have to seek Conrad out, either at his flat or at the Marlborough. It was the only way of getting hold of him if he wasn't answering his phone—she'd tried him several times but had got no response. And she needed her PC back. She could still hardly believe he would stoop so low as to get into her room and nick it, obviously worried that she might have seen what was on that damn memory stick and then determined to punish her when he found out that she had indeed transferred the Wainwright material. And what had been his plan? The *taskar* documents weren't the only ones he'd obtained, there was one called *bank*, she remembered, and another called *medical*. Details of Tessa Wainwright's private life to be pored over and scrutinised—for what end?

The thought made her feel sick. This was the guy she'd attached herself to, the guy she loved—the one her friends had warned her about, calling him a parasite and a waster, not to be trusted. If only she could feel properly angry with him the other feeling might take a back seat, but it was so hard: hard to modify let alone smother a love that had been with her every minute of the day for a year and a half. *Only a year and a half? That's nothing!* Sure, nothing. Nothing at all. Just a silly twenty-eight-year-old crush. Get over it.

What she really wanted was that he could explain it all. Maybe things weren't as they seemed, it might be that he'd taken her laptop for a good reason then been unable to communicate with her, say because he'd fallen seriously ill or had an accident—or... Well, these things could be checked. She'd just have to check them. Go to his place of work, whatever.

Meg lay down on the grass and closed her eyes. Her body was warm in the sun. The laughter of the teenagers seemed quite distant, you could almost take it for a certain sort of birdsong. On the nearby road to Wytham a car would occasionally pass. To sleep would be pleasant—a doze of forgetfulness...

Her phone rang, she was sitting up staring at the number on the screen, Conrad's number, oh God at last. At last.

'Con?'

'Hi, Meg. How are things?'

'I've been trying to call you, you never answer.'

'My phone was bust. I tripped up outside the hotel in the dark and smashed it. Had to get a new one. Sorry.'

His voice.

'But here I am again. How's your mum? You're back in Oxford, yes?'

'Yes. Mum's okay, she's fine. Look, Con...'

'What?'

'My computer.'

'What about it?'

Meg took a deep breath. 'Why did you take it? Why did you have to take it, I need that thing, Con, you can't just come into my place when I'm not there and...'

'Whoa! Who says I took your computer?'

'Elise.'

'Elise?'

'She says you turned up when I was in Bristol to get something from my room and now my computer's gone.'

'I came to get my memory stick, that's all.'

'So where's my computer? Where's my fucking computer?' Her voice was raised. *Keep calm, you have to keep calm.*

'I suppose someone must have stolen it. Maybe one of your housemates. Why don't you look in their rooms? Could be Elise, she looks the type.'

'No, Conrad, you stole it because you guessed I'd transferred what was on your memory stick and you didn't want me reading too much of the stuff you'd already stolen from Tessa Wainwright.'

The words came out clear and sharp. Anger was winning now, anger and indignation, plus the first glimmerings of a new and unfamiliar emotion, contempt.

There was a long silence. Eventually Conrad said, 'Okay. You want to know who stole your computer. I'll tell you. It was a man called Arthur. Arthur is employed by Tessa Wainwright to track down and suppress copies of documents that if they were made public would incriminate her. He somehow ascertained that there were copies of those documents on your PC—don't ask me how—so he gained entry to 27 Wharf St and nabbed your machine. If Elise didn't let him in it'll have been the other one, what's her name. Adaego.'

'Documents that would incriminate her? I see. And you somehow knew those documents existed even before you copied them off her PC onto your memory stick, is that right? Conrad Merrivale the investigative journalist, right?'

Silence.

'Bullshit. You snuck into her room and copied stuff off her computer in the hope of finding something interesting. Bank details, that kind of stuff. Not to mention a draft of volume four of *The Quest* called *taskar*.'

'Two documents, actually, *taskar(1)* and *taskar(2)*.'

'Yes, two documents...'

'And since you saw fit to nose around in the contents of my memory stick you'll now be getting a visit from

Tessa Wainwright's bully boy. I doubt that'll be a pleasant experience for you, Meg, he's not a nice guy.'

'I imagine he's just protecting her from people like you. But he won't need to pay me a call anyway since I intend to go to Tessa Wainwright and tell her the whole story. If she goes to the police so be it, this whole thing stinks to high heaven, it's the most disgusting...' Her voice was suddenly choked by tears. Their love was dying in front of them. Between them they had killed it, he by his actions, she by her words.

'Meg, Meg. You're getting this all wrong.' The soothing tone was like a hand placed on her shoulder. 'This whole affair arose out of a crackpot scheme of Pete Rowlinson's—'

'Pete...?'

'You remember, the receptionist at the Marlborough who threw himself off a balcony. He said he'd got wind of some shady dealings Wainwright was involved in, asked to borrow a memory stick so he could take a look at what was on her PC—obviously he'd have the keys to all the hotel rooms...'

'Why couldn't he use his own memory stick?'

'The thing is, Meg, he wanted to involve me. He was gay, he had the hots for me, wanted to think of us as a team, as a couple almost. It was a bit gross, but stupidly I went along with it. I ended up holding the baby, basically.'

'Oh, Con.'

'What?'

She sighed. 'I have to go to Tessa Wainwright with this. Sorry. Whether it was you or Pete Rowlinson who used the memory stick she needs to know...'

'She already knows, why d'you think she employed that tough guy to steal your computer?'

'I don't even know if that "tough guy" exists. I don't know if anything you've said is true. If you'd only been open with me from the beginning we wouldn't be in this situation and I wouldn't be forced to contact Tessa Wainwright about what looks like—looks like...'

'Meg.' He was cajoling now. 'Let's talk this over face to face, can't we? It's no good discussing it over the phone. There are a bunch of things I want to tell you actually and I thought we could... Look, what do you say to us taking a break together, you know, a long weekend—at Bwthyn Onnen? I was planning a trip there in any case, it'd be nice if you could join me.'

'Your Welsh cottage?'

'Yeah.'

Meg closed her eyes and pressed her knuckles to her temple. Her feelings were in turmoil, she no longer knew what to do, her sense of determination seemed to have crumbled. Con was inviting her to Bwthyn Onnen, something he'd never done before.

'I'll come round this evening, okay?' he said.

The warm sun shone down; Meg could hear the voices of the departing teenagers receding into the distance. She shook her head as if to clear it, though of what she couldn't have said.

'Okay.'

*

A winding trail led up the side of the hill upon the brow
of which stood a copse of firs. Although the sun shone
down it was a windy day and the two travellers were
wrapped up well as they struggled along the path, Lemula in a cloak of green, Taskar in a sheepskin mantle.
The youth limped still from the arrow wound sustained
two moons ago and he carried a staff to aid him. As they
approached the summit of the hill the princess spoke:
'Thou art weary, Taskar, and under yon firs it would
be wise for us to stay awhile and rest, methinks. There
we shall have shade from the sun and shelter from the
wind.'

'My lady, you speak truly. I only wish I could be certain that our footsteps are carrying us towards our goal;
the shepherd who pointed us hither appeared sure
enough, and yet...'

'Let us leave all such deliberations till the morrow.
It were good to rest body and mind now, the better to
tackle our problems in due course.'

They were nearly at the summit and as they approached it the wind died down and the air became
warm and fragrant with the scent of the fir trees. Underfoot were pine needles spread upon the ground as
a carpet. Soon they had arrived at the hilltop; the sun
came out from behind a cloud and at that moment the
whole plain before them was flooded in its light. Youth
and maiden gazed down from the heights upon a green
and bounteous land. And between where they stood
and the distant horizon, not more than a dozen leagues

off, they saw the walled city of Malkendron, destination and goal of all their wanderings.

*

After lunch they returned to the hotel to go off to their respective rooms, having agreed to meet up again later in the afternoon.

'Is your room okay?' asked Tessa before they separated.

'Everything's fine. I called reception a couple of days ago to make sure they had accessible rooms. They just had to do some reallocating.'

'If I'd known I would have...'

'It's cool, Mum. Don't worry about it.'

They were in the lobby. The girl at reception looked at them curiously—she knew that woman was Tessa Wainwright the famous author, whose privacy she was under strict instructions to respect and protect, but who was the boy in the wheelchair? Somebody called Delaney. Whoever it was Ms Wainwright was awfully fond of him.

'But Ben,' continued Tessa lowering her voice, 'why *didn't* you tell me? I mean... I'm sorry, I probably shouldn't be questioning you about everything all the time. It's just that—'

'Why didn't I tell you I'm in a wheelchair, you mean? Why do you think?'

Tessa looked blank. Her attachment to him now seemed to her to be so strong, though it had found its focus only three hours ago, that it was incomprehensible that it might ever have faltered in any way.

'Why?' she asked.

'Because you might not have wanted to see me,' said Ben simply.

'Oh, Ben!'

It's her son, decided the receptionist, and she congratulated herself on her powers of perception. Unless it's her nephew...

In her room Tessa lay down on her bed and stared at the ceiling in a state of bewildered contentment. What a day! Her mind teemed with the details of their time together, things he'd said, the expression in his eyes (so like Alex's), even the way he'd driven his wheelchair along the pavements while talking to her, confident and skilful. This is my son. Hard to connect him with the little bundle she had held in her arms all those years ago, the bundle they had had to remove from her embrace lest...

But I can forget about all that now, she told herself. And she continued to stare at the ceiling in a state of almost perfect contentment. Almost: for not far below the surface of her mind was the knowledge that somebody somewhere had the power to permanently mar or wreck this happiness. A snake lay coiled up in the bowels of the Marlborough Hotel biding its time. Vince must deal with it, he must put an end to it once and for all. Only that would leave her free.

Lying on her bed Tessa framed to herself the wish: *Kill him, Vince.*

She must have dropped off at around that point for when she next opened her eyes and looked at the clock on the wall it said 3.37. Must do some work, she thought. She went over to her laptop and settled down in front of it with the aim of completing the first draft of *The Homecoming* that afternoon. Tessa wanted this labour to be over, wanted the quest to be finally at an end so that she could say goodbye to a burden and a preoccupation that already seemed to belong to a previous life. Fortunately she was working swiftly and efficiently; the words came easily and it was like running the last bit of a race downhill.

An hour or so later she called Vince and left a voicemail message on his phone. 'It's finished. Done and dusted. Taskar and Lemula have come home.' Soon after that she went back down to the hotel lobby to wait for her son.

*

When Vince listened to Tessa's message he was in the Old Bookbinder's in Jericho perusing the pub menu. *Wonderful news, congratulations* he texted back. It was certainly a cause for celebration and if it hadn't been for his longstanding avoidance of alcohol he would have ordered some bubbly to mark the occasion. As it was he promised himself a slice of treacle tart with custard for dessert. Preceded by steak and chips, the whole meal washed down with fizzy water from some spa town in the west country.

After a leisurely dinner he would make his way to Wharf St, waiting till it was getting dark so as to be able to tell if the singer-songwriter was at home by inspection of the skylight. If the light was off he would come back later; otherwise he would ring the bell and ask for Meg. Yes, Tina had come up trumps—she'd asked around at the hotel until one of the maintenance men had told her the name, the very bloke she'd seen buying stuff off Conrad round by the wheelie bins. Apparently Kevin knew Meg from the folk scene—he played fiddle—and had seen Conrad with her a couple of times down at the Hedgehog.

'Tina, you've been an enormous help,' Vince told her. 'I'll have to take you out to dinner once of these days.' Squeak of delight.

Meg the singer-songwriter—with her guitar standing in the corner and her hookah and her wispy hippy drapery. How did a girl like her end up with that dosser of an Oxford student? Maybe she began as one of his customers. The folk fraternity do partake after all.

Vince went up to the bar and ordered his food. 'Well done,' he said in answer to the barman's question. 'With English mustard if you've got any.' Back in his seat he pulled out a copy of The Times from his briefcase. The briefcase also contained Meg's laptop, which he might or might not bring out during their interview. It would depend on her responses. If she denied everything out it came. Otherwise... But one thing he'd learnt in his time as a copper was that it was usually best to cross bridges only when you came to them. Don't over-plan, you never know what you'll find. Flexibility is key.

He turned to the crossword.

The steak was excellent and the treacle tart fairly good and afterwards as he strolled through the streets of Jericho Vince felt both replete and ready for action. To all appearances he was a man without a care in the world. He wore a mustard-coloured three piece suit with a red bow tie and in his left hand carried the black canvas briefcase. There was very little traffic and the street lamps were just coming on. A cat ran out from a side alley and Vince leant over to stroke it. He was not a man in a hurry.

The bell of St Barnabas, sounding as always like a saucepan being hit, chimed nine o'clock as Vince turned into Wharf St. Walking due north he heard the sound of somebody playing the piano and for a moment stood still to enjoy the music; then he resumed his course, even numbers to his immediate right, odd numbers across the road, cars parked mainly on this side. It wasn't long before he made out the skylight of number twenty-seven. A pale yellow glow shone from it, the ceiling within undisturbed by shadows. Perhaps she was engrossed in a book, or had left the light on and was in the kitchen downstairs or talking with a housemate. The light was also on in the ground floor room but not in the first floor one. Vince watched the skylight for a little longer then crossed the road. Needless to say there was no Triumph Scrambler in evidence. He lifted a large hand and pressed the bell.

XI

BWTHYN ONNEN WAS AN OLD farmhouse dating from the eighteenth century surrounded by fields and accessed by a dirt track which it was easy to miss; no signpost pointed down it and the house itself was invisible from the road, obscured by trees and hedges. The nearest neighbour was half a mile away. A white stone cottage nestling in a Welsh valley with wooded hills rising up around it—no wonder Roger Merrivale had been moved to buy the place as a holiday home back in the 1990s. The family had spent three or four weeks there every year throughout Conrad's childhood and adolescence but these days Mr Merrivale preferred to spend his summers in warmer climes, taking his wife with him to the Algarve or on Mediterranean cruises. Thus in the long vacation Conrad could be sure of having Bwthyn Onnen to himself. That he had a key to the property at all was his mother's doing. Mr Merrivale regarded his son as an irresponsible loafer who couldn't be trusted to look after the place but Mrs Merrivale, persuaded by Conrad's argument that he needed a haven of peace and quiet to pursue his studies effectively, managed to get her husband to acquiesce. And Conrad had in fact spent some valuable hours there, applying himself either to his coursework or to his novel. Or just getting stoned. Not being a party animal he had never invited friends to stay and he always left the cottage in a state which couldn't be used by his father as grounds for excluding him: tidy enough and with all traces of debauchery carefully expunged. There was an old gramophone in the sitting room and a boxed set of LPs of *The Ring* conducted by Karajan. This provided Conrad with his typical evening soundtrack. Sheep grazing in the field behind the house were treated to the stresses and strains of Wotan's relationship with his daughter and unfazed blackbirds sitting in trees blended their notes with Wagner's.

The cottage was a repository of memories, vivid, hallucinatory. Scenes from Conrad's childhood replayed themselves in his mind as he paced the rooms, evoked especially by the smells that lingered like stubborn household gods: old fabrics, woodsmoke, damp stone. Here in the kitchen his father caught and killed a rat—or had it just been a mouse? In his bedroom, the one he'd slept in as a child, knots and whorls in the oak beams danced monstrously when he lay there with a temperature of 39° one winter. Snuggled on the sofa with his mother he listened to her soft voice and drank in the pictures of the storybook which she was holding—an early one, that. The cold air which came up from the cellar brought before him as he stood at the top of the steps that time when his father had locked him down there as a punishment for stealing. All these episodes were liable to be conjured up, sharply distinct or sometimes superimposed one upon another, whenever he visited Bwthyn Onnen. He tolerated them. Occasionally he would indulge one of them, grant it an audience. On the whole however he preferred to switch them off. One must live in the present, after all.

In preparation for his sojourn at the cottage Conrad packed a bag with the usual items: laptop, whisky (the bottle at Bwthyn Onnen was probably only half full), some books, clothes, toothbrush, etc. Psychoactive substances in a Tesco's bag stuffed into the Triumph Scrambler's secret chamber. At six o'clock that evening he parked his bike by the wheelie bins in the passage at the rear of the Marlborough Hotel. He'd told them in advance that he'd have to leave early; he would put in a couple of hours and then drive to Meg's. As he ascended the stone steps to the tradesman's entrance he felt light-hearted. It was as if he were about to embark on an exciting new adventure. Bold and inconceivable experiences awaited him.

Having changed into his uniform he made his way to the kitchen where he found Hugo and Alan deep in a discussion of last night's FA Cup semi-final. Inge was instructing a newbie in the arts of slicing and dicing. Tina was nowhere to be seen.

'He should have put Bates on in the second half,' said Alan.

'You think it would have made any difference?' said Hugo.

'Up and down, keeping the tip of the blade on the board,' said Inge.

Of course he wouldn't be waiting on TW this evening, not since she'd run away. He wondered where she'd gone. He could have quizzed Bernie about it but an instinct of caution prevented him. And what about 'Arthur'? Would he be staying in the same hotel, presuming it was a hotel? Maybe they were lovers. No, that seemed unlikely; she'd probably hired him through some dubious agency specialising in 'protection'. It was more on the cards that Tina and Arthur were lovers. I could ask her when she turns up, he thought, that would be amusing. You're looking tired, Tina, don't you think you might be overdoing it with Arthur? I bet he's hung like a donkey, right? I hope you're taking precautions, you don't want to be giving birth to something that neighs.

In the dining room it was fairly quiet. The couple now occupying the Blenheim Suite were seated at table three. He was ogling his smartphone, she was staring into the middle distance. Kathy was dealing with them. As Conrad watched from the kitchen another couple appeared and he went over to welcome them.

'Table for two, please.'

'Come this way.'

Smiles, nods, gestures. In a few hours all this will be a distant dream.

As a boy he'd wanted to be able to fly. Go to the top of a tall building, lean slowly forwards with your arms outstretched, let gravity take hold of you, fall into space and flap your wings. Upwards, upwards, soaring and spinning—miles below you the people looking like ants and a sense of complete unfettered freedom.

So now he was going to the top of the building.

'Would you care for something to drink?'

The couple consulted with one another. 'How about a bottle of red?' said the man. His accent was Australasian. 'Suits me,' said the woman. Ditto.

'We have a number of reds,' said Conrad, his finger sliding down the list which the man was holding to RED WINES. 'This Shiraz is very good. It's one of my personal favourites.'

'Can't go wrong with Shiraz,' declared the man.

'Excellent,' responded Conrad.

Up the lift to the top of the building.

Behind the bar his thoughts turned to Pete's last journey up a lift. He'd gone right up to the top of the building then down again much faster by a different route. Pete's problem was that he couldn't fly—all part of his hopelessness. People have different destinies, different natures.

Conrad uncorked the Shiraz, placed it with two glasses on a tray and returned to the Ozzie couple.

'Can't go wrong with Shiraz,' repeated the man as Conrad did the honours.

'Absolutely,' agreed Conrad. *You dimwit.*

Ten minutes later he bumped into Tina.

'Evening, Tina.'

'Fuck off, Conrad.'

'Oo la la. Feeling tired and emotional, are we?'

But she was already walking away.

Conrad got out of the building at eight fifteen. He donned his helmet, zipped up his leather jacket, strapped his travelling bag to the pannier rack and wheeled his bike down the passage towards the big hedge in whose shadow Arthur had lurked before assaulting him. Near the end of the passage he slowed down, hesitated, then briskly rounded the corner of the building. It was still daylight, this nervousness was unwarranted... Well. He'd soon be out of reach of all thugs and bully boys, out of reach and far away.

The bike had a full tank of petrol—should be enough to get him from Oxford to Bwthyn Onnen without stopping. He knew the route well. A lot of motorway followed by increasingly rural B roads. There was chocolate in the bag in case he got hungry.

Down the Woodstock Road, cross over to Walton St, take a right here, this way and that way till we get to 27 Wharf St, park the bike, remove helmet. Actions performed scores of times, habitual, repetitive. The routine of eighteen months. Bye-bye, routine.

Conrad went up to the door and pressed the bell.

*

They dined in a Chinese restaurant in Summertown, the sort of place Alex had looked down on as insufficiently classy for an MP who was having an extramarital affair. Blue dragons and red lanterns abounded and the background music was pentatonic and anodyne. Tessa tried to use her chopsticks but soon gave up in the face of Ben's expertise.

'Where did you learn to do that so skilfully?'

'I shared a house for a while with someone who cooked lots of Asian food. He didn't like you using a knife and fork. Fingers were allowed, chopsticks pre-ferred, cutlery forbidden.'

She watched him eating. His appetite was healthy, nothing wrong with that at all.

'At home we never ate Chinese,' he went on. 'Miran-da's into salads and things and Dad could only do roasts. We had Indian takeaways sometimes. When I got the run of the kitchen at last I made lots of cakes and pas-tries. Put on a stone in six months.'

She laughed. 'Well, I think you could probably do with some feeding up. I recommend a regime of pasta, pizza and panforte.'

'D'you think I'm too thin?'

'You're not too anything, Ben, you're just right. I'm only playing the Italian mamma.' She paused, then said: 'Tell me about Miranda. You must be close.'

'We are close. I mean she's. . . Do we have to talk about it?'

Tessa panicked. 'No, of course not, not if you don't want to. I just thought. . . No, we don't have to talk about that or anything else.'

'I don't mind talking about Dad,' he said, clarifying. 'But I'm not sure it's a good idea talking about Miranda. Not yet.'

'Fine.'

Is it because he loves her more than he loves me? Because he doesn't love her at all? Because she was horrid to him? 'Not yet': the discussion to be postponed. We have all the time in the world, the conversation we began this morning will continue for months and years. Have patience, Tessa.

'I'm grateful to her anyway,' she said.

'Grateful?'

'For bringing you up, for giving you a home.' Bite the bullet. 'For loving you.'

Ben looked away. 'Yes.' She didn't know what he was agreeing with.

A waitress came round to take their plates away. When she'd gone Ben said: 'So how did you two meet? You and Dad?'

'How did we meet?' Tessa leant back in her chair. 'The usual story. I was working as an intern in the House of Commons. I'd gone into that straight out of university. He was an older man, charismatic—I was a younger woman, impressionable. That's all it takes.'

'I imagine you were pretty,' said Ben, blushing slightly.

'Sweet of you to say so,' she smiled. 'Anyway, I'm not proud of it. You know I never thought about his wife at all, that's what's so disturbing. I knew he was married and yet the existence of—Miranda didn't even enter my consciousness, it's as if his wife were simply a non-entity, a non-existent thing. He was married to a nothing, which is to say he wasn't married at all. That's how I felt deep down.'

'I think he was more to blame.'

'Of course. I mean I suppose so. If blame is the word.'

'Isn't it?'

He must have seen Miranda's hurt, experienced it through the years of his childhood as something grievous and unspeakable. She will have hidden it, absorbed it, and yet it will have been visible for all that.

'Dad said I was born here—in Oxford.'

'I was living here. I had a room in a shared house.'

'So you met in hotels?'

'That sort of thing.' She examined his face but saw only mild amusement. 'He thought it was better than us seeing one another in London. He must have given Miranda some reason for all those trips to Oxford, I don't know what though. Work-related, I guess. We used to sign in at hotels as Mr and Mrs Turnbull.'

Ben laughed at this and she felt she was on safe ground.

'That's why I decided to come to Oxford for this visit. It's where you were born, where I last saw you. I wanted to pick up where I'd left off.'

*

Upon the battlements one of the sentries stood looking east across the plain towards the Gamlaur hills. Two tiny figures he saw, apparently walking towards the city, the taller carrying a staff. A slow and painful progress they made of it. The sentry called one of his fellows over.

'Seest thou yonder pair of travellers?' he asked him.

'Aye,' said the other. 'A man and a woman, methinks. I will send word to our captain.'

The defenders of the city had been instructed to keep a lookout for a young man and a young woman approaching. The safe return of Taskar was every day hoped and prayed for; if he were alone a plain white flag was to be flown, while if he were accompanied a pair of red and gold flags were to be raised, one at each corner of the eastern wall. The captain was a man who knew Taskar well and would be able to identify him by sight. As soon as he arrived at the spot he looked down to where the travellers were and with tears in his eyes exclaimed, 'Thanks be to God!'

From where they stood Taskar and Lemula heard a great shout go up from the walls and towers of Malkendron. A moment later two flags were hoisted at opposite ends of the battlements, of red and of gold, and as the pair approached the city its ancient drawbridge was lowered across the encircling moat.

'Our journey,' said Taskar, 'is at an end, my lady.'

'Verily,' replied the princess. She took his hand. 'And a new life begins.'

*

'Is Meg in by any chance?'

Elise had answered the door. She looked at Vince with unconcealed annoyance, having for the second time that evening been interrupted while watching her favourite programme, a Scandi noir series called *Blodsband*. The first interruption had been courtesy of Conrad, who was probably still up there—at any rate she hadn't heard him leave. Glancing out of the doorway she noted however that his bike was gone.

Elise turned to shout up 'Meg!' There was no response so she went to the foot of the stairs and repeated the exercise. Still no response.

'Hold on,' she said to Vince and went into her room, coming out a moment later with her phone. She dialled a number and stood with the phone to her ear, right elbow cupped in left hand. Vince watched her. Eventually Elise let out a sigh and said, 'Let's see if she's in then.' Still carrying his briefcase Vince followed her up the stairs to the first floor landing. From here Elise tried again. 'Meg? Meg?' But no reply came.

Vince was familiar with the ladder which came down from the attic trapdoor having used it on a previous occasion. Now he gestured towards it and said, 'Do you think we should go up and check?' Elise vacillated. Should she let a strange man into a housemate's room without her consent? Now that she thought of it, Meg might have gone out with Conrad, leaving the room empty. In that case she, Elise, was alone with this man. Who was he anyway? And what was he carrying in that bag?

Any conclusion to which these thoughts might have been tending was pre-empted by Vince's starting up the ladder. 'Um—' began Elise but her protest got no further. She watched from below as he pushed open the trapdoor and scrambled up after his briefcase. His footsteps sounded above her head and she heard the single word 'Jesus'. There was a second or two of silence then the man called down, 'Phone for an ambulance. 999. Tell them she's unconscious.'

In the attic Meg lay on the floor with one sleeve rolled up, her pale lips parted and her eyes closed. On a small lacquered table nearby, Moroccan-looking, sat an empty syringe. Vince had already put her into the recovery position and he was examining the exposed flesh of her arm. As he did so he repeated her name.

An overdose, heroin supplied by one Conrad Merrivale.

But. But. Marks on her wrists, impressions as of… He looked round the room. Nothing thrown into a corner or hiding in the shadows. Where, then? His eyes went to the double futon. Yellow duvet, blue pillows… Reaching over he grabbed the duvet and pulled it off. There it was. The rope that had bound her, innocently coiled up in the centre of the futon, like a snake.

A wave of rage and disgust swept over him. 'Scum.' He spat the word out. Kills his girlfriend to cover up his crime, his base and contemptible crime. Kills her with his own filthy drugs. *Scum.*

But he hasn't killed her, has he. Because she's still breathing, isn't she. Fact is, he made a balls-up of injecting her, you can see that from the injection site: intramuscular, not intravenous. A long slow high rather than a big powerful hit. Which means her system won't be overwhelmed. We hope.

'Meg. Meg.'

He held her hand, rubbed it. It was lucky for her she had plump arms, hard to see the veins in. The guy was probably nervous too, and wearing gloves. He ballsed it up like the effete little ponytailed undergraduate he is.

A pretty girl, nice face. Not much makeup, just some eyeliner smudged by tears. She's no blackmailer, this one. Definitely not. Fell in love with a scumbag, that was her problem. An idiot scumbag who thought he could make it look like an unfortunate accident rather than murder, though what the hell he expected the police to make of a length of rope asleep under her duvet God only knows.

'They're coming.' It was Elise's voice.

'Good,' he replied.

Elise's head appeared through the trapdoor. 'Is she all right?'

'I hope so. I think so.'

'What happened?'

'That's for the paramedics to decide.'

'Should I do anything?'

'No, you're fine.'

The head disappeared.

Bringing his face close up to Meg's he said in a low voice, 'Wake up, Meg.' There was a quiver of eyelids. 'Meg. Wake up. Meg.' In his hand her much smaller one twitched. From deep inside her there came a sound like the wind moaning in the distance. Her eyelids were still quivering—now her head moved slightly and her mouth opened wider as if she was about to say something.

'Meg? Are you there?'

The wind moaned again, it was closer now.

'Meg, you're going to be all right. Can you hear me, Meg?'

'Uhhn...'

Her eyes were struggling to open. Vince stroked her hair and forehead, he was beginning to see her irises. The pupils appeared, contracted into pinpoints, and her lips were moving, words were forming...

'Con...'

'Conrad's not here.'

She nodded weakly.

'But we'll find him for you.'

She nodded again. 'Bth...on...'

Vince brought his ear closer to her mouth. 'What's that, Meg? What are you saying?'

'Bth...onnen...He...'

With a great effort she lifted one hand, tried to point. Vince followed the line which her index finger would have flung into space and his gaze fell on a cork notice-board hanging on the kitchen wall to which four or five notes were stuck or pinned.

He turned to her. 'Are you pointing at the notice-board, Meg?'

Again she nodded. Her hand fell exhausted at her side and her eyes closed.

'Meg, don't go back to sleep. Stay awake now...'

'Oh...okay...'

He squeezed her hand, got up and went over to the noticeboard where he scanned what was on it: a shopping list, a postcard with horses, some lines of a poem and an older-looking note headed 'Conrad in Wales' with an address underneath—Bwthyn Onnen, Ceredigion, plus a postcode. He unpinned this note from the cork board and returned to Meg's side.

'Meg...' Gently he roused her. 'Meg, is this where he's gone?'

He held the piece of paper in front of her face. The eyes opened and she spoke: 'Yes. Gone there... I...' An intake of breath like a sob.

Vince pocketed the note.

*

Collapse into space, let gravity take hold of you, you plummet downwards and the plummeting becomes a soaring, then a wheeling, higher, into orbit, and everything below is nothing. The wind in your face. Buildings, trees, people flying past, the road ahead of you. Darkness gathering: the sun has set now and you are riding towards the horizon below which it set but you won't catch up with it, it has gone for good, gone out of this world. No, that's wrong—tomorrow the light will return, but it will return for some and not for others. It will return for me. Not for her.

Careering down the A40 coke-crazed Conrad flew from the scene of a crime whose meaning for him he planned presently to scrutinise and construe, turning it this way and that way in the light and milking from it every drop of significance it might yield. He knew already that he was a different being, transformed by his deed and occupying a new level of reality. But he wished to dwell on it, ponder it, relive the actions themselves,

the gagging, the binding, the preparation of the syringe... In his memory the scene was brilliantly lit, like
a theatre stage hot under the spotlights, though only a
solitary standard lamp had illuminated the proceedings.
He was sure that in those twenty minutes the whole
meaning of his life was distilled and concentrated. True,
it had only come about as a response to her threats, was
indeed a necessary means of self-preservation; but it
was more than that, it was an apotheosis, a sacrifice.

A sacrifice to whom or what? To *her*, of course—to
Tessa. Their precious relationship would be preserved
and no third party should come between them. The
force field that united them would remain undisturbed.
She would continue to care for him, sending him the
funds he needed when he asked for them, and he in return would protect her good name, hold back her dirty
little secret from the prying eyes of the world, in this
way keeping himself always before her, lodged in her
consciousness—a part of her, inside her. Although she
doesn't know my name or identity, he thought, I am
closer to her than anyone else in the world.

His thoughts jumped sideways. Meg's mother when
she hears of it will go under. A case of collateral dam-
age. They'll start asking 'Where'd she get the junk?
Who supplied it?' and the bitch Tina will try to pin it
on me if she gets half a chance but they have nothing
on me, there's no hard evidence. Elise will say I visited,
so what? These are all details, I can just laugh in their
faces, what, are you calling me a murderer? Meg was
my girlfriend! What possible motive could I have, tell

me that? Robbery? Nothing was taken. A domestic row? Funny way to resolve it. To shut her up? About *what*? Stony silence from all and sundry including Arthur the thug. Quite.

No, I have nothing to fear and my wings only take me higher. Fear is another of the little things down below, minuscule and irrelevant. Now is the time to leave behind the yapping pygmies full of their disapproval and resentment, Tina and Arthur and Pete and Inge and all the rest of them. Let them yap! Yap-yap, yap-yap.

A little beyond Hereford he pulled into a layby—his mouth was dry and he needed a drink. There was no water to be had so he broached the whisky, Johnny Walker Black Label. As he put the bottle to his lips a car drove past in whose headlights he must have jumped out from the darkness as a shameless biker pumping up his blood alcohol for the next leg of a journey. Who cares. Turn round and arrest me. He screwed the cap back on, returned the whisky to his bag and set off again. Moon and stars were out and the temperature had dropped noticeably. In the cottage he would have to get out the electric radiators, it would be freezing. There was no central heating, just a fireplace and those old radiators—plus he ought to be able to locate a hot water bottle somewhere. He'd settle in properly tomorrow, get provisions from the village shop ('Hello, Conrad, haven't seen you in a while, studying hard I hope?'—'Yes thanks, Mrs Jones'), bring some firewood in from the outhouse, etc. etc.—all very cosy and domestic. But this evening was to be celebratory, it was to be Liberty Hall, wink wink.

Funny to think that he could have brought Meg along with him. She would have loved that, wouldn't she? A romantic getaway, lovers gazing into each other's eyes, sheep bleating encouragingly in the background. One of Mother Nature's little ploys for keeping the species going. Except that you can't turn two egos into one by entangling their bodies, the duality will always reassert itself, warfare will erupt, Daddy will hit Mummy when drunk, Mummy will cry and the little boy will stand stricken at the top of the stairs, his heart bleeding and tears running down his face. I hate you, Daddy, I hate you I hate you. Hate you. In the kitchen there he used to get down his whisky bottle and having filled his glass turn round to face her, his eyes red and vicious, preparing himself while she stood cowering, a woman half his size with hunched shoulders, he'd throw his head back gulp gulp and slam the glass down on the counter then come forwards. From the doorway of the kitchen it was four paces to where she'd be standing and once, just once, the boy ran to intercept him, come between them, protect her, and *whack* came his father's hand to the side of his head so hard that he fell onto the wooden floor at which 'What are you doing?' cried his mother and *whack* came his father's hand to the side of her head.

Conrad was huddled in an old wicker chair staring towards the kitchen. In his hand was a spliff and a few feet away a two-bar radiator glowed in the semi-darkness of the cottage. The second half of his journey from Oxford had receded into oblivion and he was now enjoying the fruits of his freedom with some of Nick's triple X skunk.

Once he'd switched off these ghosts he'd be able to concentrate on the profundity of his condition. That was the main item on the agenda, he just needed to switch off these ghosts, damn them, then he could properly contemplate the amazing leap he'd made out of one channel of existence into another. It was proving harder than usual. Perhaps the skunk was responsible.

Whack came his father's hand... He covered his eyes and murmured, 'Go away, will you.'

'Let me switch them off for you.' The voice came from the direction of the stairs. Conrad looked over and saw a man coming down dressed in biking leathers like himself. When he reached the bottom the man placed his helmet on the newel post and walked with a jaunty step into the middle of the room, stroking the hair back on his head with both hands and smiling.

'You remember me?'

Conrad nodded. 'Mr Hall.'

'Quite. And look—' He swept an arm before him. 'Are the ghosts still there?'

The room was empty, the kitchen also. Strung above the doorway of the kitchen was a row of fairy lights, festive and cheering.

'At your service, sir,' said Mr Hall bowing humorously. 'On an evening like this ghosts and memories are to be banished, are they not. It is a time for celebration, for congratulation... Congratulate yourself, Conrad, you have achieved something very special. Not many people could do what you have done.' He perched on the arm of the sofa and fumbled in a pocket, producing a pipe and a twist of tobacco. A moment later, Conrad didn't see how, the pipe was lit and a plume of smoke rose from it. It smelt of apples.

'How did you get here?' asked Conrad. He lifted himself out of his chair and headed for the kitchen to get a couple of glasses.

'Droll fellow!' chuckled Mr Hall. 'A very dry sense of humour you have.'

'No, really—how?' Conrad poured some whisky into each glass.

'I was with you, silly! Your passenger. Behind you on the bike. You must have felt me holding on to you.'

'I didn't.'

'You'll feel it soon enough.' The voice, suddenly growling, came from all around him. The walls seemed to have spoken. Conrad dropped one of the glasses and it smashed to pieces on the floor.

'Oh, don't worry about that,' chirruped Mr Hall. 'I'm happy with my pipe. You go ahead though.'

Conrad went back unsteadily to his chair holding his whisky.

'I know you're not real,' he said. 'Actually I think you're a bit corny.' He drank from the glass. 'A cliché.'

Mr Hall went off into a peal of laughter. 'Very good, very good! As if there's such a thing as objective reality. But you know perfectly well, indeed you often say it, that this stream of consciousness is all there is: a blend, a symphony of different experiences, some cohering with their neighbours, others popping out of the screen so to speak... This is all your own personal dream. And whatever happens,' he cocked his head playfully, 'you dreamt it. You're living your dream, my boy!'

Conrad was standing by the gramophone selecting an LP. He hadn't traversed the intervening space, he'd been in his chair and now he was here, that was all. He put the LP on the turntable, lowered the needle, stood back a few paces. The music started up, solemn and overpowering music coming up from the centre of the earth.

'Ah,' said Mr Hall with due gravitas. '*Götterdämmerung*. Gods' twilight, twilight of the gods. Very appropriate.' He stroked his beard and tapped a little ash off the end of his cigar. It fell on the rug at his feet. 'But to return to my own status. I suppose you wish to pigeonhole me as belonging with those other shady characters that one finds in the likes of Dostoevsky and Thomas Mann, not to mention Marlowe and Goethe, characters who hold forth portentously about this and that, symbolise something or other, and leave their poor charge in a pretty pickle, is that right? I take it that was why you referred to me as a cliché just now.'

Conrad didn't reply. He was back in his chair with one leg hanging over the side, his free hand conducting the music, eyes closed.

'Well,' continued Mr Hall, 'I have to say I rather resent the suggestion. There's *some* truth in it of course, but I feel you're being a trifle reductive. The fact is, I'm yours, specifically yours. *And you're mine.*'

The last words boomed, rolled, reverberated, cackled, it was not one voice but a thousand, a demented choir singing at all pitches and volumes at once. Conrad threw his glass away and put his hands over his ears. 'Shut up!' he screamed. One of the bars of the electric fire fizzled and went out. Mr Hall got to his feet. He was taller than Conrad remembered—perhaps it was merely that his height was emphasised by the greatcoat he wore—and he was holding something in one hand that caught the light, glinted like glass.

'What's that you've got?' asked Conrad. He was sweating despite the cold.

Mr Hall walked towards the table on which were scattered pills, powders, hash crumblings, rizlas, a couple of cardboard boxes, a Tesco's bag, a syringe. In the centre foreground of this mêlée he deposited what was in his hand with a ceremonious, almost theatrical, gesture. Then with a grin he turned to face his companion.

'You want a cliché, here's a cliché.'

In the dim light Conrad had to strain his eyes to make out what the object was. A bulbous upper section tapering in the middle then bulging out again, the whole thing symmetrical along both axes. Flat top and bottom. Sand trickled down through the narrow waist from the upper chamber to the lower. 'An hourglass,' cried Conrad and the joke of it stimulated him to an outburst of laughter, but it was a silent laughter that poured from his open mouth, deafeningly silent, and Mr Hall mirrored his mirth, his lips stretched wide and the tears rolling down his cheeks as he slapped his thighs soundlessly. Soon Conrad's face ached with laughter, he felt his whole body dissolving in a paroxysm of mute hilarity, the two men's heads lolled and wobbled on their shoulders in drunken synchrony and in the midst of this passionate hysteria Conrad heard the sound of a car door banging. In an instant Mr Hall was gone, the hourglass had disappeared and the opposite wall was whitened by beams of light entering the cottage through the window behind him. He turned in his seat to be dazzled by the glare of headlights. Across this glare the silhouette of a body moved.

'Mr Hall,' whimpered Conrad. 'Mr Hall, where are you?' He pushed himself up out of his chair and faced the front door. Footsteps approached, slowed down—stopped. He watched as the doorknob turned. Then with a swift movement the door was pushed open to reveal a large man with a gingery moustache wearing a red bow tie.

XII

THE MAN WITH THE BOW tie stepped over the threshold and closed the door behind him. He wore brown leather driving gloves and was carrying a black canvas briefcase which he placed on the floor by his feet. Conrad stared at him. That face—he'd seen it before, seen it in a series of glimpses by moonlight, like the film from an old cinema reel, jumpy, discontinuous. Now it was uninterrupted and open to view and it returned his gaze. A large pockmarked face with bright blue eyes and a ginger moustache.

'You're Wainwright's thug, aren't you,' said Conrad. 'Arthur. The one who attacked me round the back of the hotel.'

Arthur inclined his head a little as if in acknowledgement. Neither of them moved.

'What do you want from me? And how did you know I was here?' Conrad was trembling but he didn't know if it was fear or drugs or the cold. All three, probably. *Adrenaline*, he thought. I'm going to need that. Fight or flight...

'I have to inspect your personal computer,' said his visitor unexpectedly. His voice was level, there was no hint of violence in it. The gloved hands hung by his sides relaxed and unthreatening.

'Is that so?' replied Conrad. He attempted a smile.

'Yes,' said the other. 'There are some documents on it that need deleting permanently. You know the ones I mean.'

He looked around the room and his eyes came to rest on Conrad's laptop sitting on the floor amid a jumble of clothes next to an open backpack. 'That'll be it,' he said nodding towards the PC.

'And you came all this way for that?'

Arthur looked at him steadily. 'That's right.'

'She must pay you well.'

The man took a step forward and Conrad jumped back, getting behind the wicker chair and placing his hands on it in a posture of readiness. 'Happy to co-operate,' he said quickly.

'I'm glad to hear it. Now would you care to bring the PC to the table or shall I?'

'I can do it,' said Conrad. He went over to the pile on the floor and picked up the laptop. He was thinking of the memory stick. *Delete all you want, you old fool.* Under the man's gaze he carried the laptop over to the table and pushed back packets, sachets and rizlas to make a space for it. Then he drew up a chair and gestured with his open palm by way of invitation.

'Thank you,' said Arthur coming forward. 'You—' He pointed at Conrad, then at a position on the other side of the table. Conrad obeyed, moving round to where Arthur would be able to keep an eye on him. Arthur lowered himself into the chair and opened the PC. As he did so he sniffed the air. Without looking up from the screen he said simply, 'Skunk.'

'Yes,' said Conrad. 'Would you like some? You're more than welcome.'

Arthur ignored the joke. Conrad was having to shield his eyes from the glare of the undipped car headlights which were still beaming into the cottage from outside. 'Your lights are on,' he remarked. 'Battery'll go flat.'

'This won't take me long,' murmured Arthur. 'I'll just finish this job then I'll be out of your hair.' He leant in a couple of inches towards the screen. 'What's all this?' A crooked smile was playing beneath the moustache. '*Conflagration, a novel*. A novel, eh, Conrad? So we're a secret writer, then? Been hiding our light under a bushel, have we?'

'Don't read that!' shouted Conrad.

Arthur's eyes were going from left to right, the smile still on his lips, a sardonic eyebrow raised.

'I said don't read that!'

Conrad started coming round the table but halted when Arthur shot him a fierce glance and half raised himself from his chair. For a moment the two men were frozen in a tableau of unfulfilled violence, a couple of tomcats holding each other in the glare of their hatred. Gradually the tableau melted; Conrad returned to his post, Arthur resumed his seat.

'Not much to read, is there though,' he said quietly. 'A few paragraphs, a list of names, some phrases and half-finished sentences...total word count 2,513. Don't know why you're so excited.'

'It's a sketch,' said Conrad. 'Merely a sketch.' He was filled with murderous hostility towards this man. Bully-boy emissary, thug, peasant. His mind reeled with delicious images of smashing and slicing the life out of the bastard, of burying the body somewhere, of washing the blood from his hands...

Arthur was tapping and scrolling. He had found what he was looking for. 'And...delete.' A final triumphant click. 'Flushed out,' he concluded. 'All evidence of theft destroyed. You should be thanking me.' He closed the lid of the laptop and stood up.

'Thank you, Arthur,' said Conrad smiling sweetly.

Arthur went over to the sofa and threw himself into one corner, stretching his long legs out in front of him. A few feet away the electric radiator with its single bar did its best to mitigate the cold. A sort of knocking or clicking came from one of the walls, probably Deathwatch beetle.

'Take a seat,' said Arthur. 'No need to keep cowering over there. I thought we could have a little chat, Conrad. Man to man, you know. It's always interesting to find out more about a person, get an idea of what makes them tick. As a novelist I'm sure you'd agree?' He smiled his crooked smile. 'And since you're such an exceptional person it'll be more than usually educational to hear about what makes *you* tick.'

Conrad had moved back to the wicker chair. Though still a little shaky he felt calmer now, the thug's purpose in visiting having turned out to be such a modest one and (by the thug's deluded lights) so easily attained. I needn't murder him after all, he thought. He'll be off before long, galloping back to his mistress with the good news, too stupid for it to occur to him that a memory stick must have been involved somewhere. I'll wait a few weeks then turn the screw on her again. But how did he know where to find me? The question rankled.

'Nice place this,' said Arthur benignly. 'Nice little holiday cottage. Somewhere you can get away from it all. Surrounded by nature. You can go for long walks in the day and get smashed in the evenings, right, Conrad? No one around to stop you getting completely off your face on drink and drugs, Mummy and Daddy don't know and your nearest neighbours are a flock of sheep. Perfect for someone of your refined sensibility I would say.'

'How did you know I was here?'

'And if you run out of coke or heroin,' Arthur went on as if he hadn't heard, 'you can always hop on your bike and motor over to Aberystwyth or even tap into one of the county lines, right?' He glanced over at the table strewn with drug paraphernalia. 'Though it doesn't look as if you'll be running out any time soon, I must say.'

'How did you know I was here?' repeated Conrad.

'The key point being that you don't have to *worry*. Money worries are so unpleasant, aren't they? And not knowing if you'll have enough to pay the bills or buy the skag must be so nerve-wracking, especially for one of such a refined sensibility. But fortunately you don't *need* to worry! And the reason is you've got an income, right, Conrad? A nice little earner, a source of revenue, a bountiful milch cow called...' Arthur paused for effect. 'Called Tessa Wainwright. Except that now I've deleted those documents you don't anymore. That oil well has dried up. Now the cupboard is bare and you'll have to think of something else, some other scam. What's it going to be, Conrad? I'd have thought pimping might be your line, what do you think? You could do a bit of underage grooming, get the girl or girls hooked on your drugs, sell their bodies and come out making a profit. Or closer to home there's always your girlfriend, you could always pimp for Meg, couldn't you, she's an attractive woman...'

'Did she tell you? Did Meg tell you I was here?' Conrad's voice was urgent. The horrible thought had struck him: could it be that he hadn't—that she hadn't...

'Let's not talk of *her*,' said Arthur as if he found the subject boring. 'It's your character that intrigues me, Merrivale. But it's thirsty work chewing the fat like this. How about a whisky? I can see from that tumbler over there that a bottle's been opened. I wouldn't mind something for the road—just a wee dram and I'll be out of your hair, I promise you.'

'The bottle's in the kitchen. Help yourself.'

Conrad watched as Arthur got to his feet and made for the kitchen. He's playing with me, he thought. If Meg told him I'm here Meg is alive and if Meg is alive she will have told him I tied her up and injected her with a

whack of heroin and left her to die, ungagged and un-
bound and lying on the floor of her attic, the silly fool.
But I'm the silly fool for failing to kill her. Never attempt
what you're not 100% sure will succeed.

Only Meg knew he was coming to Bwthyn Onnen.
Only Meg could have told Arthur where to find him.

In the kitchen Arthur was pouring himself some
whisky. Conrad heard the clink of glass on glass followed by the glug of liquid—then Arthur's voice: 'Any
ice around? I prefer it on the rocks.'

'Let me find it for you,' replied Conrad getting out of
his chair. 'The freezer compartment is in a funny place.'

As he passed by the table he picked up a knife which
he'd used earlier to nip the top off a plastic vial. Arthur
was at the counter by the sink with his back to the living
room; in front of him was the kitchen window. Beyond
the window hung a curtain of blackness. Conrad felt he
was moving between worlds, crossing galaxies—his feet
were as light as feathers and he could see his own reflection, a figure sidelit by offstage headlights emerging
out of the blackness beyond the window, and he knew
he would have to act fast before Arthur looked up so he
lunged and thrust the knife into Arthur's flank, blood
spurting from his side while he cried out in agony, but
the vivid images wobbled and sank back to where they
had come from inside him and Conrad was left staring
at the knife in his raised hand, dazed and stupid, the galaxies congealed into a few inches of stainless steel. Pain
exploded in his face as Arthur's elbow smashed into it.
The knife flew from his hand and landed somewhere and

now Conrad was putting out his hands to protect himself but Arthur pushed his arms down and got him in a bearhug, shoving him back into the living room hissing 'Oh no you don't, you piece of filth' into his ear. A punch in the stomach turned him to jelly and the floor came up to meet him. A hefty kick to the head followed. He must have passed out for a few seconds because when he came to Arthur was lifting him up into a chair and was fumbling with something, passing it around Conrad's arms which he twisted behind the chair and tightening it. A rope. He was being tied up... In a panic he started kicking his legs, yelling and thrashing, but the other man was in control, the rope was pulling his legs back, it was being wound round them then round the back of the chair, pulled tighter and tighter. The yelling dissolved into whimpering. Soon Conrad had ceased to struggle and the other man stood looking down at him.

'Bad idea,' he said. 'You obviously need restraining, young man. Just as well I brought some rope with me, don't you think?'

Conrad looked over to the black canvas briefcase sitting by the door. He felt like saying something but nothing came. His right eye was puffing up and he could taste blood on his lips.

'Not very hospitable if I may say so,' continued Arthur. 'There I am, about to enjoy a whisky on the rocks, and you decide that it might be a good idea to knife me from behind! Not very friendly at all. But you didn't manage it, did you. You screwed up. Second screw-up in twenty-four hours, that's not so impressive, is it Conrad?'

'Where did you get that rope?' The words emerged almost inaudibly from Conrad's battered face.

Arthur laughed. 'I'm sure you can guess. It's your property after all.'

He went back into the kitchen to fetch his whisky.

The Deathwatch beetle was beating time, knock knock, knock knock. Conrad shivered.

'Getting cold, are you?' said Arthur returning. 'What you need is some of this. Hold on a minute and I'll let you have some.' He placed the tumbler on the table. 'But first I think I'll follow your advice and switch off those lights.'

He went out by the front door and a moment later the headlights were extinguished. Conrad heard the car door slam. The room was darker now, only a lamp in one corner and the light from the kitchen kept out the blackness of the night. Arthur came into the room bringing a cold draught with him and strolled over to the table. He sat down. In front of him was spread a cornucopia of mind-altering substances, a lighter and a Tesco's bag. He regarded the spread for a few seconds, idly curious, then picked up a cardboard packet and inspected it. He shook it experimentally and there was a soft rattling sound. Opening the top he poured out the contents onto the table, twenty or so light blue tablets from which he selected eight, sweeping the remainder away from him. Conrad observed him listlessly.

Arthur took a sip of the whisky. 'Mm—not bad,' he said, holding the glass up to the light. He took another sip then brought the base of the tumbler down onto the tablets and began to push down and twist, grinding the tabs with controlled movements of his right hand so that in a short while he had produced a small pile of whitish powder. To this he added a few final grains with a fastidious wipe of the tumbler's base. He lowered the glass to a position where its rim was below the level of the table and swept the powder into the glass.

'What... what are you doing?'

'Didn't you say you were cold?' said Arthur standing up with the tumbler in his hand.

'But what have you...'

Arthur was walking towards him. He was smiling.

There was nothing Conrad could do when Arthur brought the glass to his lips, leaning the chair back on its hind legs and squeezing Conrad's mouth open with his other hand. Vainly the boy struggled, vainly he pushed against the rope that bound him. He tried to turn his head away but the fiery liquid kept finding its way into his mouth, he was choking and spluttering, a gloved hand squeezed his cheeks and he felt the whisky passing down his gullet bearing its load of obliterating sleep.

'Good boy, we're nearly finished,' said Arthur pouring the last drops into his victim's mouth. He righted the chair, put the empty glass back on the table. 'Nearly but not quite.'

'Why... why...' The boy was weeping, tears were streaming from his eyes.

'Why indeed. *Why* is always the question,' said Arthur. He was seated at the table and had Conrad's laptop open, was fiddling with it. '*Why* must have been the question on that poor girl's lips when you put the gag in her mouth and stopped all her questions. *Why* must have been shrieking in her head when she saw you preparing that syringe for her.' Suddenly he turned on Conrad. 'And why was it? Why was it, eh? What were you getting off on, you piece of shit? She loved you, didn't she?'

The boy was silent, the silent tears flowed down his cheeks.

'Anyway, it's too late for *why* now,' said Arthur turning back to the laptop. 'Much too late.'

He fiddled some more then said, 'Here we are, this'll do. You've got a good connection here, that I will say. Wonderful how they've rolled out broadband across the country. There you go.' He rotated the PC so that it faced towards the boy. Conrad raised his head slowly. Through the blur of his tears and distorted by the swelling in his right eye he made out writhing flesh, heard the gasping and moaning of simulated pleasure, saw a lipsticked mouth enveloping an erect cock...

Arthur was on his feet again. He was holding the Tesco's bag in his left hand. With his right he pulled a length of string out of his jacket pocket. The image of a conjuror at a children's party floated through Conrad's mind.

'You're a connoisseur of self-pleasuring, aren't you Merrivale? You must know all about the quest for the ultimate high, the climax of climaxes, the moment when Heaven and Hell rush together and copulate in your brain. It's a question of treating your own body as a chemistry lab. We all know the role oxygen plays in the modulation of biological functions, how it influences inputs and outputs, secretions, all that stuff. Not surprising that all sorts of interesting things can happen if you meddle with the oxygen supply. Perverts like to enhance their orgasms that way. I'm sure I don't need to tell you the word for it, you must have come across it in your researches.'

Arthur raised the Tesco's bag above the boy's head.

Knock knock, knock knock went the Deathwatch beetle.

'Autoasphyxiation. That's the word for it.'

He lowered the bag over the boy's head, wrapped the string around the neck, tied it in a knot. Raising his voice so as to be heard he went on: 'Of course I'll be untying the rope in a bit. But not just yet. And I suppose to make it realistic we need to—' He unbuckled the belt of Conrad's jeans and wrenched at the jeans and the boxer shorts beneath them, sliding them away from the boy's genitals, over his knees and down around his ankles. A metallic glint caught Arthur's eye peeping from the pocket of the jeans. 'Well well, what do we have here?' He extracted the object. 'Looks like a memory stick. That's handy, I thought I might have to search the place for it.' He put the stick in the inside pocket of his jacket. Raising his voice again, though he might have been talking to himself as much as to the boy, he went on: 'And if you really want to know *why*, well—if I just overdosed you it might not work, that's why. With your lifestyle you'll have a higher than average tolerance: a quick stomach pumping could leave you right as rain. Then you'd live to tell the tale. And we know how annoying that can be, don't we Conrad?'

The body in the chair was motionless. The exposed skin on the calves and thighs had come out in goosebumps from the cold; the arms were tied stiffly behind the body, the head had slumped forward onto the chest. Arthur considered it for a moment, glanced at the laptop screen where a man was ejaculating over a woman's face and checked his watch. One thirty-five. It had been a long day and he had to drive a three-hour journey. Best not to hang around any longer than was necessary. He counted to a hundred then gave the boy's shoulder a light shove; there was no reaction. Bending down to inspect the plastic bag he could see no changes in its surface, nothing to indicate inhalation and exhalation. Okay, time to unbind. He undid the knot, unwound the rope from the body and looped it round one hand to make a coil. As he watched, the body leant slowly to one side, its supports withdrawn, the arms free, gradually picking up speed, slipping, sliding off the chair till it tipped and fell into a heap on the floor. A hand twitched a couple of times. Then all was still.

Arthur walked over to the black canvas briefcase. He stuffed the coil of rope into it, took one last look around the room and at the body on the floor and went out by the front door, closing it behind him.

*

The hand twitched again, lay still, twitched some more. Slowly the elbow bent, bringing the hand up to the plastic bag and the string that secured it. A finger fumbled at the string, plucked feebly—lay still. It fumbled again, met with the thumb, together they pulled, nothing gave...A moan oozed from the bag like blood from a wound. Suddenly with the force of a spasm the arm shot out across the wooden floor, a random movement pushing away despair, but the hand at the end of it encountered something, cold metal and wood, a familiar shape. The intelligent fingers were already feeling it, interpreting it. Instinctively they gripped the haft of the knife; obediently the elbow bent, joints and muscles working together to bring the blade up against the string, all these servants of the brain busying themselves with the task of releasing it and preserving it, all responding to its frantic commands. The rest of the body was coming alive, a new energy was being tapped in readiness for action, after some cutting the string was severed and now the other hand reached up and grabbed at the bag, pulling it away from the gasping head.

Conrad was swimming in a sluggish sea, he needed all his strength to fight against the downward pull, the warm gravity of near-death, bliss-kiss of extinction. Crawling towards the kitchen he made himself focus on the image of what he was about to do and in this way encouraged himself, fortified his intention: he was going to, he was about to, yes here he was in the kitchen doing, *doing* it—struggling to his feet, his jeans and boxer shorts around his ankles, opening a cupboard, pouring salt into a tumbler, filling the tumbler with warm water from a tap...Action, motive, cause, effect. Drink, swallow. Fingers down the throat, push those fingers, now the gagging starts, here comes the gagging, eject, eject the poison, out it comes, obedient reflex of stomach and throat to bring forth the deathly mix. Vomit, boy, vomit as you have so often done before. Purge, cleanse, make yourself a clean slate, a tabula rasa. Retching he bent over the sink, eyes watering and body shaking, till no more would come and he sank exhausted to the floor.

Breathe now, breathe deep and calm. Deep. Calm. Soon we shall drink cold water, the water that replenishes, but for now we breathe. Dear oxygen, dear blessed oxygen! Bit by bit the fog disperses. The lungs dilate, the blood courses around the starving body. A million UN parcels are delivered to a million grateful refugees. On Conrad's face a smile was emerging, a crease of relief and triumph in the sweaty flesh of his face. His eyes glittered beneath their heavy lids.

*

Tessa woke with a start. Disoriented, she thought at first she was in her bed at the Marlborough; she could visualise around her the pink furnishings of the Blenheim Suite bedroom, sense intuitively the space of the living room next door. Putting out a hand she felt a wall where there should be nothing and the room promptly metamorphosed: she was back in her bedroom at the Zenith. Her heart was beating fast, scraps of the dream still hung about her. There is a black metal box, shut tight, from which sounds are coming, ominous, unearthly sounds... *knock knock, knock knock*... the lid of the box starts shaking, it's about to open, she knows she has to stop it from opening but she's too far away, or perhaps her limbs are paralysed—she watches as the lid trembles, sees the edge of it rise and a crack appear, something is inside pushing upwards... trying to get out... suddenly the lid bursts open and out of the box comes a snake's head, baring its fangs and lunging at her, the forked tongue quivering and flickering.

That was when she woke up, her own screams echoing in her ears. She was fairly sure she had only dreamt the screams. Even so, she was reluctant to go straight back to sleep. Turning onto her side she peered at the bedside clock; its illuminated face told her 2:07.

She pushed aside the bedclothes and sat up. From the door into the bathroom came a faint glow. Guided by the night light Tessa made her way into the bathroom for a drink of water. I hope Ben is sleeping soundly, she thought. I hope he has no such dreams. God preserve him from such dreams. She drank from the plastic cup and looked at herself in the mirror.

After a while she went back to bed.

*

Narrow B roads, scarcely wide enough for two vehicles to pass one another, hedges on either side. Can't go faster than forty on such roads in the daytime but by night you can step on it: undipped headlights tell you the layout of the road ahead and you don't have to dip them for oncoming traffic since there isn't any. Not in Wales.

Vince drove with a clear head and a firm grip. His mind was less on what was behind him than on the coming hours and days. Tessa could rest easy now though he wouldn't be able to tell her that till the thing was in the papers. 'That chap who was blackmailing you—seems he killed himself with an overdose. Some sort of drug addict. Explains why he wanted the money I suppose.' Soft-hearted Tessa would sigh and express sorrow at the waste of a young life. And would secretly rejoice.

And Meg? He wanted to know that she was all right. She'll be kept in hospital for a few hours, he thought, then be sent home. At some point she'll have to hear about her boyfriend's death. They'll tell her all the details—or maybe they won't, she isn't next of kin, but in any case it'll come as a blow, even though he did try to murder her. Will she remember telling me where the little scumbag had taken himself off to? Even if she does that shouldn't be a problem. And she may not remember.

Another clear night, moon and stars out, those hills there very distinct against the sky. Definitely picturesque. Not a bad country, Wales. Not too many people and plenty of space. You could do worse than retire here—get some little cottage like that Merrivale place, give it a proper English name, perhaps go in for a bit of farming on the side. I'd prefer it any day to a fancy Italian villa like the one Tessa's spent half her life in. Decent food too...

His thoughts were interrupted by a flash of light in his rear view mirror. It lasted only a split second but he knew he'd seen it. He was on a bendy stretch of road with woods on one side and the flash had come just before he took a bend. Wales isn't completely deserted, then. Someone's up and about at two in the morning, some guy driving home from a pub lock-in or a vet called out to do an emergency caesarean. He maintained his speed and pretty soon the flash recurred, for a bit longer this time. It was a single headlight—must be a motorbike. Pubgoer not vet, then. A minute later there it was again, he was on a straight stretch now and the light was steady, keeping its distance, in no hurry apparently and Vince thought Okay, I'll accelerate, get some space between us, the glare from my mirror is beginning to be annoying. He pushed down on the gas and the light began to shrink. The road curved round and the light disappeared—ahead there was a T junction. He slowed down as Ms Satnav gave him his instructions: *In 300 metres turn right*. He turned right at the T junction. For a few minutes there was nothing to report and Vince was beginning to think of other things when there it was again, it had cropped up out of nowhere and was closer behind him now, the single headlight focused and deliberate, he was being tailed, no doubt about it, and at this point Vince changed gear mentally, he accepted that he might have to deal with something awkward, something bad. But, but... one thing it was impossible he should have to deal with was... He was forced to cast his mind back to the cottage, that little whitewashed cottage in the Welsh valley, family getaway and holiday home with its field of sleeping sheep outside and its drugged corpse inside. Surely no one could...

The roar of an engine scattered all thoughts and the glare in the rear view mirror expanded rapidly. Vince realised the bike was aiming to get past him. It came up on the outside, disappeared into his blind spot and reappeared again on his right overtaking him, it was alongside him, both vehicles going at 60 mph and the road only just wide enough for the two of them. On the motorbike the leather-jacketed driver stared ahead of him and holding onto him from behind a man in a yellow jumpsuit turned his head to look at Vince. He grinned and brought up his hand in a middle-finger salute, keeping it there as the two vehicles went neck and neck. Then with a spurt of power the Triumph Scrambler shot ahead. Vince watched it disappear into the distance, the red of its rear light contracting to nothing. He was sweating. Dropping his speed to forty he began mumbling to himself, a hollow in the pit of his stomach, gloved hands gripping the steering wheel hard. Impossible. Impossible. How had?... And who was that—what was that –

In the far distance the headlight was visible again. The bike had turned around and was facing back. At first it didn't move, it was merely a pinpoint, a glimmer, and Vince slowed the car right down, he was doing twenty-five now, his heart racing, eyes fixed on the light ahead. Still it didn't move; Vince was crawling in second gear. The long straight road had hedges all along both sides and a tree loomed up two hundred yards off on the left, branches and trunk pale in the moonlight.

Vince remembered passing a turnoff not far back, a farm track or something, probably just leading into a field. As he watched the light he brought the car to a standstill. Then he put it into reverse, for in his bones he knew what was coming, knew that the light would start growing, that the bike would begin on its return journey, and sure enough the pinpoint was expanding—Vince was backing down the road, picking up speed, but the light was growing fast, the bike was accelerating and the distant roar of its engine was getting louder. He stepped on the gas, his left arm over the seat while he twisted round to look out of the rear window, careering between the hedges towards the turnoff—hell, where was it?—but the bike was going at sixty, seventy, there was no way... Vince turned in his seat to see the headlight exploding like a star, the glare and the roar of the bike ate up everything and a second later a splintering flesh-crushing impact

XIII

ELISE PUT A MUG OF camomile tea down in front of Meg.

'I always think it smells of hay,' said Elise seating herself opposite. A plate of digestive biscuits was between them on the kitchen table. Meg picked one up then changed her mind and put it back. Her stomach wasn't ready for much beyond hot liquid.

'So you say you didn't know this guy?' said Elise.

Meg shook her head.

'Weird. And calling round in the evening like that. Nine o'clock or something. He just went straight up to your room without asking, it's as if he knew something was wrong. And then when the ambulance turned up he just melted away again. Weird.'

'Weird,' murmured Meg in agreement. And yet in a way it seemed to her far from weird that someone had stepped in at that moment, when such a gratuitous rent in the fabric of her world had been made. The world surely couldn't stand by and watch! Some agent of normality would have to appear to restore equilibrium, erase the obscenity. And so he did, whoever or whatever he was. She recalled as if from a dream the large face with blue eyes and a moustache, warm hand stroking her forehead, a deep voice repeating her name. He had taken down the note with Conrad's address in Wales on it, held it before her face and asked 'Here?' Then later there had been other people; someone had shone a light into her eyes and she felt an injection in her arm, then they had carried her down, all the way down to the street where an ambulance was waiting for her. She could remember Elise saying 'Will she be all right?' and a woman in green mumbling something in reply. They drove her to the John Radcliffe Hospital where she spent a few hours undergoing treatments and tests; now she was back in Wharf St.

She sipped her camomile. It was six in the evening. Birds were singing outside. They had a small garden with a buddleia at one end, perhaps a blackbird was sitting there. Meg felt the tears rising. So much beauty in the world.

'Do try and eat a little,' said Elise, 'they said that would help. When you feel up to it.' She smiled encouragingly. 'Just a little bit.'

Meg reached for a biscuit. Dear Elise. It can take a catastrophe to bring two people together. She hoped she would be as solicitous if Elise ever suffered a similar calamity—though she hoped she never would. Splitting up from your partner, losing a parent, these are the ordinary sorts of blow ordinary people are meant to endure in life. Not having your boyfriend try to kill you because you know too much.

He's gone to Bwthyn Onnen. Did that man go after him? Perhaps he's a policeman or a detective on Conrad's trail, after a drugs tip-off, say. Finding Conrad's flat empty the detective pays a visit to the girlfriend's place, her address already supplied by whoever gave the tip-off, and stumbles upon the scene of an attempted murder. Except that he wouldn't know it was that: it probably looked like any other overdose scene. In hospital she'd told the doctors what had happened and they had listened impassively to her lurid story, expressing neither belief nor disbelief. She had no idea whether they would contact the police. Perhaps she'd get a call later that evening. But even if the man who'd saved her was a policeman he was on other business, that was for sure. He had melted away, in Elise's words, disappearing into the night with the address of Bwthyn Onnen in his pocket.

Elise was looking at her. Meg knew what she must be thinking: my housemate is a junkie. I can't tell her yet, thought Meg, not yet, it's too horrible. In time I will. But not yet.

She finished her camomile. 'I think I'll go up now. Thanks for the tea and biscuits, Elise. You've been really kind.'

'Do you want me to come up with you? You mightn't be steady on your feet yet, I could stand at the foot of the ladder...'

'No. I'll be okay,' smiled Meg. 'Thanks again.'

'Remember I'm here if you need anything.'

Meg climbed the stairs to the first floor. Looking up at the trapdoor into the attic she hesitated; up there was the room where she'd so often had Conrad round to stay, where they had talked and made love, had lain naked together under the summer stars, and where last night he had tied her up and injected her with enough heroin to kill her, albeit incompetently. She would have to own the space again, enter it and reclaim it. No dithering. She ascended the ladder.

The room looked different, things had been moved away from the central stage on which the drama of her resuscitation had been played out—the beanbag tossed to one side, the lacquered table placed for some reason on top of her futon, her laptop sitting on the kitchen counter next to the sink. Paramedics don't stay to tidy up a room. Meg dragged the beanbag back to where it lived and put right the other stray objects, then she put on the kettle for some more camomile. A step towards normalisation. As the kettle boiled she opened her laptop where it sat by the sink. She was concentrating on keeping busy, doing all the little things that fill up one's time, the humdrum things which take up just enough attention to stop it from slipping into dark places. She got down a packet of teabags, took a mug from off the draining board, put a teabag into the mug. Now pour on the boiling water. Elise thinks it smells like hay.

This'll take you to a lovely place, Meg. Those were the last words he'd spoken to her, holding up the needle in his gloved hand to inspect it. Before that he'd said: *You should never have tested me.* Tested him? Put him to the test? No, she should never have done that, that was certainly a mistake. Look how he'd failed.

She realised she was shaking. Focus on the ordinary, Meg, drink your tea. Don't think about the terrible things.

He's still out there, he could come back at any time. When he returns to Oxford he'll find out I'm still alive. Then he'll try again.

She went over to the trapdoor, knelt down on the floor and pulled up the retractable ladder for the first time in many months. Then she closed the trapdoor and went back to her ordinary tea and her ordinary laptop.

*

'Someone to see you, Mr Parker.'

The nurse withdrew and a stocky man in a raincoat came into the room. He stopped for a second or two, looking down at the bed and its inhabitant. As if satisfied that he was in the right place he went over to the NHS armchair by the side of the bed and sat down on it. On the bedside cabinet stood a plastic jug of water with a beaker and a papier mâché receptacle. The man glanced knowingly at the receptacle then turned to the person sitting propped up by pillows in the hospital bed.

'Hello Vince.'

Vince regarded him with his left eye, the unbandaged one.

'Jack Gregson. Hello Jack, what brings you here?'

'I heard you'd been in the wars. Thought I'd pop in to see you.'

'Is this an interview?'

Jack chuckled. 'Don't be paranoid now. Am I wearing my uniform?' He leant forward in his chair. 'How're you feeling, Vince? The doctor out there said you were a sorry sight when you were admitted, cuts and bruises all over, broken bones... Wasn't there a ruptured spleen?'

'Yes. They took it out. You don't need it.'

'One less thing to worry about, I suppose!' Jack chuckled again. 'Anyway, you're on the mend, that's good, that's very good. As for the other chap... well, I guess you know about the other chap.'

Vince looked at him. 'The other chap? You mean the guys on the motorbike? I haven't been told, no. What's—'

'Only one guy, Vince. Name of Conrad Merrivale. He didn't survive. Dead on arrival.'

'Dead.' He paused to digest the proposition. 'But there were two, weren't there. Merrivale had a passenger. Right?'

Jack shook his head slowly. 'No passenger. Why would you think that?'

Vince was silent.

'You were a bit concussed at first, that's what the doctor said. Seem all right now. But perhaps you think you remember...'

'A man in a yellow jumpsuit. There was definitely... Could he have been thrown clear of the crash? That must be it. He must have...'

'There was just the two of you, old boy. The ambulance arrived pretty quick, someone in a nearby house heard the crash, came out and had a look and phoned 999. You should be grateful, you could have bled to death if they'd taken any longer. Anyway the young man died.' Jack cleared his throat. 'It seems he was on his way from Oxford to a little cottage his family owns. As usual the reg numbers identified the accident victims, that's why I knew it was my old friend and colleague driving the car.' He smiled broadly. 'So I thought to myself, if it isn't old Vince Parker of the Met! Wonder what he's doing in this neck of the woods. Must be twenty years since I've seen him. Think I'll pay him a visit if he's languishing in hospital. It's my parish, after all. I'll tell you what, Vince—' Jack's tone became intimate and confidential. 'Dyfed-Powys is a bloody sight better to work for than those idiots in London. We both of us got out in time, didn't we? Though maybe for different reasons. But it's good to see you again, that it is, even if it's in rather sorry circumstances. And I know you won't mind if I just ask you one or two questions about—well, about what you were up to that night.'

'This is feeling like an interview, Jack, whether or not you're in uniform. I'm not aware of any crime that's been committed. It was a head-on collision.'

'It was indeed a head-on collision. With Merrivale driving towards his cottage and you driving away from it.'

'How do you know where I was driving from?'

'The address of the cottage was written on a slip of paper found in your jacket pocket. Unless you're going to say you'd been somewhere else in the vicinity? You were a long way from home, Vince, Oxford is a long way from Ceridigion and you were driving back, weren't you, though God knows what you'd been up to in Wales at midnight.'

Vince reached for a wire hanging by the side of his bed. He fumbled along its length till he found the buzzer, which he pressed.

'What are you doing?'

'I've got a headache. I'm going to ask for some painkillers.'

'This won't take long, Vince. You know I'm just doing my job.'

'You still haven't mentioned any crime. If I can't assist you in connection with a suspected crime why don't you bugger off.'

'You know what it's like. When there are class A drugs in the picture we have to take it seriously. That cottage was chock a block with class A drugs, freshly opened packets, freshly cut coke, a sinkful of vomit...'

'That was all his stuff.'

'And yet he hadn't arrived there. He was still on his way there from Oxford. Facing towards it, not away from it.' Jack leant over to the bedside cabinet and poured some water into the beaker. 'Unlike you.'

'Hello, what can I do for you now?' The nurse had come into the room. 'More pain relief, is it?' She spoke with a Welsh lilt.

Vince said, 'Yes please.'

'I'll be right back.'

'Where were we?' said Jack once the nurse was gone. 'I think you were going to tell me what you'd been doing in that cottage.'

Vince sighed. 'I went there looking for Merrivale. When I found no one at home I decided to drive back. I thought I might meet him coming and I did, didn't I.'

'What did you want with him?'

'I'm not sure I have to tell you that.'

'People go long distances to buy drugs...'

'But since you ask,' Vince said firmly, 'I suspected him, with good reason, of having tried to murder his girlfriend in Oxford. And if you doubt me you can ask the girl herself.'

Jack sat with his mouth open. 'Murder his girlfriend?'

'Yes.'

'That's quite a thing you're saying. Quite a thing.' He sat back. 'Look, Vince, we know each other, we're old friends—if there's bad stuff happening in your life I can be compassionate. You don't need to do a smokescreen on me, I understand how addiction works...'

'Shut up, you idiot, I'm not a bloody addict. I'm telling you straight. That little scumbag tried to kill his girlfriend.'

'I've got some paracetamol here. A couple of tablets should help with the pain.' The nurse had come back. She held out a paper cup to Vince, standing on the other side of the bed from Jack at whom she looked through narrowed eyes.

Jack pointed at the beaker. 'I've poured you some water,' he said to Vince.

Vince took the plastic cup with his left hand and brought it to his mouth, tipped back his head and transferred the tablets from cup to mouth. Still looking up at the ceiling he groped with the other hand for the beaker; Jack gave it to him and Vince swallowed some water, then sat back again with a grunt. Jack relieved him of the beaker and returned it to the cabinet. The nurse took back the plastic cup.

'There's teamwork for you!' said Jack smiling all round. The nurse left without a word and Jack turned once again to his old friend.

'Now then. This is serious. This is bloody serious, Vince. You're alleging that the deceased had come fresh from an attempt on the life of a young woman, is that right? And that you were pursuing him? Despite the fact that you got to the cottage first?'

'He must have stopped somewhere for a bite to eat.' Vince had closed his eye.

'How did he try to kill her?'

'By giving her an overdose of heroin and making it look like an accident. Tied her up first.'

'Where did this take place?'

'In her room. She lives in an attic room. I paid her a visit because I was after Merrivale for something else and thought she might know his whereabouts.'

'You stopped being a copper years ago. What's all this chasing after criminals? Is someone employing you?'

'Old habits die hard, Jack.' Vince looked as if he was ready for a doze.

'Old habits die hard,' repeated Jack thoughtfully. 'That's true enough. I remember some of your habits from the old days. Some would call them—unconventional. Your superiors took rather a dim view I seem to recall. I hope you haven't been indulging in any of those particular old habits, Vince?'

Vince spoke slowly. 'I'll give you the girl's name and address and you can go and interview her for yourself. But since the bastard's dead it won't be much of a murder enquiry.'

*

It was a Wednesday morning when the news of Conrad's death broke at the Marlborough. Tina was coming in from having a cigarette break and she saw Maria with her hand to her mouth listening to Hugo, who had just received the news from Bernie. As she approached she caught the tail end of Hugo's account: '...somewhere in Wales apparently. A head-on collision—you don't stand a chance on a bike unless you're thrown clear.'

'What's all this?' asked Tina.

'Conrad's dead,' said Hugo.

'So sad,' said Maria shaking her head. 'And him just a young one.'

'Dead?' said Tina. 'Conrad?'

Hugo nodded.

Bernie appeared out of nowhere looking anxious. 'Could people keep their voices down on this, we really

don't want to alarm any guests. I know it must come as
a shock to those of you who...'

'Why would it alarm the guests?' asked Tina.

'He's worried they'll think the place is jinxed, aren't
you Bernie?' said Hugo. 'Two deaths within a month.
Both violent.'

'Oh my God,' murmured Maria.

'How did he die?' said Tina ignoring Bernie's gestures.

'Crashed his motorbike. He was on a country road.
Crashed into a car, right, Bernie?'

'Sadly, yes. Now if people could please go back to
their...'

'Okay, okay,' said Hugo turning to go. 'But let's face it,
the guy was a prick.'

Tina chatted for a while with Maria then made her
way to the kitchen. She wondered whether Arthur
knew. He'd have no more need of her assistance now.
Case closed. But maybe he didn't know and she could
do him one final service by informing him. They could
meet on that bench in St Giles to talk it over and there
was a coffee shop nearby if they wanted to continue
their discussion...

I'll give him a call, thought Tina. But when later in
the day she dialled his number the line was dead.

*

In the lobby of the Zenith Hotel the boy and the girl
were following the movements of the fish in the aquarium, standing side by side, her blonde head a couple of
inches higher than his. Tessa watched them from her

armchair. An empty coffee cup sat on the table beside her. She'd already had breakfast and was now reading a magazine while waiting for Ben to appear. Ben was a bit of a late riser, something she vaguely attributed to his disability; she didn't know what sorts of routines he had to follow, what private intricacies of washing and dressing marked his mornings. She didn't know, but she hoped by gentle means to acquire such knowledge. All in good time. Of course he wouldn't want to be mothered, he was a young man after all and she had discerned a note of proud independence about him that was only natural. On the other hand it would surely be unnatural in *her* not to care for him with a mother's care. He had had no real mother up to now, the poor boy. Miranda didn't count.

They were planning a trip to Blenheim that afternoon. She especially wanted to show him the grounds, with their landscaped hillocks and meandering paths, birds sitting on top of their reflections in the artificial lake. It would, she supposed, be ideal terrain for his wheelchair. Tessa had discovered Blenheim when still staying at the Marlborough Hotel, a prey to that horrible blackmailer whom Vince had had to see off. Where was Vince? It was odd of him not to have contacted her before now—the finished version of *The Homecoming* had been in his inbox for several days and she hadn't heard a thing from him. Very unusual. Perhaps she should give him a ring.

Tessa smiled to herself. So Taskar and Lemula have finally come home. What further adventures await them no one knows, not even their creator. Thousands of fans will have to say goodbye to the indomitable duo, making do with whatever characters and creatures presently come to take their place. If their creator continues to write fantasy, that is.

She looked at her watch. Ben was more than usually late in coming down this morning. I'll have another coffee, she thought. Those two children have drifted off somewhere, I didn't notice them going, and the unobserved fish in the aquarium continue on their ceaseless round like imprisoned sleepwalkers. Sleepswimmers, I mean. Asleep with their eyes open, like certain human beings.

She got to her feet and at the same moment Ben appeared, moving towards her across the parquet floor from the direction of the lift.

'Good morning, sleepy head,' smiled Tessa. 'Do you want to have breakfast?'

'Hello mum. No, I'll skip breakfast I think. A coffee would be good though.'

'I was on the verge of getting myself one. Milk and no sugar?'

He nodded. Tessa went over to the coffee machine humming. The girl at reception watched her with mild interest; it was a slack morning at the Zenith.

'So a quick lunch in town followed by a trip to Blenheim Palace—yes?' said Tessa bringing the coffees over. 'Perfect weather for it.'

Ben smiled at her and picked up his cup. There was something stiff in the smile, something constrained.

Tessa was vaguely troubled and she scanned his face carefully.

'Is everything all right?'

'Yeah, everything's all right.' He took a sip of coffee, paused, then immediately took another. He was avoiding her gaze.

'No it isn't,' said Tessa. 'What's the matter, Ben?'

He cleared his throat and managed to look her in the face. 'Mum—I hope you don't mind but... I've been on the phone to Miranda. That's why I'm late down, we had quite a long chat. About things.'

'Things?'

'You and me. The past. Miranda wanted to tell me stuff she thought I ought to know now that we—you and I, are... are reunited.' He blushed. 'Stuff about when I was a baby, you know.'

Tessa felt cold all over. Her heart was beating fast. She found that she couldn't speak.

'And mum... what I want you to know is...' The constrained smile appeared again. 'It doesn't matter. It absolutely doesn't matter. Really. You were sick, you had depression. You couldn't help it. Even Miranda...'

'Even?' interrupted Tessa. 'Why *even*?'

'Mum.' Ben looked as if he were in pain, there was a frown of anguish on his face.

'Why did she tell you this? Why? Does she hate me?' Tessa's voice was trembling, ready to break. 'She didn't have to tell you this. God! How could she be so...'

'Mum! I said it doesn't matter. Didn't you hear me? Maybe if I'd been told as a child it would have mattered, but now that I've met you and got to know you—how *could* it matter? Really?'

'Oh Ben.' The tears were coming, she couldn't help it. 'Ben, I'm so sorry.'

'What for?' He sounded exasperated but when she looked up she saw that he too was crying. 'What for? What on earth have you got to be sorry for?' He took the hand that she held out to him, took it and kept hold of it.

*

Broken ribs and femur, a fractured pelvis, one eye damaged, multiple lesions and a missing spleen. 'We'll have to keep you here for a while,' said the doctor. No kidding. At least my hands and arms aren't too badly hurt, thought Vince. Bruised and painful but essentially intact. And my brain still functions. It could be worse—a lot worse. I'll probably get bed sores lying here for ages but if you can't put up with bed sores you must be pretty feeble. The main thing is I'm still alive, unlike that lunatic.

The last thing he could remember was seeing the distant headlight facing his way. The crash itself and the seconds that led up to it had been erased from his memory. Just that glimmer of white light sitting there in the darkness, pointing at him like a gun, a held breath before the descent into madness... Hatred intense enough to embrace self-destruction: *I'm going to pull you down with me, pull you down to Hell.* But the lunatic failed, as he had failed with the girl and again with that knife. He was an all-round failure was Conrad Merrivale, like so many criminals and wasters, even if he did regard himself as some sort of superman. A superman dressed as a hotel waiter. Vince smiled grimly. And the little fool thought he could get the better of me!

Without warning the image of a yellow jumpsuit popped up, a man riding pillion on a motorbike raising his middle finger and grinning. Black eyes in a white face. He shook his head to rid himself of it. Jack was probably right—it was a post-concussion effect, confabulation arising out of physical trauma. The ambulance had picked up two bodies, no more, no less. Forget about it, Vince.

Through the slats of the blind he could see the darkening sky. They'd be bringing round the evening meal before long, such-and-such with mash or maybe a curry. Good institutional fare. Not that he was hungry. He raised his right arm, bent and unbent it, flexed his fingers, then did the same with his left arm. The strength was still there, it was his legs that were going to need building up, hours of physiotherapy no doubt, tottering around with a walking frame and getting dunked in pools by burly nurses. Well, those are the risks that come from being a soldier. He'd entered the fray and come off the battlefield wounded, that was all. And hadn't he succeeded? Hadn't he dealt with the threat to Tessa's name and reputation? He'd dealt with it fully. Target terminated with extreme prejudice.

Tessa. She'll be wondering where I am, he thought. Incommunicado for a week or so, not answering the phone or replying to emails, very unlike old Vince especially at a time like this when another book is done and dusted and ready to be sent off. And not just 'another book' but the crowning volume of the tetralogy, possibly even the crowning volume of Tessa Wainwright's whole career. I suppose it's in my inbox waiting to be read. We need to get a move on with this. I'll ask the nurse for a phone to ring Tessa on.

'Steak and kidney pie?'

The words were uttered by the person pushing a trolley who now entered Vince's room. He was a small thin man of indeterminate age whom Vince judged to be Filipino.

'Fine,' replied Vince.

The man set about laying out the food on a hospital table next to Vince's bed. He lifted a metal cover off the plate, placed utensils and a paper napkin beside it and manoeuvred the table top over Vince's inert knees. Vince looked down at the food without relish.

'Cup of water?' asked the man.

'Yes please. Oh, do you think you could ask the nurse if I might use a phone? I have to make an important call.'

The man smiled and pointed at the buzzer beside the bed.

'Righto, Signor Jobsworth,' muttered Vince and he leant over to press the buzzer. In due course the nurse came round. She promised him the use of a phone. 'But eat your dinner first,' she said. 'And we'd appreciate it if you'd ask the other person to call you back if it's to be a long conversation.'

'Naturally,' said Vince broaching his pie.

Half an hour later he was talking to Tessa. She was alarmed to hear about the accident, relieved to know he was on the mend.

'I tried ringing you but the line was always dead.'

'I think we can assume my phone was part of the mess that got swept up after the accident. Sorry I couldn't contact you sooner.'

'Oh Vince, don't apologise, I'm just glad you're all right. Have you got a room to yourself?'

'I have.' Comrade Jack might have had something to do with that, he thought to himself. 'It's quite comfortable. I'll be here a while so some reading material would come in handy. Have you by any chance...'

'Sent you *The Homecoming*? Yes I have, I emailed it to you a few days ago.'

'I'll get hold of a PC.'

'I could bring you yours. I could bring you that and anything else you needed from your B & B, it would be no trouble at all, really it wouldn't.'

'My dear Tessa, please don't think of it. All I need is a PC and I'm sure they'll let me have one. If not I'll let you know, rest assured.'

'So Vince...I can't help being curious. What were you doing in the middle of Wales—if you don't mind my asking?'

He sighed. 'It's a long story. A woman I used to know lives in these parts; she got in touch, wanted me to visit. Her life's turned upside down recently, it's a real mess... Maybe I shouldn't go into details...'

'No, of course not. I understand. Sorry for prying, Vince.'

'Not at all. But tell me: how is young Ben? How is all that going? Have you been seeing a lot of one another?'

'It's kind of you to ask. You're a kind man, do you know that?'

'Oh come...'

'No, you are, you ought to admit it. You've done so much for me, I've got so much to be grateful to you for. Really. Don't think I don't appreciate all the efforts you've made and are still making on my behalf. I've been seeing a lot of Ben, yes. And there's one thing I wanted to tell you which I hope will come as a relief, though you might at first feel doubtful. It's to do with that blackmailer.'

'Blackmailer?'

'You know, the person who was putting notes...'

'Yes yes, I know who you're talking about—but what have you... I mean, what—'

'I think I've solved our problem. And it's the most obvious solution, the one we should have adopted from the outset. I've been too cowardly, too scared of—of shame and humiliation I suppose, but actually, as I've come to see thinking it over, and Ben has been a great help to me in this, there isn't any cause for shame and humiliation, what happened all those years ago is nothing to be ashamed of, it was just a horrible, a ghastly thing, a symptom of clinical depression not an act of wickedness. You see? So there's no reason why the world *shouldn't* know about it. I should never have felt it had to be covered up. So if... if... Vince, are you still there?'

'I'm still here. Still here.' His voice sounded remote.

'If the blackmailer contacts me again, asking for more—which anyway he may not do—but if he does, I'll be able to say "Go to hell." Because it's going to be made public anyway. I'm going to tell the world myself. People *ought* to know about such things, they ought to realise what some mothers go through, the ones who get post-natal depression, how awful it is and how... especially if someone well-known can say she's had it; if someone as famous and successful as Tessa Wainwright has suffered from post-natal depression then any stigma that attaches to the condition, unjustly attaches to it, will be reduced in people's minds. So I feel it's almost my duty to speak out. Do you see? Vince, do you see what I'm saying?'

She was talking rapidly, almost breathlessly, the words tumbling out.

Sitting propped up against his pillows Vince had closed his unbandaged eye. He still held the handset to his ear. His mouth was slightly open.

The voice continued to come to him through the handset but he no longer listened to it.

*

Two police officers were at the door, a man and a woman. The woman officer said, 'We're hoping to speak to Margaret Owens if she's at home.'

'That's me,' said Meg. It was a grey day and there was a light drizzle falling. 'Do you want to come in?'

'Thank you. I think that would be a good idea.'

They stepped over the threshold and followed Meg through the house and into the kitchen. Elise and Adaego were out. Meg had been about to make herself some lunch but that could wait. She knew what they'd come about and she felt both relieved and nervous; if the police were involved that meant her story had been taken seriously. They'd surely have to offer her some sort of protection.

'Did the doctors at the JR tell you about me?' she asked as the three of them sat around the table. It was a bit of a squeeze—the policeman was a big guy, he'd had to stoop coming into the kitchen and the chair he was sitting on seemed too small for him. It wasn't completely obvious why he was there since his colleague did all the talking.

'No, as a matter of fact,' said the woman officer in reply. 'The police in Wales have passed this case on to us.'

'In Wales?'

'Yes. I take it you haven't heard from your boyfriend recently?'

'You mean Conrad?' Wales: the cottage. Bwthyn Onnen. 'No I haven't. Has he been. . . ? Sorry, could you tell me what this is about?' She was confused, the scene wasn't being played out in the way she'd expected it to be.

The two officers exchanged glances and the woman went on: 'You may be unaware of the fact that Conrad was involved in a motor accident on 28 July as a result of which he is... I'm sorry to have to tell you this, Margaret, but Conrad is now deceased.'

Deceased. Conrad was *deceased.* Dead. The boy she had loved more than anyone else in the world was dead. And she was safe.

Meg found that she was sobbing. She felt the policewoman's hand on her arm, gentle, comforting, but under that touch her vulnerability was inflamed and the weeping overwhelmed her, tears mourning all the hours spent with him, the love she had wasted on him, the part of her he had ripped out and trampled on. Eventually she calmed down enough to say, 'Where is he? Have they... has he been...'

'The funeral is due to take place this Saturday. I can give you more details later, but—Margaret—we do need to ask you some more questions if that's all right. It has to do with the night Conrad left Oxford. Do you think you could tell us a bit about that?'

Meg nodded. She reached for some kitchen towel, wiped her eyes and blew her nose. She took a deep breath. Then she told them how Conrad had tried to kill her. This second telling was different from the first, more detailed, less crazy sounding. What she said to the doctors had come out like vomit, it was a drugged-up woman wailing on a hospital ward, whereas here in her own kitchen she was able to bring out each fact like an exhibit, assemble the data in cold daylight before the gaze of her audience and allow them to judge according to their own lights the nature of what they heard and saw. For how could they fail to see as if with their own eyes the scene she painted for them, the backpack thrown carelessly on the floor from which he drew the coiled rope, the table knocked over during their struggle, the latex gloves he put on before handling the syringe? And when he stuffed the handkerchief in her mouth, forcing it in, how could they fail to hear her stifled cries and the music he put on to drown them, the same music they used to listen to sitting hand in hand or lying side by side on the futon in the days when... The weeping broke through again but it was not enough to stop her tale and even when she had to describe how he pulled up her sleeve and felt for a vein, how he knelt down and brought the needle towards her, his eyes glittering strangely, she didn't break down or falter but pressing on came at last to the slow dropping of the curtain, the dimming and blurring of her world and the sinking into an oblivion from which after an interval that lacked all duration she was roused by the touch of a stranger.

'Can you describe this person?'

'Ginger moustache. Blue eyes. He was wearing...' She paused. '...a red bow tie.'

The officers nodded to each other.

'And did he say who he was?' asked the woman officer. 'Or what he was doing in your attic?'

'No he didn't,' answered Meg. 'I've no idea why he was there. And later he just disappeared. It was as if he was...was some sort of angel, come down specially to save me.' She looked at them and smiled weakly. 'Don't you think?'

The male police officer raised his eyebrows. His colleague said, 'That man's name is Vincent Parker. It was his car that Conrad's motorbike crashed into. Or rather they crashed into each other.'

Meg drew a sharp breath. Then she said, 'So he did go after him.'

'What do you mean?'

'I told him Conrad had set off for Wales. To his cottage. I gave him the address.'

'Written on a slip of notepaper?'

'Yes, he took it down from the noticeboard where I'd pinned it.' She frowned. 'Did he—did Vincent survive? The crash, I mean?'

'Yes, he survived, he's recovering in hospital now. He was quite badly injured but he'll be all right.'

Meg considered for a moment. 'Do you know if this man was connected in any way with Tessa Wainwright? The author? Conrad once said… But no, that was someone else. With a different name, something like—like…'

'Vincent Parker is her literary agent,' replied the officer. 'At least that's what we've been informed. But I don't think Tessa Wainwright has anything to do with this case.'

Meg was thinking of the documents she'd transferred from Conrad's memory stick, with names like *taskar(1)* and *house* and *bank*, documents which she knew to be Tessa Wainwright's property and which she had recently discovered to be missing from her PC, leaving no trace behind them. It was as if they had never existed. But they must have existed in order for Conrad to have

had a pretext for murdering her. Without those documents she wouldn't have argued with him, he wouldn't
have tried to kill her and Vincent Parker wouldn't have
pursued him as far as a country lane in the middle of
Wales. Without those documents Conrad would still be
alive.

The front door slammed. Elise must have come in.

'Well, Margaret,' said the woman police officer, 'I
think that's about all for now. You've been extremely
helpful. We may need to ask you to make a statement at
some point, I hope that's all right?'

'Of course,' said Meg as the three of them got to their
feet. Elise appeared at the door of the kitchen holding
a bag full of shopping. 'Is everything okay?' she said
with a worried expression, looking from one person to
another.

'Everything's fine,' answered Meg. 'Absolutely fine.'

Then as if to explain what she meant she added:
'Conrad's dead.'

*

Taskar and Lemula were to be married on Midsum-
mer's Day. The nuptial preparations could not but be
tinged with sadness given the death of the old king. It
was in widow's weeds that Queen Alumel came to speak
to Taskar one morning as he was tending to his steed,
Flamehoof, in the royal stables.

'Your majesty,' said Taskar. 'What brings you hither?
Let us go out into the fresh air. The close atmosphere of
these stalls must offend your nostrils.'

'Not so, dear Taskar,' replied the queen. 'I am a horse-woman as well as a noblewoman. But for the sake of privacy let us do as you say.'

They left the stables and made for the avenue of elms to walk along which was one of the queen's habitual pleasures. Here she addressed Taskar in these words: 'We each carry within us our own origin, as the oak carries within it the essence and nature of the acorn from which it grew. The soil plays its part, nurturing and fostering the living thing, but another seed in that same soil brings forth another tree. So it is with a human being. You are who you are, dear Taskar, because of what you grew from, the acorn out of which you sprouted.'

She smiled at him.

'But you will berate me with talking in parables. Let me then be as clear and direct as the subject demands. You have a right to know your own origins, and also to know those of your beloved bride to be, the princess Lemula. It is of these matters that I must speak.'

They had arrived at a seat beneath one of the great elms and here they rested. Taskar prepared to listen earnestly to all that the queen would relate to him. Her eyes appeared to fix upon some spot in the far distance as she sought for the words that would most aptly broach her topic. At last she began.

'When you were but a newborn baby. . . '

*

Several months after his death Conrad's college set up a prize in his name, the Merrivale Prize, funded by his parents. On the college website the conditions are stated as follows: *In memory of a young and promising scholar, this prize is to be awarded in Hilary Term to the student whose essay on the subject of 'Respect for Others' (6000-8000 words) is deemed best by a panel of judges.* The first person to win the prize was a girl from Hong Kong who wrote about the genetic basis of altruism.

The Merrivales sold Bwthyn Onnen to a neighbouring farmer who within twelve months demolished it in order to erect a wind turbine in its place.

Vince Parker now walks with a stick. He has retired from his job as a literary agent. Tessa Wainwright rarely sees him. The fourth volume of her tetralogy, *The Homecoming*, was published to a predictably rapturous reception. 'Wainwright has outdone herself,' wrote one reviewer. 'A fitting conclusion to an epic tale,' wrote another, while a third expressed the opinion that 'it is going to be hard to say farewell to that royal couple, Prince Taskar and Princess Lemula.'

As for Tessa Wainwright herself, she has moved to Canada. She lives in Ottawa with her son Ben.

NEXT BY
ROGER TEICHMANN

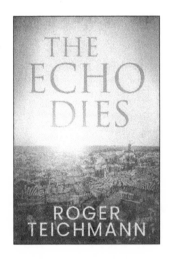

JULIUS DURWARD, 64-year-old author of the cult book *Pandora's Mirror*, is visiting the French town of Uzès hoping to meet up with old friends. His memory failing, haunted by a past tragedy, Julius finds himself being pressured to support two wildly different causes, the Utopianism of an aging American billionaire and the radical extremism of an underground environmentalist group. As the mistral blows and civil unrest everywhere increases, Julius's world appears on the verge of disintegrating.

ABOUT THE AUTHOR

ROGER TEICHMANN is a writer and philosopher. He teaches at Oxford University and has written several books on philosophy in addition to the two novels *Dog's Twilight* and *The Echo Dies*. He is also a keen musician and has composed music for various forces including a chamber opera, *A Practical Man*. He lives in Oxford.